Would Mary leave her rich boyfriend for her bodyguard?

Trace shifted the phone and listened to Jonathan Regent talk about a business trip that would keep him out of D.C. for the next few weeks.

"Trace," Mary's fiancé finished, "I want you to move into her spare bedroom."

Live with Mary? Didn't Regent see what he was doing, throwing them together like this? It was too dangerous. "Mr. Regent, I don't think that's such a good idea," Trace said softly.

"Why?" Johanthan said sharply. "Is there something you're not telling me?"

Plenty. But nothing Regent would want to hear. "No, nothing like that. It's just that..." *I'm attracted to your fiancée.*

Trace considered his options. He could resign from his position as Mary's bodyguard. But if he quit, who would protect Mary from the stalker? And if he moved into her apartment, who would protect her from *him?*

ABOUT THE AUTHOR

Judi Lind and her husband, Larry, live in a suburb of San Diego, California, where they have a large extended family of six children and three dogs. The children somehow grew up and left home while Judi was busy writing.

Books by Judi Lind

HARLEQUIN INTRIGUE
260—WITHOUT A PAST

Veil of Fear

Judi Lind

Harlequin Books

TORONTO • NEW YORK • LONDON
AMSTERDAM • PARIS • SYDNEY • HAMBURG
STOCKHOLM • ATHENS • TOKYO • MILAN
MADRID • WARSAW • BUDAPEST • AUCKLAND

With love and affection for the Thursday Group who
always challenge me while bolstering my confidence.
Te adoro.

ISBN 0-373-22310-2

VEIL OF FEAR

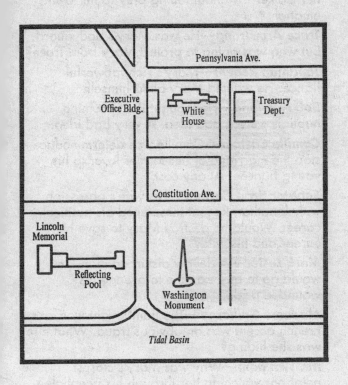

Pennsylvania Ave.

Executive
Office Bldg.

White
House

Treasury
Dept.

Constitution Ave.

Lincoln
Memorial

Reflecting
Pool

Washington
Monument

Tidal Basin

CAST OF CHARACTERS

Mary Wilder—Could she save herself from her stalker—without falling prey to her own emotions?

Trace Armstrong—He was Mary's bodyguard. But who was going to protect Mary from Trace?

Jonathan Regent—Mary's rich, powerful fiancé. He wanted Mary all to himself.

Bob Newland—He thought the upcoming nuptials were a bad idea. A very bad idea.

Camille Castnor—Camille was determined to stop the marriage of her former lover to his young fiancée. At any cost.

Senator Brad Castnor—His wife's obsession with Jonathan Regent threatened his political career. Would he destroy Mary to save his career and his wife?

Mark Lester—A deeply disturbed man, he would go to any extreme to avenge his wounded pride.

Madame Guillarge—The flamboyant woman's French accent was an obvious fraud. What else was she hiding?

Mr. Waltham—Why was Mary's closest neighbor watching her through his peephole?

The Man in the Purple Cap—A shadowy figure who was always around when trouble started.

Prologue

It was only by chance that the reader even picked up the *D.C. Diplomat* newspaper. But there, on the society page, the boldfaced caption read: *HOTEL MAGNATE JONATHAN REGENT ANNOUNCES ENGAGEMENT*.

The reader sank into a chair and pored over the small print. Little was said about the bride-to-be, only that prior to her engagement she'd been a clerk at a rare-books store in Georgetown. There was no shortage of information, however, on the prospective groom. Jonathan Regent was well known in Washington society. A self-made multimillionaire who'd gone from manager of a small inn to CEO of the huge conglomerate Regent Hotels International in just under twenty years.

Jonathan, apparently bored with adding more money to his already burgeoning coffers, had recently taken to dabbling in local politics. The newspaper article hinted that Jonathan was expected to enter the congressional race for the small northern Virginia suburb where he resided.

The insinuation was that every budding politician needed a wife. Hence the engagement.

But was it a politically correct decision to ally himself to a nobody little shop clerk?

The person reading the article held it up, scanning the accompanying photograph of the smiling couple.

Mary Wilder, the bride-to-be, appeared considerably younger than her fiancé. She had shoulder-length blondish hair, wide dark eyes, and a disarming smile. Not a classically beautiful woman, but she was imbued with a sweet expression evident even in the fuzzy newspaper photo.

Yes, the reader thought, Mary Wilder had a vulnerable prettiness that would appeal to any man.

But the image of the woman's guileless eyes staring into the camera like those of a frightened doe suddenly made one thing clear: she wasn't the right wife for Jonathan Regent.

He needed a woman with a boldness of character who could withstand even the most strident opponent. A society matron beyond reproach. A social hostess who could dine with sharks and not sustain a nibble. Mary Wilder was too innocent, too naive. She would be eaten alive by those power-hungry congressional wives.

The reader took a pair of large shears from the desk drawer and neatly cut out the photograph.

No, Miss Mary Wilder wouldn't do at all. She was a mistake, but one that could be eliminated.

Chapter One

Mary Wilder tapped her fingers on the desk top, barely able to contain her excitement. At last, the somber voice on the other end of the telephone line droned his usual greeting, "Good morning. Mr. Jonathan Regent's office. Robert Newland at your service. How may I—"

She cut off his practiced patter. "Hi! This is Mary. Is Jonathan available?"

"I'm afraid he's quite busy at the moment, but I'm sure if it's important he won't mind being interrupted."

"Oh, it's not that important, Bob."

"Robert."

"Sorry. Robert. Anyway, I know Jonathan is used to this kind of publicity, but have you seen the cover of—"

"Of practically every magazine and newspaper in the country, Ms. Wilder? Yes, I have."

Mary frowned, her enthusiasm deflating with every second she spent talking to Bob—*Robert*—Newland. Jonathan called him a perfect assistant, but Robert Newland was so...so stuffy he made her want to say something outrageous just to shock him out of his pomposity.

Giving in to that devilish urge, she continued, "Gee, Robert, since Jonathan's tied up, I'll chat with you. How many magazines do you suppose—"

"Oh, Ms. Wilder, I see Mr. Regent's off the phone now. One moment and I'll connect you."

A moment later, the deep stentorian tones of Mary's fiancé boomed over the line. "Mary, darling! You haven't forgotten about our luncheon date, have you?"

"No, of course not. But I just had to call you. Our picture was on the cover of *Newsweek* this morning!"

"As a matter of fact, I just cut off the cover for your scrapbook. It's right here on my desk." Jonathan chuckled. "Mary, my sweet, sweet innocent. You'd better get used to seeing your lovely face in the media. As Mrs. Jonathan Regent, you're going to become something of a celebrity."

"This is going to take some adjustment, Jonathan. I mean, everything is happening so fast, I feel like I can't catch my breath."

"Speaking of fast," Jonathan cut in, "I have to leave here in five minutes if we're going to make our lunch reservation. Is Camille with you?"

"No," Mary said. "She and the senator are going to meet us at the restaurant. I'm on my way out the door right now."

"Good. I'll see you there. Oh, and Mary?"

"Yes?"

"I know you still have some misgivings about Camille, but, darling, she's doing us a tremendous favor. There's no woman in Washington who knows more, who gives better parties, who always has the correct assortment of guests and who—"

"I know, I know. And who is always dressed with impeccable style. I told you that I'd listen to her advice, Jonathan, and I will, but . . ."

"But what?"

Mary chewed on the edge of her fingernail and blinked away a sudden tear of frustration. Jonathan had been so generous, so wonderful, that she always felt an ingrate when she refused his largess. But his apparent wish to transform her into a duplicate of Camille Castnor made Mary feel...deflated, somehow.

Oh, she knew Jonathan wouldn't understand. They'd been over this ground a dozen times already. And he was right, really he was. Not many women would complain because their fiancés wanted them to wear designer clothing and have their hair done by a celebrity stylist. So why did Mary feel as though she were losing herself?

"Mary? Are you all right?"

She knuckled away the single tear and took a deep breath. She was being silly. Silly and immature. "I'm sorry, Jonathan. I'm fine. Truly."

"Good." Relief was evident in his voice. Jonathan prided himself on running a smooth ship, as he called his corporation. "See you at the Pepper Tree in half an hour. And, Mary?"

"Yes?"

"Don't worry so much, darling. Everything's going to be just fine."

After they broke the connection, Mary went into her bedroom for a last-minute peek in the mirror. The sleek image that stared back at her seemed alien, bearing little resemblance to the Mary of a few short months ago. Her hair was several shades lighter than its natural honey-blond color, and this Mary wore her hair in a trendy, asymmetrical pageboy that skimmed her shoulders. This Mary's makeup was applied with a light but polished hand. And her simply cut suit cost more than the old Mary earned in a month.

She dabbed on a bit more lip gloss. Finally satisfied that Jonathan would approve, she picked up her handbag and left her hotel suite. Just two weeks ago, the same night that he'd proposed, Jonathan had urged her to move into a two-bedroom apartment suite in one of his hotels. He couldn't sleep nights, he'd said, worrying about her safety in that dingy studio she'd rented in Arlington.

Part of his reasoning, Mary acknowledged as she waited for the elevator, was Jonathan's eagerness to separate her from Mark Lester, the man she'd been seeing casually pre-Jonathan. Not that she could blame her fiancé. Mark hadn't handled the breakup very well, even though they hadn't had a serious relationship to start with.

Jonathan had been right, Mary admitted as she exited the elevator and strolled across the sumptuous lobby. Her moving into the hotel, and making a clean break from Mark, was best for everyone.

And she loved living in the Georgetown Regent Hotel. There was an old-world style and dignity about the red brick building that spoke of an earlier, more genteel era. The lobby and hallways were spacious and papered in pale gold brocade. Even the elevator cabs were made of fine cherry wood, the fixtures polished brass. Although Jonathan often bemoaned the fact that the Georgetown Regent was so small, and held so few guests, Mary loved the feeling of intimacy the hotel fostered. Only eight floors high, it was a far cry from the chrome and glass monstrosities that were popping up all over the metropolitan D.C. area.

She smiled at Rick Carey, the day desk manager, as she passed. Just walking through the lobby with its huge bowls of fresh cut flowers made her feel cheery and warm.

When she stepped outside into the balmy April afternoon, Mary still had nearly twenty minutes before she was due at the Pepper Tree. No need to take a taxi. She had plenty of time to walk and enjoy the warm spring weather.

Spring was absolutely her favorite time of year. Especially here in D.C. The shrill, icy winter had faded into memory, while the sultry heat of summer was still a distant promise. And because tourist season hadn't yet commenced in full force, one could still amble comfortably through the pleasant Georgetown neighborhood and admire the glorious old brick houses that lined the cobbled streets.

Mary had walked only a few blocks down Wisconsin Avenue, when a prickly sensation began inching up her spine. Keep walking. Don't turn around, she told herself. There was no one behind her, no one following. There never was, even though she'd checked often enough in the past few days. Yet ... yet she couldn't escape the feeling of unseen eyes following her every move. Boring into her with a white-hot intensity.

The day was suddenly, ominously, quiet. Only the click of Mary's heels on the pavement broke the menacing stillness. Then, she heard it. The soft thud of a footfall.

Someone *was* behind her. Close. Very, very close.

Mary eased her fingers into her handbag and pulled out her key ring. Gripping her door key tightly between her fingers, its sharp end pointing outward like a small but lethal weapon, she took a deep breath and whirled.

The quiet street was completely empty.

Mary waited for a long moment, willing her battering heart to stop hammering. What was wrong with her? When had she developed this ... this paranoia? But even as she argued with herself, she scanned the recessed doorways, looking for anything unusual. A shadow too deep. A curtain suddenly swaying.

Just as she started to walk on, a darting movement caught her peripheral vision. Someone was there! A shadowy form had scurried around the corner.

Was it someone hurrying to return to work or an unseen stalker? She rubbed her fingertips across her temple, as if somehow, she could summon the truth.

Lost in her confused thoughts, Mary stood for several minutes on the deserted sidewalk until the roar of a delivery truck broke her concentration. She glanced at her watch, and realized that her dawdling would make her late for her luncheon date. With a growl of vexation, she hurried toward the Pepper Tree.

Walking briskly, Mary tried to ignore that heavy curtain of apprehension that pressed in on her with each step. She forced herself not to look back, yet with every step, she half expected a hand to grab her. Once, unaccustomed to the high heels she wore, she stumbled on a crack in the sidewalk. Flailing her arms wildly in an effort to maintain her balance, she almost screamed as her hand encountered something solid.

A lamppost.

Mary hung on to the iron post for a moment until her wobbly knees stopped shaking. She was being ridiculous, working herself into a panic like that. She had to learn to ignore these sudden, eerie feelings that overtook her lately. Obviously, her intuition wasn't working and she was only scaring herself.

Taking deep, calming breaths as she walked toward her destination, she managed to release the fear and even regain a feeling of ease before she arrived at the Pepper Tree.

Inside the restaurant, Jonathan and his friends, Senator and Camille Castnor, were already seated. When the maître d' showed Mary to the table, she kissed Jonathan lightly on the cheek and slid into her chair. "Hi, everybody. Sorry I'm late."

Jonathan patted her hand. "No problem, dear. What happened? Did your taxi get snarled in traffic?"

A light flush crept up her cheeks. Jonathan had been bedeviling her for weeks about walking alone in the city. Mary was willing to make some changes in her life to please her fiancé, but she wasn't about to give up walking. Instead of answering directly, she took a drink of water and murmured, "The time just got away from me. Sorry."

In an effort to change the subject, she turned and teased the rotund senator seated across the table. "So, Brad, what's new with you? Have you voted yourself any new pay raises lately?''

"Mary!" Jonathan blurted out in consternation. "Really, dear, your sense of humor—"

"Oh, leave her alone, Regent. She's probably the only straight-talking person left inside the Beltway." Brad Castnor leaned back in his chair and roared with unabashed delight. "Voted myself any pay raises, that's rich! Wait till I tell that one up on Capitol Hill this afternoon."

Camille Castnor, the senator's wife, took a tiny sip from her glass of chardonnay and gave Mary a wan smile. "I hope I'm not speaking out of turn, Mary, dear, but after you and Jonathan are married, you will have to watch your...little witticisms. Someone might overhear and misunderstand."

It was on the tip of Mary's tongue to remind Camille that her husband's voting history was a matter of public record, and he had, in fact, been one of the ringleaders involved in the latest senate pay hike. She was saved from her own candor by the waiter who approached their table, glistening white cloth draped over his arm.

"May I bring *ma'mselle* a cocktail before her meal?"

"No, thank you. Water will be fine," Mary said, and picked up the menu.

After they ordered, the mood became more festive when Brad proposed a toast to celebrate the announcement of Jonathan and Mary's engagement.

"Ah, yes," Camille said, holding her glass for her husband to fill. "I saw the happy couple made the cover of *Newsweek*. I'm impressed." Her tone implied she was anything but impressed.

"Is that so?" Brad boomed. "Hope you saved it for me."

Camille smiled sweetly. "I cut the article out for my scrapbook, but you can read it. Let's have the toast now. To Jonathan and Mary, an unusual but adorable couple."

"So when's the big date?" Brad asked after the four-some had clinked glasses.

"We haven't set a date yet," Jonathan answered. "Probably sometime in the early fall. I was willing to wait until we could book the cathedral, but Mary said she'd rather have a small, more intimate ceremony."

Camille raised an eyebrow. "A small wedding means some important people will be left out. That could come back to haunt you at election time, Jonathan."

He shrugged. "Perhaps. But this was Mary's decision."

Mary set down her salad fork and took a deep, calming breath. "That's not fair, Jonathan. We discussed this and I thought we'd agreed."

He reached across the snowy linen cloth to take her hand in his. "Why so prickly? I was just having a bit of fun with you, dear. Your feathers are ruffling awfully easily today. Are you sure you're all right? I mean, you seem a bit... edgy."

He'd hit the nail squarely on the head, Mary conceded to herself. She *was* tense. That incident on Wisconsin Avenue was bothering her more than she wanted to admit. She hated to bring up the subject in front of the Castnors but felt she should at least explain her sudden moodiness.

Mary ran a fingertip around the rim of her water goblet, trying to find the right place to begin. "Do you remember last week when I told you that I had the oddest impression that someone was watching me?"

"Certainly." Jonathan smiled. "And I told you that I didn't want to let you out of my sight, so I was having my imagination follow you around."

Camille rolled her eyes. "Oh, God, that's just too, too sweet for words."

Ignoring Camille's sarcasm, Mary continued. "Anyway, I've had that feeling several more times since then. When I was walking here today, suddenly I just knew someone was behind me."

"Good heavens, Mary, I thought we discussed your walking around the city by yourself."

Mary raised her chin and stared into Jonathan's pale gray eyes, now dark with irritation. "Yes, Jonathan, we discussed it, but the day was so beautiful I decided to walk."

"But you see what happens? There probably *was* a mugger trailing you, just waiting for the right moment to snatch your purse. I wish you'd listen to me, Mary. I know this city."

"Jonathan, whether or not I should walk around Washington on my own isn't the issue here. Besides, you've said all along that this... this feeling is nothing more than premarital jitters."

The senator hooted. "I wonder what Freud would say about the symbolism—she's engaged to one man and fantasizing about being pursued by another!"

"That's not funny," Jonathan snapped.

"Sorry. It was meant to be."

Mary stifled a grin. She rather enjoyed the senator's sense of humor. People in politics tended to take themselves quite seriously, if her recent introduction into the Washington social strata was any indication. In fact, it sometimes seemed she and Brad Castnor were the only people within the Beltway who *had* a sense of humor.

Apparently satisfied that his friend's apology was sincere, Jonathan turned back to Mary. "Darling, exactly how often have you had this feeling of being watched?"

She closed her eyes and considered. "At least five or six different times. And they weren't all when I was out in public. Once when I was at the hairdresser's, I sensed someone staring at me through the front window."

Camille leaned forward. "Mary, how horrible! Why didn't you say something? I could have asked Henri to give you a more secluded booth in the rear."

Mary shook her head. "I can't go through life riding in taxis and hiding in the back rooms of beauty salons. If someone is following me, then I need to take some *reasonable* precautions." She placed a strong emphasis on reasonable. "In fact, I'm thinking about buying a gun."

Jonathan threaded his fingers together and stared at her. "I don't think that's wise. I believe statistics will bear me out here, Mary. Unless you're completely prepared to use that gun and perhaps take another person's life, owning a firearm is more of a liability than an asset. Besides, I really don't believe a weapon is necessary."

"I'm surprised to hear you say that, Regent," the senator interjected. "If someone is really following Mary, she could be in danger."

Jonathan shook his head. Rather than respond directly to his friend, he continued addressing his remarks to Mary. "Forgive me, my dear, but I'm still not convinced that what you've been experiencing isn't merely a case of nerves. But if someone *is* lurking around beauty shops, I'm sure it's that unemployed waiter you used to date."

Mary stifled a grin at Jonathan's description of her previous boyfriend. Despite her continued protests that she and Mark Lester had never had a serious relationship, Jonathan still acted jealous whenever Mark's name came up. And he knew perfectly well that Mark had only worked as a waiter a few nights a week to help cover his graduate-school expenses.

She couldn't seriously believe that Mark was skulking around behind her, watching her every move. He hadn't been that interested when they were dating.

Camille, as if annoyed that the conversation was centered on Mary's welfare, pointedly shifted the subject. "Well, I'm sure Mary will take every precaution just in case some lunatic is out there. But let's talk about the wedding! Mary, when do we get to go look at wedding gowns? You know, my dear, I'd be more than happy to help you plan the wedding. An event of this magnitude takes a certain amount of . . . social experience, you know."

The rest of their meal was punctuated with merriment as the two women discussed color schemes and honeymoon locales. The men groaned frequently and made obligatory macho comments about the cost of the upcoming nuptials exceeding the national debt.

Just before they broke up their lengthy luncheon, Jonathan raised his hand. "Brad, Camille, I asked the two of you to dine with us today for a reason. You're my oldest friends and I wanted both of you present for the occasion." Jonathan reached into his jacket pocket and extracted a small, blue velvet jeweler's box. He pushed the unopened case in front of Mary. "For my beloved bride. I'm afraid it pales compared to the purity of your smile, but it was the best I could do."

With a trembling hand, Mary opened the tiny box and gasped in astonishment. Nestled in the midnight blue lining was a twinkling diamond solitaire. Quite possibly the largest diamond she'd ever seen outside the Smithsonian. "Jonathan, it's lovely. But... but it's so... enormous!"

Immediately, his eyebrows dipped and a scowl took command of his handsome features. With an incredulous shake of his head, he asked, "Don't you like it?"

Mary lifted the glittering band out of the box and slipped it on her left ring finger. The stone was much larger, and more ostentatious than what she would have chosen for herself, but she knew that to Jonathan the size of the diamond was comparable to the depth of his devotion. She was swamped with a surge of tenderness for this complex man who'd breezed into her life and swept her into a world she'd never dreamed existed.

Raising her hand so everyone could see the exquisite stone dominating her delicate fingers, Mary turned to Jonathan. "It's the most impressive ring I've ever seen. Thank you so much, Jonathan. Truly."

His gloomy expression lightened immediately. "Only the best for my bashful bride."

Camille stood up and clasped her clutch bag. Her already pale face looked pinched and drawn. "All I can say is, if Mary wasn't being stalked by muggers before, she will be in the future. Jonathan, that ring is about one carat shy of being a diamond mine unto itself. Brad, are you ready to go? I have an appointment with my personal trainer at three."

Stuffing a last bite of dinner roll into his mouth, Brad heaved his bulk out of his chair. "I suppose you know, Regent, that I'll never hear the end of this. For the rest of my life, Camille is going to be griping about that 'chip' on Mary's finger."

Jonathan laughed and clapped the senator on the shoulder. "As my candid bride would say—vote yourself another pay raise and buy your wife a bigger one!"

With that rejoinder, the foursome parted company. At Jonathan's insistence, Mary accompanied him in the limousine until it dropped him off at his Alexandria, Virginia office. Then the chauffeur reversed his route, taking the George Washington Bridge back across the Potomac River, and threaded his way along the Washington streets. It was over an hour later before he finally dropped Mary off at the Georgetown Regent Hotel.

As she crossed the lobby, pausing only to check for mail at the desk, she paid scant attention to the luxurious surroundings. Her mind was on the details involved in planning a society wedding. She wondered what Jonathan would say if she told him she'd rather exchange vows in her mother's living room in northern Michigan than go through all the hoopla Camille had recited at lunch.

Reaching her apartment door, Mary fumbled in her bag for her key, unlocked the door and stepped across the threshold. Suddenly, she stopped.

There it was again. That creepy sensation of something being wrong. Out of place.

No, it couldn't be. Not here in her home.

Forcing herself to take several calming breaths, she turned to lock the door behind her, when her foot crunched on something on the carpet. Moving her foot, she saw that she'd stepped on an envelope that apparently had been slipped under the door.

Relief flooded through her.

Something *had* been out of place. Her subconscious had simply picked up on the envelope lying on the floor.

It looked like an invitation. Must have been hand-delivered, she mused. Plucking the envelope off the rug, Mary engaged the dead bolt and kicked off her shoes. She hated wearing high heels every day, but Camille insisted that a woman of "Mary's station" should always wear heels in public. Wriggling her toes in the thick pile carpet, Mary crossed into the living room and nestled on the shell pink damask sofa. She curled her feet beneath her and opened the envelope.

For a moment, she stared with perplexity at the single sheet of paper. After reading the brief message for the third time, she watched the paper slip from her numb fingers. Acting purely on instinct, Mary picked up the telephone and punched in Jonathan's office number.

"Oh, Ms. Wilder, it's you. Again." Robert Newland sighed, as if her telephoning twice in one day was a tremendous trial for him.

Swallowing a biting retort, she said quietly, "May I speak with Jonathan? It's quite important."

"Of course. I'm certain Mr. Regent won't mind another interruption."

"Thank you."

When Robert finally transferred her call, Jonathan's voice sounded harsh, impatient. "What is it, Mary? I'm in the middle of a meeting."

Briefly, her voice as cold and hard as the chunk of ice forming inside her, Mary told him about finding the note inside her apartment door.

"So? I'm afraid I've missed the point, dear. What did th
note say?"

Mary didn't have to retrieve the note to recite the ugl'
words cut from magazine articles and pasted onto the shee
of white bond paper. They were already branded into he
soul.

"Oh, Jonathan, it's so awful. It said, 'Life isn't like ;
fairy tale where Cinderella lives happily ever after wit)
Prince Charming. If you marry Jonathan Regent, you wil
not live happily... or ever after.'"

Jonathan sighed. "Damn that Mark Lester. I told you h·
was behind all this. Mary, darling, the idiot is only tryin;
to take his petty revenge because you dumped him. He ob·
viously wants to frighten you into breaking our engage
ment. Don't give him the satisfaction of responding to hi
childish game."

Mark? She could imagine Mark storming over to he
apartment and shouting at her through the door, but send
ing anonymous threatening letters? Mary desperatel'
wanted to believe it was Mark's wounded pride causing hin
to act so horribly and not some madman pursuing her. "D·
you think that's all it is? Mark, acting out?"

"Of course. Now, just throw the silly thing in the trasl
and forget all about it. And, by the way, sweet, I'm goin;
to have to cancel dinner tonight."

"Oh, Jonathan, I'd looked forward to it."

"Me, too, but it can't be helped. Have to take care o
business, you know. But if you're so upset that you reall'
feel I should cancel this meeting, then, of course..."

Mary's nerves were so jittery that she hated the idea o
spending the evening alone. Still, Jonathan had so mucl
responsibility with his corporation that she felt guilty ever
considering asking him to cancel his business appoint
ment. After taking a few seconds to rationally evaluate th·
situation, Mary responded, "Don't worry, Jonathan, I'l
be fine. You go ahead with your meeting. Maybe I'll call ;

friend from the bookstore. I may go to a movie, or something."

"If you think that's wise," he responded tartly. On several occasions, Jonathan had hinted that Mary should drop her friends from Arlington. He felt she should cultivate new friends in his social circle. Jonathan didn't understand that his social level was as unfamiliar to Mary as a foreign culture.

Interrupting her thoughts, Jonathan said, "What I think you should do, honey, is to take a long nap. Then soak in a bubble bath and order up room service. Leave Mark Lester to me."

Mary bit her lip. She didn't want Jonathan to get into a fight with Mark, but she also wanted to defuse this disturbing situation before it got worse. Reluctantly, she agreed.

"Good. Now, don't you worry your pretty little head another minute—"

"Jonathan! You make me sound like a Barbie doll."

There was a long pause before he continued, "I see you're still distraught. I can understand that. But really, dear, you have to stop finding offense in every minor comment. Now, you take a nice nap and I'll speak with you later."

Mary felt less than satisfied with the outcome of their discussion but she was too emotionally drained to continue. After double-checking the lock on the apartment door, she went into her bedroom and pulled the drapes shut.

That king-size bed *did* look awfully inviting.

Ten minutes later, Mary was fast asleep.

"AH, ARMSTRONG! Glad you're able to give us a hand on this." Robert Newland ushered the newcomer into the conference room. Tossing a thick manila file folder on the polished teak conference table, Jonathan's personal assistant raised a hand, offering Armstrong a seat.

The tall, slender man lowered himself into one of the swivel chairs and faced Newland. "What's up? Another possible industrial spy you want us to run a check on?"

Newland seated himself across from Armstrong and steepled his fingers. "No, nothing like that." He broke off and stared into space for a long moment, as if to gather his thoughts. "This is something that's more of a...a personal nature."

Armstrong leaned forward. "You know I can keep a confidence. Why don't you just spit it out?"

Newland reached for the file folder he'd thrown on the conference table and pulled a sheaf of papers from it. The first item he passed to Armstrong was a color photograph of Jonathan Regent and his fiancée—taken from the cover of *Newsweek* magazine. "Did you happen to see this?"

Trace Armstrong glanced at the photo. "I haven't been in Antarctica for the past two weeks. Of course I knew Regent was engaged. Kind of cute, isn't she?"

Newland raised an eyebrow. "Cute like a fox. Crafty, shrewd and devious are words that come quickly to mind."

"I gather you don't care for the woman. Why not?"

Newland raised a hand. "Oh, it's nothing personal, understand. It's just that I can recognize a brass-plated gold digger when I see one. And believe you me, this Mary Wilder is a gold digger with two shovels!"

Trace retrieved the magazine photo and took a second look at the woman. Interesting. From the soft, guileless expression the photographer had captured, he would never have suspected the sweet-faced Mary Wilder of being after Regent's money. "And you want me to dig around in her background, come up with a little dirt for your boss?"

Newland hesitated, then said, "Actually, that's not a bad idea. But let's hold off. Things may work out on their own."

"How's that?"

"It seems our sweet Mary is being followed. Stalked. Mr. Regent wants me to hire a full-time bodyguard for her. Of course, I thought of you."

Trace shrugged. "No problem. I can put one of my people on it right away. Or did you want round-the-clock protection?"

"No." Newland shook his head. "Right now, we think just someone to stay with her during the day. When she's out and about. She's staying at the Georgetown Regent. I think she's pretty secure at night, but, of course, we'd like you to double-check the security."

"Of course."

Newland drummed the tabletop with his fingertips. "The other thing is, I don't want one of your operatives on this job. I'd like you to handle it personally."

"Wait a minute!" Trace's head popped up. "You know that I don't do fieldwork anymore. I'm retired to a desk, remember?"

"I know, and normally I wouldn't ask you but . . ."

"But what?"

Newland paused, appearing to weigh his words. His slight, rabbitlike features were more pronounced than usual. "I want you to do more than protect the young lady. I want you to watch her, form your own opinion."

"On what?"

Again, Newland paused. He glanced around the large office as if searching for listeners hiding behind the empty chairs. "Remember, this is in confidence?"

Trace Armstrong frowned. "You don't have to ask, you know that."

Leaning forward, Newland continued in a conspiratorial manner. "I think the whole thing is some kind of a con. I don't think there's a stalker. I think Mary Wilder is playing a game. Manipulating Mr. Regent into moving up the wedding date so she can get her hooks into his money that much quicker.''

"I see," Trace said, not sure what else to add. He'd done a half-dozen jobs for Regent Hotels in the past year or so. They always paid well and promptly. Yet in all that time, Trace had never seen the slight personal assistant so riled. So agitated. This Mary Wilder must be some piece of work.

Trace rose to his feet. "I think I can free myself for a couple of weeks. Let's see what our Miss Wilder is up to.''

MARY HAD NO IDEA how long she slept, but the insistent ringing of the bedside phone finally brought her to wakefulness.

Wiping the sleep from her eyes, she yawned into the receiver. "Hello?''

"Mary? What took you so long to answer? I was starting to get concerned.''

"Oh, Jonathan. I decided to follow your advice and take a nap.''

"Still sleeping? Oh, well, it really doesn't matter. Listen, dear, I've been doing some more thinking about this problem. Even though I'm convinced that Mark Lester is our culprit, there's no sense taking chances. Anyway, Bob Newland knew of a private bodyguard who has an excellent reputation and I've decided to hire him.''

"A bodyguard? That seems a little extreme, don't you think?''

"More extreme than your buying a gun?''

"No," Mary admitted, "I guess not." But the very word *bodyguard* conjured up an image of a hulking brute about the size of a tractor trailer with bulging biceps and corded muscles where his neck should be. In the movies, bodyguards always had names like Moose or Tank. And their intelligence quotients usually matched their names. Nevertheless, right now she needed protection, not someone who read the *Encyclopedia Britannica* for pleasure.

As if taking her lack of argument for concurrence, Jonathan went on, "Anyway, this guy—his name's Armstrong, by the way—should be at your place any minute now. Tell him everything that's been going on. Show him the note. I realize I told you to throw it away, but you haven't yet, have you?"

"No, I haven't. But...do you really think I need a full-time bodyguard? It's not like I'm a rich rock star, or something."

Jonathan's sigh was long and deep. "You still haven't grasped the changes yet. Mary, sweet, you may not be wealthy but I am. This whole business stinks of Mark Lester, but I could be wrong. Someone could be using you to get to me. There could be a kidnapping in the works, who knows? I'll just feel better if I know you're protected."

Mary heaved a sigh of her own. She was the one who had kept insisting that her intuition be taken seriously. She was the one who kept jumping at every shadow. So why was she now trying to decline the very help she'd been asking for?

At that moment, the doorbell rang. Mary raised an eyebrow. To Jonathan she said, "Well, at least your bodyguard's prompt. What did you say his name was—Armstrong?"

"That's right. Be sure to see his identification before you let him in."

"Jonathan, I'm not a child," she said through clenched teeth. Honestly, sometimes his protective nature was a little confining. Before she could protest further, the doorbell buzzed again. And again.

This Armstrong might be prompt, but apparently patience wasn't one of his virtues.

After finally breaking the connection with Jonathan, Mary ran her fingers through her hair, then grabbed her robe off the bed and stuffed her arms into the sleeves as she hurried into the living room.

The hulking bodybuilder in the hallway had punched the doorbell twice more while she was en route.

"I'm coming, I'm coming," she called as she tiptoed up to look out the peephole. "Who is it?"

"Name's Trace Armstrong. Sent by a Bob Newland."

Mary couldn't see anything through the peephole but a vague shadow. She unlocked the dead bolt, but left the brass safety latch in place and peered out the small slit. The man stood between Mary's vision and the soft lighting behind him, casting his form into a backlit silhouette. But he sure didn't look as large as she'd imagined. "Could I see some identification, please?"

"At least you have some common sense," he grumbled as he handed her a plastic card case.

Mary looked at the state-issued identification card and shrugged. What was she supposed to be looking for? The card was issued to a Trace Armstrong and it *looked* official. Still, from his ID photo, Armstrong looked like an escaped felon. She passed his card case to him through the slit. "Just a moment," she murmured as she shut the door in order to undo the security latch.

The door opened. Expecting the muscle-bound hulk of her imagination, Mary started when the lean figure eased across her threshold. As the diffuse light from the overhead lamp illuminated his face, Mary's breath stopped. Trace Armstrong wasn't pretty-boy handsome, but he literally reeked of raw, masculine power.

Closing the door softly behind him, he thrust his hand in her direction. "Mary Wilder? I hear you've been having a little problem."

Mary slipped her hand into his and looked up, losing herself in the most incredible pair of eyes she'd ever seen.

Chapter Two

Trace Armstrong leaned casually against the doorframe. Mary was caught in time, her gaze locked with his. His hazel eyes, reflecting golden light like those of a panther, flickered over her, cataloging and assessing.

Trace wasn't as large a man as she'd expected. Instead of blatantly protruding muscles on an apelike frame, he was as lithe and sinewy as a jaguar.

Spare and rangy, yet wide-shouldered, he exuded a powerful catlike aura. A lush head of pitch-black hair fell in shaggy abandon, the ends curling against his collar. He wore black Levi's, a creamy shirt and a charcoal sport coat. Mary thought the sport coat was a rare concession; like a tiger wearing a bow tie. He looked uncomfortable and a little surprised every time he moved his shoulders.

When he tilted his head, Mary noticed sooty stubble darkening the bottom of his face, framing an angular, aggressive jawline. But his most arresting feature were those startling eyes that continued to study her with laserlike intensity.

There was a gritty hardness about the man, a rugged unsparing toughness that made other men fade by comparison. And made Mary's nerves jangle with an ominous premonition.

She wrenched herself away from her thoughts and finally recaptured her voice. "Please, come into the living room, Mr. Armstrong. We can talk there."

She led the way into the dark room and flicked on a table lamp. Then two. She needed to flood the room with enough light to dispel this trance that had ensnared her ever since she'd opened the door.

Mary curled in the corner of the sofa and waved a hand toward a pair of easy chairs a safe ten feet away. "Have a seat, Mr. Armstrong. I suppose you'll want to ask me some questions."

Moving with the casual grace of the jungle cat he resembled, Trace tread lightly toward her, poised on the balls of his feet as if ready to pounce on unsuspecting prey. Mary had the fleeting sensation of being a field mouse, caught in a trap, unable to escape the advancing danger.

Not taking the proffered chair, Trace asked without preamble, "Is that door the only access into this apartment?" His voice was low-pitched, velvety and shot with a hint of menace.

Mary pushed a wayward lock of hair from her eyes. "No. There's the balcony. But we're on the eighth floor. I can't imagine anyone scaling an eight-story brick wall to break in. There's also a connecting door to the suite next door, but—"

"Show me."

Taken aback by his brusque, almost rude manner, Mary decided two could play his game. Wordlessly, she uncoiled from the sofa and led the way down the hall, to her bedroom. Without turning on the light, she leaned in the doorway and pointed to a pair of white doors set in the pale blue wall. She didn't bother to mention that one door connected with the adjoining suite, the other led to her closet.

He strode through the maze of her shadowy bedroom, looking neither to the right nor left, yet avoiding the dresser, the foot of the bed, even the jumble of clothing she'd dropped on the carpet. Again, Mary had the image of a jaguar weaving its way through the underbrush without disturbing a single leaf.

Trace grasped one of the door handles and tugged, pulling open the closet door. Undeterred, he entered the small walk-in and made a careful inspection of the interior. Then he stepped back outside and tested the connecting door to the adjoining suite.

"We'll need to put a reinforcing dead bolt on this side of the door," he said. "A child could pick this lock."

Mary shook her head. "Jonathan—Jonathan Regent, my fiancé—owns this hotel. Both of these suites are reserved for his private use. No one ever uses the adjoining apartment. It's always empty."

Trace snorted in disbelief. "If that's true, it's even more dangerous."

Mary's forehead crinkled in confusion. "What do you mean?"

"Anyone who knows that room is never occupied would feel pretty secure about using it without permission. How many people know about it?"

Again, Mary shook her head in protest. "Hardly anyone."

With a cock of his eyebrow, Trace held up his hand and began ticking off possibilities on his fingertips. "Let's see, you know it's empty, and now I know, as well. Then, there's Mr. Regent and his key people. Not to mention the entire hotel staff, and probably most of their friends and relatives. Any other people live full-time in this hotel?"

Mary shrugged. "There are six penthouse apartments on this floor. Jon—my fiancé—retains two of them, there's an old man who has a long-term lease, and a Japanese corporation keeps the fourth for when their executives visit the area. That leaves two penthouse units for visiting dignitaries. You'd have to ask the manager about the other floors."

Nodding, Trace counted along on his fingertips. "So, in addition to the old man and the Japanese corporation, we could add Regent's friends and business associates, and former hotel employees, as well. All in all, I'd say more than a few people are probably aware of the easy access to that vacant apartment."

"Perhaps," Mary said quietly. "But none of those people would want to harm me."

He continued to watch her from across the room. The only illumination was the dusky light that seeped in through the window. Yet from the intensity of his stare, Mary had the strongest notion that Trace possessed powerful night vision like that of his feline counterpart.

Then, with a quick, decisive movement, he stepped forward. Within a few strides, he closed the distance between them. He eased his body close to hers in the doorway, bringing his face only inches away from hers. Inexplicably, her breath caught in her throat and her heart started to pound.

A shock of ebony hair fell over his forehead as he shook his head in disbelief. "You can't be so naive that you think you're safe in a city like Washington. Maniacs and stalkers thrive on sweet young things like you."

She wanted to cover her ears against his words. Against all the ugliness he'd seen in his life that was now mirrored in those gold-flecked eyes. Instead, she whispered, "I'm not that young. And certainly not that sweet."

Wordlessly, he raised a finger and reached toward her face as if to brush aside a strand of hair. For an eternal instant, his fingertip hovered just over her cheek. Mary's skin flamed and she stood breathless, anticipating his touch.

Then, with a sudden jerk, Trace yanked away his hand as if he'd been stung by a scorpion. "I'd say you were sweet. You have an air of virginal innocence that makes you vulnerable to that kind of creep. And you *are* an innocent, aren't you, Mary Wilder?"

When she refused to take his bait, Trace stalked past her, heading toward the living room and leaving a faint waft of musky scent in his wake.

She felt weak with fear. Nothing in her existence had prepared her for the strength of her reaction and the sure knowledge that this man held the key that could unlock her innermost thoughts and release her very essence.

But she was engaged to Jonathan. Steady, stable, reliable Jonathan. Even back in school, she'd never been tempted by the "bad boys" the way most of her female classmates had been. Mary had always been old for her years, more mature than her friends. This purely physical response to Trace had to be a case of delayed puberty. Raging hormones.

Hauling her rebellious pulse back under control, Mary followed Trace into the front of the apartment.

He was standing in the middle of the room, legs splayed widely, fists planted on his hips. "Let's check out the balcony."

Afraid her own voice might betray her, Mary mutely nodded and jerked open the drapes.

Twenty minutes later, Trace had managed to make Mary feel as if her apartment was wide open to anyone who wanted to trespass. Not only did he consider the balcony accessible, he also pointed out the false ceiling where someone could gain entry through the air-conditioning shaft.

Mary stood in the middle of her living room, her arms wrapped across her chest as if to protect herself from the horde of intruders Trace's graphic description had conjured up.

"Now, before I get the details about your stalker," Trace continued, "I need to lay down a few ground rules. For your protection. First, you're not to leave this apartment unless you're accompanied by either me or your fiancé, and preferably me. Second, I'm going to screen all your tele-

phone calls and mail. I'll give you my beeper number in
case anything happens when I'm not around—use it. Then
we're going to arrange a telephone code system so that
anyone calling—''

"Just a minute, Armstrong." Mary held up her hand,
halting him in midsentence. Trace's abrupt manner and
bossiness had finally broken through the fog she'd been
wallowing in since Jonathan's phone call had snatched her
from sleep.

"The first thing I'm going to do," she declared, "is go
in the kitchen and make myself a cup of coffee. After that,
we can either sit down like civilized human beings and discuss which of your *suggestions* I may or may not want to
implement to enhance my security. But what we're *not* going to do, Mr. Armstrong, is continue this little power play
where you try to scare the living daylights out of me and
then start telling me how I'm going to live my life. Do I
make myself clear?"

"What's clear is that you're the one who's apparently in
danger—not me. You arranged for your sugar daddy to hire
me, Ms. Wilder. You need me, not the other way around."

Sugar daddy! Mary's palm itched with a sharp need to
slap the knowing smirk off this Neanderthal's handsome
face. Wrapping her anger in a coating of sarcasm, she said
slowly, "Nevertheless, Mr. Armstrong, my 'sugar daddy'
will be paying your salary. *If* I decide to engage your services—and that's a very big if. Now, I'm going to fix that
cup of coffee. Should you still be here when I return, then
we'll discuss the possibility of your employment—on my
terms."

With that she whirled and strode out of the room in what
she hoped was a confident, assured manner.

Trace stood in the living room, moored in her wake.
Whew! Ms. Mary, Mary Quite Contrary had a long fuse,
but once it was ignited, that woman went off like a neu-
tron bomb. Not that he hadn't deserved the resulting ex-

plosion, Trace thought ruefully. From the moment Bob Newland had referred to his employer's fiancée as "something of a gold digger," Trace had felt the first pang of enmity.

Too often in this business, he'd seen rich, powerful men brought down by "helpless" women whose only goals were to separate their lover from his money. Careers, families and even lives had been lost when private affairs suddenly became public fodder.

Once, Trace had guarded a presidential candidate whose career was ruined by a single indiscretion. He'd been a decent man, and Trace had been an unwilling witness to the man's shame and humiliation.

Remembering that sad time, Trace's first instinct had been to turn down this assignment. That would have been the smart thing to do. And he would have if he hadn't been so busy playing head games with himself that he'd blotted out common sense.

Still, there was no denying that by the time he'd arrived at this penthouse suite, he had built up a full head of steam.

Then Mary Wilder had opened the door and her ingenuous face had pushed him over the edge.

You should have walked out right then, Armstrong, Trace chided himself. He was no match for wide brown eyes glowing in an angelic face. Eyes that could make the strongest man bend to their will.

It wasn't too late. He should leave right now. He could send any one of a half-dozen competent ex-secret service agents to Bob Newland for this job. But even as the thought whispered through his mind, Trace knew he wouldn't do it.

Mary Wilder was afraid. He'd seen it in the faint blue smudges beneath her eyes. Seen it in the way she kept hugging herself, as if to ward off harm. Trace had seen the fear even when she'd lifted her chin in defiance just before she'd darted into the kitchen.

Whatever he felt about Mary's motives in becoming engaged to the wealthy and much older Jonathan Regent, one
thing was clear: someone was terrorizing the bride-to-be.
And Trace had had his fill of a world where the bullies ruled
by intimidation.

Turning on his heel, he followed Mary into the narrow
galley-style kitchen. "Got any more of that coffee?"

To her credit, she didn't gloat at his capitulation. Taking a stoneware mug from a wooden stand, she raised a
questioning eyebrow. "How do you take it?"

"Black."

She handed him a steaming mug and pointed to a plate
of sandwich fixings on the counter. "I didn't have supper.
Would you care for a sandwich?"

Trace's salivary glands shifted into overdrive. He hadn't
eaten dinner, and had only taken a couple of bites of a
greasy burger at lunch. When *was* the last time he'd sat
down and eaten a complete meal? Sharing a late snack with
Mary suddenly sounded very appealing. "Here," he said,
setting his mug on the counter. "Let me give you a hand."

While Mary rustled up plates and condiments, Trace
slapped together a small platter of sandwiches. By silent
accord, they carried their bounty into the dining room and
settled across from each other at the glass-topped table.

For a time, they ate without speaking. Then, as Mary
leaned back to sip her coffee, Trace polished off his third
sandwich and wiped his mouth on the soft linen napkin.
With a replete sigh, he picked up his own mug. "So, tell me
about your stalker."

After a long pause, Mary lowered her gaze and recited
dully. "I don't really remember the first time I felt like I was
being followed. A couple of weeks ago. Just after Jonathan and I announced our engagement."

"How many times has it happened? That feeling of
someone watching you?"

She frowned. "Five. Six. I'm not really sure."

"What did you do about it?"

"I talked it over with Jonathan and he said I should ignore it."

Trace's coal black eyebrow lifted. "Ignore it? Strange reaction for a man whose future wife is being threatened."

Feeling it her duty to defend Jonathan, Mary sat up, and insisted, "Oh, no! It wasn't like that. I mean, you see, at first Jonathan thought it was just my nerves."

"Are you prone to nervousness?"

"No, but... but so much has happened in my life so quickly that... that I haven't really been myself lately."

"I see. So if Mr. Regent thought you were a little overwrought, what changed his mind?"

Mary raised her hand, lifting a thick fall of hair and letting it drift through her fingers back onto her shoulder. "Today I was certain I saw someone. Jonathan seemed to believe me, but..."

"But what?" Trace prodded.

"Jonathan was convinced that if I *was* being spied on, that it was an old, uh, friend of mine. Mark Lester."

"Friend? Or old boyfriend?"

Mary shrugged. "We dated, but nothing serious."

It was on the tip of Trace's tongue to ask if Mary and this Mark Lester had been lovers, but he sensed that she'd hate the intrusion. Besides, why was he so interested in her love life, anyway?

Instead, he asked, "Is this the kind of stunt your former boyfriend would pull?"

Mary squirmed in her chair, looking decidedly uncomfortable. Again, Trace had the impression that she was a very private woman, unused to divulging details of her personal life. Finally, she looked up and slowly shook her head. "I don't think so. I mean, Mark was really angry when I broke off the relationship, but I think that was just his pride."

"Nobody likes being dumped."

"I guess you're right," Mary agreed. "And Mark does have an overgrown ego."

Trace reached into his pocket and pulled out a small black notebook and ballpoint. "Do you know Mark Lester's address? Phone number? What's he do for a living?"

Clearly relieved by Trace's professional manner, Mary filled in the details about Mark.

When she was finished, Trace flipped the notebook closed and dropped it on the table. He finished off his now-cool coffee and pushed the mug aside. "Did you ever actually see anyone when you thought you were being followed?"

Mary's forehead furrowed in concentration. "I'm not sure. A couple times I caught a blurred movement out of the corner of my eye. I had the impression of someone ducking around a corner or into a doorway."

So far, all he had to go on were some shadows Mary might or might not have seen. Jonathan Regent was a busy man, obsessively ambitious, according to Bob Newland. Was this shadow man of Mary's her way of trying to get more of her fiancé's attention?

Lost in thought, Trace rubbed his chin with his fingertips and was surprised to encounter stubble. Surely he'd shaved that morning. Great. Now he was forgetting to eat *and* shave. Why the hell couldn't he get his life back on track?

Not wanting to deal with his own screwed-up life, he turned again to the woman who was watching him with quiet absorption. "Okay, Mary, now I want you to think very carefully about the last two weeks. Close your eyes, it might help. Try to recall where you were and what you were doing when these events occurred. Visualize all the people standing around. Was there anyone, a bum, a traffic cop, anyone you can remember seeing on more than one occasion?"

She hesitated, then followed his instructions. The moment her eyes drifted shut, it was as if she had removed a lovely mask, revealing a vulnerability that was almost painful to behold. Mary Wilder was a woman without artifice, without contrivance. Her lessening fear and her growing confidence in Trace were clearly etched on her features. The inner beauty, inner honesty she had unwittingly exposed was rare among the women of Trace's acquaintance, and utterly beguiling.

He watched her mobile face as the memories flitted through her mind. Suddenly, she chewed her upper lip and frowned. "Yes! A man."

Her eyes popped open and she stared at Trace in wonderment. "I remember now. I didn't really get a good look at him, or even particularly notice him at the time, but I saw the same man at least twice. Once when I was coming out of Jonathan's office in Alexandria. Then, a few days later, that same man was standing across the aisle from me in a department store."

Trace reached across the table and enveloped her hand in his. She had good mental recall—if it wasn't her imagination painting a very vivid picture. "Now, take your time. Don't rush it and don't let your imagination manufacture any details. But try to remember everything you can about this man. How tall was he? What color hair? What was he wearing? How do you know it's the same man?"

Leaving her hand tucked in his, Mary closed her eyes again and tried to conjure up a mental picture of the man who'd looked so out of place in the lingerie department of Woody's. "He was wearing blue jeans. Old jeans, patched. And work shoes. The kind that lace up."

"You're doing just fine, Mary. Now keep that picture in your mind. Don't open your eyes." Trace lowered his voice to a smooth monotone so as not to divert her attention. "Try to visualize his features. Can you remember what he looked like? Did you see his face?"

Shaking her head pensively, Mary murmured, "No. I couldn't."

"Why couldn't you?"

"The bill of his cap covered his face. That's it!" Her eyes blinked open. "That's why I noticed him. It wasn't the work clothes. He was wearing a cap, like a baseball player. But it wasn't a Redskins cap or one from the Baltimore Orioles. You see those all the time around here. No, this one was different but I can't remember—"

"What color was it?"

"Purple," she answered promptly. "Bright purple with a huge gold insignia. Some kind of animal, I think, but I can't really recall." Her eyes darkened with disappointment.

Trace patted her hand. "Don't push it. It'll come back to you when you're not concentrating so hard. You did just fine. One last question, then we'll move on. Think about this man's overall size and appearance. Could he have been Mark Lester? Maybe wearing work clothes as a disguise?"

Her eyebrows dipped as she considered his question. "I suppose so. He was about the same size as Mark but I never had the impression that it was Mark. I just don't know."

Trace picked up his pen and scribbled a note in his pad. "That's okay, at least we know not to rule him out. Tomorrow I'll start a background check on Lester."

She cocked her head. For the first time, he noticed a faint inch-long scar running from the edge of her upper lip into her cheek. Somehow, the small imperfection only highlighted her gentle loveliness. Made her more vulnerable, softer. He had an urge to touch his lips to the scar, and kiss away the long-ago pain of her injury.

Mary must have felt his gaze fasten on her lip because she raised a hand to her mouth, covering the scar. The gesture was almost automatic and told him how sensitive she was to the flaw.

"How do you go about checking into a person's background?" she asked. "Are you like a private investigator?"

He smiled mirthlessly. "Not really. But I've still got a few friends with connections. Computer connections."

"Oh. So, how does one become a bodyguard, in the first place? Most boys want to be a doctor or fireman when they grow up. Maybe a policeman. Did you always want to be a bodyguard?"

"No. I wanted to be a Mafia hit man or a jewel thief," Trace answered with a straight face. "Just joking," he added when he saw her stricken expression. "Actually, I planned on going into the FBI after college but somehow I got sidetracked and ended up in the secret service."

"Why did you leave?"

Trace felt his back go rigid. How had they meandered into such dangerous territory? He didn't want to talk about the near-fatal shooting that had left him lying in a hospital bed for months, wondering if he'd ever walk again. Hell, he didn't even want to *think* about those endless weeks. But her words had already evoked the nightmare. A bead of sweat tickled his forehead as he vividly recalled the agonizing hours of physical therapy. And the million disappointments before the first small flare of hope.

Now, he felt Mary's eyes on him, studying him with curiosity. After nearly two years he should be able to come up with some cute quip to explain his early retirement. He'd even thought of a cocky rejoinder—something about being shot by a jealous president. Trace should be able to laugh the whole thing off and keep his private hell locked away, but he couldn't find the bantering tone necessary to pull it off. When he finally answered, his voice was tense and guarded. "Retired. Disability." He stood up.

All business once again, he asked her for the anonymous letter she'd found earlier.

The note Mary handed him was typical of hundreds of others Trace had seen during his eight years with the secret service. The words were cut from magazines and newspapers and glued to cheap paper.

The perp in this case, however, fancied himself witty. Usually, threatening letters, written by depressed and deeply disturbed people, were terse and to the point. This jerk used word games—*the bride won't live happily*—or *ever after*—to intimidate his victim as if he was enjoying himself.

Trace dropped the note onto the table and looked up into Mary's trusting eyes. He felt unaccountably compelled to reassure her. He couldn't offer any real hope, so he resorted to platitudes. "Sounds innocent enough. Mr. Regent's probably right, just your ex-boyfriend out to wreak a little revenge."

"Oh, do you think so? Truly?"

He couldn't lie—not when she asked him directly like that. "I hope so, Mary. That's the best I can tell you right now."

The crestfallen expression that claimed her features lasted only a moment. Proving herself a true Pollyanna by nature, she immediately forced a quavery smile. "But you'll be able to stop this creep, won't you? Can't you send that note to the FBI? I took a tour of FBI headquarters, it's amazing what they can do with a shred of evidence like this."

Trace ignored her first question and responded to the easier one. "I'm afraid we can't involve the FBI in this. No federal laws have been broken and no real harm's been done. Besides, I doubt if their lab could be much help."

Mary tapped the tabletop with an impatient fingertip. "Why not? During the tour, they told us how they'd tracked down criminals with partial fingerprints and DNA testing, and ink samples and...and all kinds of tiny clues no one would ever think about."

Civilians! They were so used to seeing cases neatly resolved in an hour on television that they couldn't understand that criminal investigation was rarely as clear-cut in real life. Trace hated to be the one to do it, but Mary was about to get a lesson in reality.

Choosing his words with care, he began. "First of all, fingerprints. How many people handled this envelope? You? The doorman? Did the perp bring it to your room himself or did he tip a bellboy to slip it under the door?"

"I don't know," she murmured.

Trace shook his head emphatically. "It doesn't matter, anyway. That letter's been handled so much, any prints it may have held have probably been obliterated."

"I'm sorry," Mary said. "I never thought about fingerprints when I opened it."

He smiled to soften the implied rebuke. "You had no way of knowing. You also mentioned ink samples. What ink? The guy cut the words out of magazines. As for DNA testing—what're we going to test? Okay, *maybe* our letter-writing friend actually licked the envelope and left traces of saliva. Do you have any idea how expensive DNA testing is? The amount of time it takes to process? More important, we have to have a suspect to compare against the results—assuming we get any conclusive evidence to begin with!"

"But what about Mark?" she argued.

Trace was impressed. Mary wasn't going to give up easily. He was glad she had a strong fighting spirit. She was going to need it.

He stood up and slipped the note into his pocket. "Mark Lester is certainly a viable suspect. But even knowing that, what can we do? Go ask your ex-boyfriend to lick an envelope and give it to us so we can charge him with harassment?"

Mary pushed away from the table, her dark eyes flashing. "Your sarcasm is cute, but unnecessary. What do you propose we do, Mr. Know-It-All, wait until he tries to kill me?''

Trace busied himself with recapping his ballpoint and closing his notebook. He couldn't look into Mary's eyes just yet for fear she'd see the truth.

Nearly ten years of protecting people who were targets of deranged criminals had taught Trace one lesson: there really *wasn't* much that could be done until and unless the criminal actually got bored with writing letters and decided to follow through with the threats.

Mary Wilder was absolutely right. Other than increasing security, there wasn't much more they could do.

The next move was the stalker's.

Chapter Three

The easy camaraderie Trace and Mary had enjoyed over their sandwiches had vanished like morning mist on the White House lawn. She tried a couple of times to draw him out, to find that genial companion of a few short moments ago. It was no use. Trace had retreated into his shell and locked the door firmly behind him.

He paced across the living room, as if suddenly ill at ease, pausing only to check and recheck the patio-door lock. His charcoal jacket swung away from his hip, and Mary saw for the first time that he was wearing a gun.

She felt weak and trembly all of a sudden. If Jonathan had hired an armed guard, then surely she'd been underestimating the danger. Suddenly, Mary was very glad to have the arrogant Mr. Armstrong around.

When he started toward the front door, she asked, "Are you leaving?"

He paused with his hand on the doorknob and nodded. "For tonight. So far, Mr. Regent's authorized me to accompany you only when you're outside this apartment. He doesn't feel that you need twenty-four-hour-a-day protection. He thinks you'll be safe here as long as you keep the door bolted."

"And what do *you* think?" Mary asked, trying once again to reestablish the earlier rapport she'd felt with this enigmatic man.

Trace shrugged. "He's probably right. I'll check the roof access before I leave the hotel tonight, and tomorrow I'll get a dead bolt for that adjoining suite. You should be safe enough for tonight. Besides, we don't have any reason to believe this kook is going to do any more than send nasty letters."

Mary crossed her arms and stifled a yawn. Even after that long nap she'd taken, she was still exhausted. "So, what's the game plan for tomorrow?"

"I'll be back early in the morning. You just go ahead with your normal plans and whither thou goest, I'll tag along. Then, in the evenings, I'll lock you up in your tower like Rapunzel."

"Sounds exciting. Do I ever get to let down my hair?"

Trace groaned and walked to the door. "On that really awful pun, I'll say good night. And, Mary—"

"I know, I know. Lock the door behind you."

He nodded and disappeared into the hallway without a backward glance.

She followed behind him and bolted the door, then flipped on the security latch. Turning around, Mary faced the empty foyer. How much larger, and lonelier, her apartment seemed without Trace here. She went through the rooms turning off lights, and tried to ignore the way Trace's presence still dominated her thoughts.

Now, she understood the lure of the perpetually bad boy. Suddenly, she felt more alive than she'd ever felt in her life. Every nerve ending was sparking. But all that raw, blatant sensuality he exuded was bad news. *He* was bad news. Men like Trace deprived a woman of her reason and self-control. If Mary had a lick of sense, she'd call Jonathan right now and demand a replacement bodyguard. An old one. Or a fat one. Even a muscle-bound hulk. Anybody but Trace Armstrong.

But even as the thought flitted through her mind, Mary knew she wouldn't make that phone call.

LIKE A RECURRING nightmare, a thunderous pounding on the apartment door awakened Mary. She sat up with a groan. It seemed as though she'd just dozed off.

"Just a minute," she called as the knocking continued nonstop. "Hold on."

She stumbled into the bathroom for her robe and took a moment to quickly brush her teeth before hurrying down the hall to the front door.

She already knew who was at the door; only Trace's "knock" sounded like a battering ram. After peeking through the peephole, she unlocked the dead bolt, disengaged the security latch and opened the door. Trace surged in, two large containers of what smelled like fresh coffee in each hand.

"Took you long enough," he grumbled in lieu of a greeting. "I was starting to worry."

Mary shoved her hair out of her eyes. "What time is it?"

He balanced one container of coffee on top of the other and looked at his watch. "Quarter after seven."

"In the *morning?*" Mary squeaked.

"Yeah, I'm late." His eyes raked her length, from unkempt hair to bare feet. "Sorry to get you up so early, Your Highness. But some of us have to work for a living."

Arghh! He was starting already. The last thing she felt like was more sniping and sarcasm. She'd hoped he would have slept off his surly mood of last night, but no such luck.

Not up to his brand of repartee this early in the morning, she muttered, "I'm going back to bed. You stay out here and . . . and continue working."

She went to her bedroom and slumped into bed, pulling the mound of blankets on top of herself. But after ten minutes of turning, tossing and punching the pillow, Mary gave up. It was impossible to get to sleep with Trace just on the other side of the bedroom wall.

BY EIGHT O'CLOCK, Mary was seriously considering shooting Trace Armstrong.

He hadn't even given her time to get dressed before he started making his demands. He wanted a key to her apartment, the addresses and phone numbers of all her friends and a list of every man she'd dated since she'd moved to the D.C. metropolitan area.

For the past half hour, Trace had prowled around her apartment, asking rapid-fire questions and muttering under his breath. Finally, her patience snapped.

She slammed her coffee mug on the counter and stalked into the living room. He'd gone out onto the balcony and was staring into the distance with a pair of binoculars.

Following him out into the chilly morning, Mary said, "I don't know how you expect me to answer you when you're grousing under your breath and then walking off in mid-sentence. What are you griping about now?"

He pointed toward two high-rise apartment complexes across the park. "Do you realize that you'd be an easy target for anyone over there with a high-power rifle? We're going to have to keep your blinds drawn all the time."

"Are you serious? You expect me to live in the dark and only leave my cavern if I'm escorted by you?"

"Yeah," he said. "And you shouldn't go out any more than necessary."

Mary snatched the binoculars out of his hand. She lifted them to her eyes and adjusted the focus. To her amazement, occupants of apartments a quarter mile away appeared as close as if they were standing on her patio. She shoved the glasses back at Trace. "My God, I feel like a Peeping Tom with those things. We'll be lucky if someone doesn't call the police on *us!*" She turned and stalked back inside.

Trace followed on her heels and pulled the vertical blinds closed behind him.

With an exasperated sigh, Mary switched on all the lamps and plumped down on the sofa. Scowling at the man who was now testing the ceiling tiles, she asked, "When do I get my bulletproof vest?"

Trace glanced down at her. "Do I detect a note of sarcasm in your tone this morning, Ms. Wilder?"

"If I had a hammer, you'd detect a knot on your head!"

"Tsk, tsk. A bad temper and prone to violence. Not a good combination."

The man was maddening. He refused to acknowledge what drastic sacrifices he was asking her to make in her lifestyle. Worse, he flicked aside her complaints as easily as if he were swiping aside an irritating mosquito. Nothing seemed to ruffle him.

Trace glanced at his wristwatch. "All right, Mary Sunshine, what have you got planned for the day?"

She looked down at her disheveled appearance. "Take a shower and change my clothes."

"Good start," he agreed. "And then?"

"I have some phone calls to make this morning. Then I don't have anything scheduled until after lunch. I need to meet with a bridal consultant at two this afternoon."

Trace's eyes darkened inexplicably. "Do you have a car?"

"No. If I don't walk, I generally take a cab or Jonathan sends his limo."

"Not anymore," he told her. "Do you have an assigned parking spot in the hotel garage?"

She shrugged. "I imagine so. Why?"

"Because I'm going to park my car downstairs. We'll take it when we need to go out. It's too unpredictable having to rely on public transportation."

Mary nodded. For the first time, one of his suggestions sounded reasonable rather than paranoid. "I'll call the desk and arrange for you to pick up a parking pass."

"Good. Since you have your morning planned here in the apartment, I'm going to run some errands. I'll pick up the dead bolt for the connecting door and then I'm going to arrange for a locksmith I know to come install a special lock on that glass patio door."

With a slow shake of her head, she said, "Isn't that overkill, Trace? I mean, do you seriously think someone's going to climb up seven balconies—outside occupied rooms—to reach mine? Without being seen?"

"No, I don't think someone is going to scale the building, and no, I don't think I'm being paranoid. I'm concerned someone could gain access to the roof and drop a rope over the side and slide down *one* floor to your balcony."

"Oh. I didn't think of that."

Instead of the snide rejoinder she expected, he replied with a hint of modesty, "Well, this is what I do for a living. No one would expect you to think of things like that."

He slipped on his windbreaker and started for the door. "Are you sure you feel okay about staying here alone for a while?"

She rolled her eyes. "Yes, I imagine I can struggle through by myself for a couple hours."

"You'd better have another cup of coffee. I think you need the caffeine."

Mary slammed the door behind him and snapped the bolt with unnecessary force. What a pain in the... The man was more irritating than sand in a bathing suit.

She sighed and started for the bathroom. Turning the hot water on full force, she stripped off her robe and nightgown. She stepped under the relaxing, steamy flow and thought about Trace Armstrong—and her reaction to him. What was it about that man that made her want to punch his lights out one minute, only to find herself laughing at his droll humor the next?

It wasn't just that he was annoying. Bob Newland was annoying and she didn't like him.

Nor was it simply that Trace was so drop-dead gorgeous that he made her tummy wobbly. Heck, Jonathan was a very attractive man in his own right. More sophisticated. And certainly more...gentlemanly. But, although Jonathan's kisses sometimes made her pulse race, she'd never felt that warm liquid rush in her insides when Jonathan walked into a room.

There was no doubt about it—Trace Armstrong was a sorcerer, a snake charmer. And if she wasn't careful, Mary knew she could easily succumb to his brand of magic.

A harsh shaft of guilt shot through her. She was acting and talking to herself as if she were unattached, available. There was no need to concern herself with Trace's raw magnetism, because she was promised to another man. She was going to marry Jonathan Regent.

Grabbing the shampoo bottle, Mary poured a lavish amount on her hair and kept repeating the little speech she'd just given herself. Maybe she could convince herself it was the truth.

After finishing her shower and blow-drying her hair, Mary went into the bedroom and deliberately selected the most unattractive outfit she owned. One of those tweed skirt and mud-colored sweater combinations she'd worn most of her life. Before Jonathan and Camille had helped transform her. Somehow, Mary hoped the unflattering outfit would make her feel less attractive, and maybe help repress her purely hormonal responses to Trace.

She'd just walked into the front of the apartment, when the doorbell buzzed. She frowned. She wasn't expecting anyone, and the hotel maids always serviced Mary's apartment in the afternoon.

Feeling a chill of apprehension, she padded softly to the door and looked out the peephole. Camille Castnor's distorted image stared back.

Mary quickly opened the door and stepped aside. "Camille! Come in, please. Did we have plans that I've forgotten?"

Camille entered the foyer and smiled. Even before nine in the morning, not a glimmering blond hair was out of place. Her black Donna Karan suit was perfectly suited to Camille's tall, slender form. A simple gold brooch was her only adornment. Even though Mary thought the pale sable coat draped over her shoulders was a bit of an overstatement for a warm spring day, Camille was, as always, perfectly attired.

Mary sorely wished she'd chosen a different outfit. Even when she looked her very best, she felt frumpy beside Camille.

"I'm sorry to disturb you so early," Camille said with her perfectly modulated voice. "And, no, we didn't have an appointment. Actually, I had a yen to go over to Alexandria for some shopping. There's a marvelous new boutique that Julie Stennard says is just too divine. Anyway, after I dropped the senator off, I decided on the spur of the moment to see if you wanted to go."

Camille was the only person Mary had ever met who habitually referred to her husband by his title rather than his given name. "I'm afraid I have other plans today, Camille, but thanks for asking." Leading the way into the living room, Mary asked, "Can I get you a cup of coffee? I was just about to make myself some toast."

Camille took a few steps inside, then hesitated. "I'd love to, but maybe I'd better pass. As I said, I just stopped by on the spur of the moment. My car's in the loading zone out front. Are we all still on for dinner tonight?"

"As far as I know," Mary said.

"Then I'll see you tonight. Have you and Jonathan decided yet on a date for the big event?"

"No. I imagine we'll pick one pretty soon."

"Well, my dear, you'd better get moving. You cannot imagine the million details we'll have to attend to right away. Besides, you can't even book the reception hall or the church until you've decided on a date."

"I know. And I promise, we'll make a decision soon." Mary opened the door and Camille walked out into the corridor.

"Oh, I almost forgot!" Camille reached into her oversize handbag and extracted a package. "This is for you."

"Why, thank you!" Mary said, totally surprised. She'd recognized the extravagant packaging immediately. It was her favorite brand of chocolates. The forty-dollar a pound variety. She had always thought that Camille merely tolerated her because of Jonathan. And here Camille was, giving her a gift. What a lovely gesture. Mary made an immediate mental vow to try her best to warm up to Camille Castnor. "Please, let me fix you some coffee and let's dive into this box."

"No, thanks." Camille laughed. "I've been a chocoholic ever since Jonathan bought *me* my first box of Splendoras. If I eat even one, I'll snatch the entire package out of your hands."

"I know what you mean. But I certainly appreciate this."

Camille pulled her sable around her shoulders, and slipped her purse under her arm. "No trouble. I'll see you this evening then."

"Bye."

Mary locked the door and carried the beautiful goldfoiled box into the dining room. Her lips curved in an eager smile.

Feeling like a naughty child, Mary untied the midnight blue ribbon. She hadn't even known such things as Splendora Chocolates existed before Jonathan presented her with a two-pound box on their second date. It had been love at first bite.

Mary could hear her mother's voice in her head, chiding her for even thinking about eating candy for breakfast. Laughing out loud, she decided that was one of the best things about being an adult—she could darn well eat chocolate for breakfast if she wanted. And she wanted.

Mary lifted the sparkling gold lid and selected one from the center—hazelnut liqueur, her favorite.

Carrying her gilded box into the living room, she curled up in her customary spot in the corner of the sofa and bit into the delicious confection. Heaven. Pure unadulterated heaven. Although a little sweeter than she remembered. But then, she'd never eaten Splendora Chocolates this early in the morning before.

Feeling totally decadent, Mary decided to delay her phone calls for a while. She topped off her coffee from the carafe on the end table, picked up a half-finished novel and draped a woolly afghan over her lap. One hour. She'd be a sloth for just one hour.

Mary licked a smear of dark chocolate from her fingertip. She could do serious damage to this box of delight in an hour.

FOR SOME inexplicable reason, Trace found himself whistling as he ambled down the hallway to Mary's apartment. In complete contrast to his initial reaction to this assignment, Trace found himself looking forward to the next few weeks.

Since he'd gone into the private security business, he'd found himself guarding a half-dozen beautiful women. But their beauty had all been artifice. Faces surgically sculpted, individually applied false eyelashes, and fake nails an inch long. Mary Wilder, on the other hand, was a refreshingly natural beauty.

Twice now, he'd seen her looking...*scruffy* was the kindest word he could think of. But she hadn't apologized or made excuses. She was who she was. That was a rare quality in a Washington socialite.

It was just too damn bad she had that five-pound diamond on her ring finger.

Burdened with packages of security devices, Trace paused outside her apartment. Lifting his foot, he lightly kicked the bottom of the door. "Mary! Open up. It's Trace."

There was no answering grumble from the other side of the door.

Deciding that she must not have heard him, he leaned over and punched the doorbell with his elbow.

Still, a full minute passed and Mary didn't respond.

Annoyance rapidly mutating into concern, Trace dropped his bags and fumbled in his pocket for the key she'd given him. For once, he hoped she'd forgotten his standing order to keep the security bolt engaged.

While he was feeling for the loose key, Trace used his other hand to pound on the door. "Mary? Are you all right? Answer me!"

Not a sound emerged from the too-quiet suite.

Finally finding the key, Trace inserted it into the lock and pushed against the door. Thankfully, Mary *had* neglected to lock the security bolt and the door swung open.

Trace stepped inside and paused. "Mary? Are you in here?"

Only silence greeted his call.

Easing the door closed behind him, Trace drew his service revolver from the concealed holster beneath his windbreaker.

His senses were on full alert now and he moved into the dim apartment one careful step at a time. Slowly, stealthily, he made his way into the living room. Empty. As were the dining room and kitchen.

His back almost skimming the wall, Trace started down the hall to Mary's room. Stopping outside the guest bedroom, he eased open the door. Dropping low, he jumped into the room, his gun held at arm's length. After a quick but thorough check of the vacant room, he headed back toward Mary's bedroom.

Her door was half-open and he could see that her rumpled bed was unoccupied. Using his shoulder, he pushed the door fully open, until the knob made contact with the wall. Then he stepped inside.

This room, too, appeared deserted.

At that moment, Trace detected the sound of running water in the adjoining bathroom. A shudder of relief rippled through him and he realized he'd been holding his breath.

Dropping his gun hand to his side, he crossed the room and rapped on the bathroom door with his knuckle. "Mary? Are you all right in there?"

Almost instantly, the door opened and she stepped out.

Trace sucked in a deep breath of alarm. Instead of the perky, somewhat contentious woman he'd been expecting, a wan and frightened Mary Wilder slumped against him.

Shoving his revolver into its holster, Trace lifted her weak body into his arms. He carried her to the bed and laid her head on the soft pillow and pulled the covers up to her chin.

He knelt beside her and took her trembling hand in his. "What is it, honey? What's happened?"

"I . . . I think I've been poisoned."

Chapter Four

A jolt of rage, heavily laced with fear, shuddered down Trace's backbone. Until now, he hadn't truly believed Mary was in real danger. He'd attributed her vague feeling of being followed to premarital jitters. Nor had he taken the note left under her door too seriously, dismissing it as a spiteful but harmless missive from her former boyfriend. No, from the moment Bob Newland had phoned him, Trace had expected this assignment to be mere baby-sitting duty.

He'd done his job, of course. Taken the usual precautions. But in Trace's experience, only rarely did an anonymous note writer come out of the shadows to harm his prey.

Poisoners, however, were different. Far more twisted, and in Trace's mind, far more evil. Usually closely associated with the victim, a poisoner was a deadly cold bastard who could stand and watch his target writhe in agonizing pain.

A trickle of sweat beaded down Trace's cheek. Praying that Mary was wrong, that her stalker hadn't made that horrible leap to attempted murderer, Trace leaned closer. With a gentle hand, he swept a damp strand of golden hair off her forehead. "Why do you think you've been poisoned? Maybe it's just nerves. You've been under a terrible strain lately."

Mary pushed his hand away and sat up. Her face was pale, ghostly pale and her lower lip trembled. As if overcome with the effort of sitting, she dropped back against the pillow. "It was the candy. I...I ate just a few pieces and became horribly ill. It *had* to be the candy. I was feeling fine before."

Trace frowned. "What candy?"

Mary lifted an arm and pointed toward the living room. "Camille brought me a box of candy. Splendora Chocolates. My favorite."

Dropping her hand, Trace leapt to his feet and bounded into the living room. A few moments later, he stalked back into the bedroom, bearing the gold-foil box. "I've called for an ambulance. It should be here in a couple minutes. How are you feeling?"

"Better, much better. Maybe...maybe I don't need to go to the hospital." To her amazement, Mary realized it was true. Now that the horrible surges of nausea had passed, she was feeling stronger by the minute.

Trace ran his fingertips along the ridge of her jaw, feeling the clamminess of her flesh. Mary's voice was stronger but her skin was still ghastly white, tinged with rings of blue and lavender beneath her eyes. Trace shook his head vehemently. "We're not taking any chances." He laid the box of chocolates on the bedside table. "How did you receive this?"

Mary closed her eyes. "I told you. Camille Castnor."

Trace's eyebrows furrowed in surprise. "The senator's wife?"

"Uh-huh. They're both good friends of Jonathan's. We see quite a lot of them."

"When was the package delivered? How? A hotel clerk? Messenger service?"

Screwing her face into a frown, she raised herself onto wobbly elbows, tucking the sheet under her chin. "You're not listening to me. I told you already. Camille brought them herself."

Trace picked out a piece of dark chocolate candy and raised it to the light so he could examine it more closely. He didn't see any signs of tampering, but a tiny puncture left by a hypodermic needle would be easy to erase. The poisoner had only to heat the candy slightly and smear the slick chocolate over the small hole. No one would suspect a thing.

He tossed the candy into the box and turned his attention to Mary. "This doesn't make sense. If Mrs. Castnor wanted to poison you, she wouldn't bring the candy herself."

Mary scooted up against the headboard and pulled the blanket over her bare legs. "Camille? Oh, Trace, I can't believe she'd do anything like this. I mean, why? And, for crying out loud, she's a *senator's* wife! She'd never risk the headlines, even if she hated me."

"Does she?"

"Hate me? No, of course not." Mary paused for a long moment, considering the outlandish suggestion. Camille wasn't exactly her closest friend...but why would she want to harm her? Just because Camille and Jonathan had once dated was no reason for Camille to—

Mary's troubling thoughts were interrupted by a pounding at the front door, immediately followed by a long blare of the doorbell.

"Must be the ambulance," Trace said. "I'll let them in."

FOR MARY, the next two hours passed in a blur of white uniforms, bright lights and unpleasant medical procedures.

The paramedics took her vital signs and had a brief, whispered conversation with Trace. One of the technicians approached the bed and with a reassuring murmur, inserted an IV needle into the tender flesh on the top of her hand. Acting quickly yet gently, the two men lifted her onto a gurney. Within minutes, Mary was staring up at the vaulted, gilded ceiling of the hotel lobby as they wheeled her through.

Catching the eye of the day manager, Mary watched him recover from his shock and grab a telephone. No doubt he was calling Jonathan who would be chagrined at his fiancée being a public spectacle in one of his hotels. *Get over it, Jonathan,* Mary thought, dropping a hand over her eyes to shield them from the bright sunlight as the paramedics pushed the gurney out through the glass double doors. She had more to worry about right now than Jonathan's injured dignity.

Could it really be true that someone had tried to kill her? Now that her queasiness had finally subsided, the idea seemed impossible. Ludicrous. Yet deep in the darkest recesses of her heart, Mary knew her first reaction had been right.

It was too much of a coincidence that only moments after eating a few pieces of chocolate, her stomach had turned inside out. Mary had never had a nervous stomach and there was no reason to assume that this violent attack of nausea had been suddenly brought on by "nerves."

Even Dr. Keller, the young resident in the emergency room, was openly skeptical. Nonetheless, he sighed deeply and ordered a full battery of tests.

Fortunately, Mary's earlier bouts of vomiting saved her from the indignity of having her stomach pumped. Several more doctors came into the curtained cubicle and probed and poked every conceivable inch of her body. A lab technician entered with a metal basket filled with medieval instruments of torture, then departed after obtaining a healthy sampling of Mary's blood.

Finally, the room was quiet and she was alone.

Mary fidgeted on the narrow examining table, wishing they'd given her a better-fitting gown or a sheet. Every tiny movement exposed some portion of her anatomy.

She looked around the sterile cubbyhole and felt unaccountably lonely. Suddenly, she realized that she'd lost track of Trace in the flurry of medical activity. He'd probably been banished to the waiting room. She was surprised how much she missed his warm comfort. His calm, reassuring voice.

Then, the curtain surrounding the bed moved and Trace was beside her, as if he'd felt her need. He reached down and took her hand.

"How's it going, kiddo?"

Mary shrugged. "I've been better." Now that her stomach was relatively calm, she didn't feel sick. Or even frightened. She felt embarrassed. Foolish at having made such a fuss.

Lying here, under the bright glare of the emergency-room lights, her fears of poisoned candy seemed...melodramatic. Who could possibly want to harm her, anyway? No one.

Jonathan was right. In all probability, it was Mark Lester who had been following her around like a sulking teenager. And no doubt, it was Mark who'd slipped the note under her door. But try to kill her? No, she couldn't believe that. Her imagination had simply got the best of her.

All she wanted now was to get into her clothes and slink out of the hospital with as little fanfare as possible. Clothes! With a groan, Mary remembered that she'd stripped down to her underwear after being taken ill. What was she going to wear home?

Again, as if in direct response to her thoughts, Trace dropped a brown paper bag on the foot of the narrow bed. "Just in case the doc decides not to keep you overnight, I brought you some stuff to wear home."

Mary ignored his eerie mind-reading ability and rummaged gratefully through the bag. If Trace hadn't kept his wits about him enough to gather her a pair of slacks and T-shirt, she'd be leaving the hospital in her bathrobe.

That provoked another disconcerting thought. What if the media got wind of her trip to the emergency room and plastered a photo of her on the cover of every supermarket tabloid? "REGENT'S FIANCÉE CLAIMS SHE'S BEING STALKED BY CRAZED POISONER!"

Mary shuddered as she imagined Jonathan's reaction to such sensational press. The best thing to do was get out of here before anyone discovered she'd been hospitalized.

Looking up at Trace, she couldn't contain the surge of anxiety in her voice. Her words fell over one another in her haste to get them out. "Can we leave now? I—I didn't mean to make such a fuss. I mean, I'm sure that I overreacted," she rationalized, feeling a little guilty for her gluttony. Eating chocolate for breakfast would make *anybody* sick.

Trace shook his head. "I don't know that you did overreact."

A sudden chill crept through Mary's body. What was he saying? What did he know that she didn't? Whatever it was, Mary wasn't at all sure that she wanted to hear it. In a self-protective gesture, she wrapped her arms around her chest. The crinkling of the paper gown was the only sound in the small cubicle.

Finally finding her voice, she asked, "Why do you say that?"

Still holding her hand, Trace ran the edge of his thumb over her trembling fingers. "I checked with the front desk before I came to the hospital. They don't know who that candy was from. It suddenly 'appeared' on the counter early this morning. Mrs. Castnor saw the box sitting there when she stopped at the desk to see if you were in. She offered to bring it up. Since the clerk knew her, he didn't think there could be any harm."

Mary eased up on her elbows. Pulling her hand from Trace's grasp, she tucked the paper gown firmly beneath her. "Well, that lets Camille off the hook. I mean, she could hardly have stopped in the ladies' room and steamed open the package, poked something into the chocolates and rewrapped the cellophane before bringing the box to me. Not that I suspected her in the first place."

"I'm sure you're right. But I'd still like to talk to her."

The green curtain draped around the bed fluttered and Dr. Keller stepped inside, carrying a clipboard of lab results.

"You certainly look better," he said, glancing at her before turning his focus to the clipboard.

Mary and Trace watched in rapt attention as he flipped from one form to the next. When he let the last sheet of paper drop back into place, the doctor crossed his arms and frowned at Mary. "This is the damnedest attempt at poisoning I've ever seen."

Mary sat up. "So it was all my imagination, right?"

"No-o-o. I wouldn't say that exactly."

"What exactly would you say?" Trace cut in. "Has she been poisoned or not?"

As if noticing him for the first time, Dr. Keller arched an eyebrow and asked pointedly, "Are you a family member, sir?"

"No, but—"

"Then I suggest you keep quiet and allow me to speak with my patient. Otherwise, I'll have to ask you to wait outside."

Trace felt his back stiffen at the doctor's patronizing tone. Obviously, Dr. Keller knew who Mary was—or rather, to whom she was engaged. He probably thought Trace was her chauffeur. Quelling the urge to shove the doctor's condescending tone down his ivy-league throat, Trace said quietly, "I've been hired by Mr. Regent as a security consultant for his fiancée."

"Oh. Her bodyguard. I see." He made bodyguard sound like the social equivalent of a ragpicker. Turning his back on Trace, totally dismissing his presence, the doctor said to Mary, "All right, then. The lab report shows that several of the chocolates *had* been tampered with. Someone, Ms. Wilder, has an ugly sense of humor."

Forgetting the short paper gown she wore, Mary slid her legs over the side of the bed and stood up. Lifting her chin so that she was at eye level with the doctor, she asked, "What do you mean? That this was some kind of joke?"

Dr. Keller nodded. "Yes, I'm afraid you've been the victim of a very crude practical joke. Those chocolates were laced with ipecac syrup."

Mary frowned. "What's that?"

"It's an emetic," Dr. Keller said.

Seeing Mary's bewilderment, Trace explained, "It makes you throw up. People with small children keep it on hand in case the kid eats something toxic. Is that correct, Doctor?"

"Simply put, but accurate. Your poisoner didn't want to kill you, Ms. Wilder. Someone was playing games with you."

AN HOUR LATER, Trace opened the door of Mary's apartment and followed her inside. She was exhausted and imagined that she looked worse than she felt. Not that she really cared at this moment. She wanted nothing more than to drop onto her bed and—

"Why don't you go in and lie down?"

Mary blinked. That was three times in as many hours that Trace Armstrong appeared to have the uncanny ability to read her mind. It was disconcerting to have a man know what you were feeling even before you did. It made her nervous, very nervous. Jonathan never invaded her mind like this.

When she realized that Trace was still waiting for a response, she shook her head. "I really should eat something. All I've had today was a handful of chocolates. And those didn't sit well."

Trace laughed. "No, I guess they didn't."

Mary glanced at the credenza in the corner of the foyer where the telephone answering machine rested. To her surprise, there was no flashing red light announcing a message. She thought Jonathan would at least have called to check on her condition by now. Unless, of course, she'd been mistaken and the desk clerk *hadn't* been phoning Jonathan. Maybe her fiancé didn't even know that she'd been taken to the hospital.

"Did you happen to think to call Jonathan's office?" she asked Trace. Mary didn't want to think about the ugly little part of her brain that said *she* should have thought of phoning her future husband.

Trace frowned. "To tell the truth, I didn't even think of it. Do you want me to phone his office?"

Mary debated whether she should call Jonathan now or just wait and tell him the whole story tonight. Tonight! The embassy party. She'd forgotten all about that highbrow affair. But there was no way she was going to attend. She was still feeling too weak to stand on her feet all evening and listen to lobbyists argue about their special interests. Jonathan would be annoyed, but for once, Mary wasn't going to cave in to his wishes. It would take a crisis of catastrophic proportions to make her budge from her room tonight.

"No," she said at last. "He'll be over later. I'll tell him then."

When she looked up and saw Trace's dark eyebrows dipped in a scowl, she hastened to explain. "There's no point worrying him needlessly. What more could he do? He's already hired a bodyguard for me."

"Yeah. Some bodyguard. If those chocolates had contained arsenic instead of ipecac, you'd be laid out on a marble slab in the morgue right now."

Mary cringed at the graphic and chilling description. "It wasn't your fault, Trace. Even if you'd have been here, you wouldn't have thought twice about my eating chocolates that were delivered by the wife of a U.S. senator. You'd probably have eaten a few, yourself."

"Maybe. But that doesn't change anything. My job is to keep you safe, and in less than twenty-four hours, I've already allowed someone to get close enough to possibly harm you. Believe me, I won't be that careless again."

Mary wanted to argue, to convince Trace that it wasn't due to any lack of dedication on his part that the doctored chocolates had gotten into her possession. Her stalker, whoever he was, was very cunning. Mary had the horrible feeling that if her stalker wanted to harm her badly enough, no force on earth could keep her safe.

Knowing that it was useless to pursue the issue, she rubbed her weary eyes. "I'm going to fix a sandwich. Then I'm going to take that nap you prescribed. The tranquilizer the nurse gave me just before we left the hospital is starting to kick in."

Trace intercepted her on the way to the kitchen. "Good, you need the rest. I'll fix you something to eat. Why don't you go on and lie down?"

Suddenly, being pampered sounded like a very good idea. She was so emotionally and physically drained that she doubted she'd have the strength even to slice a tomato. "I'd love a sandwich, Trace. Thanks." With a wave of her hand, she started down the hall.

When Trace carried a cloth-covered tray into her room fifteen minutes later, Mary was sprawled on top of the bed, sound asleep. Still dressed in the slacks and T-shirt she'd worn home from the hospital, she looked like an innocent waif lying there with her fist curled under her cheek.

He hated to wake her, but she should get something in her stomach. She was too thin already. Trace laid the tray on the bedside table and lowered himself onto the edge of the bed. In a minute. He'd let her sleep just a little longer.

As he sat watching her slumber, Trace found himself mesmerized by the sweetness of her expression. She was such a genuine person, with a fresh, old-fashioned sweetness of spirit. Yet it was that very unworldliness that made her so vulnerable.

Without thinking, he reached over and stroked her cheek with the edge of his finger. Her skin was soft. Kissably soft, just as he'd known it would be.

Mary stirred in her sleep and curled toward him, trapping his hand between her cheek and the pillow. "Mmm," she murmured, as a lazy smile curved her lips.

Trying not to awaken her, Trace started easing his hand from beneath her face.

Mary moaned softly and tossed her head in a nestling motion against his palm. A tiny responsive thrill shivered in the pit of his stomach. She moaned in her sleep again, like a woman delighting to her lover's touch.

That innocently enticing moan was almost Trace's undoing. The small spark in his stomach ignited like a wildfire, sending a trail of white-hot flame through his loins.

Taken aback by the strength of his response, Trace knew he had to get out of there. Away from Mary. At least until he could regain his equilibrium.

Pressing his hand against her shoulder, he tried to raise her slightly so he could free his hand. Without warning and still sound asleep, Mary lifted an arm and hooked it around his neck, pulling him to her. Her soft, enticing lips were so close he could feel the soft puff of her breath. Too close. Way too close. Before he could extricate himself, Trace heard the bedroom door open.

Swiveling his head free of Mary's grasp, Trace swung around to face the tall, well-dressed man who stood in the doorway.

"Just what the *hell* is going on here?" the stranger boomed.

Hastily jumping to his feet, Trace ran his sweaty palms against the sides of his jeans.

Taking two steps toward the shadowy figure silhouetted in the doorway, Trace thrust out his right hand. "Jonathan Regent, I presume?"

Chapter Five

Trace kept his voice barely above a whisper so as not to disturb Mary. "I'm Trace Armstrong, Mr. Regent. The bodyguard you hired?"

The air was palpable with tension as the man continued to ignore Trace's outstretched hand. The only sound in the bedroom was the soft rustle of sheets as Mary stirred in her sleep.

A fractional easing of Jonathan's tensed shoulders was his only reaction. He glared at Trace, his eyes glittering with fury even in the dim lighting. With a quick glance at the still-slumbering woman, Jonathan muttered between gritted teeth, "Bodyguard, huh? I believe we may need to redefine your duties, Mr. Armstrong. May I see you in the living room?"

Without awaiting a response, he turned on his heel and stalked down the hallway.

Trace strolled out of the bedroom and found Jonathan waiting in the living room. The man had opened the small bar that was set into the ebony-wood entertainment center and was pouring a dark amber liquid from a decanter into a faceted tumbler. He watched Jonathan toss down a deep swallow, then roll the glass in his palms while he assessed Trace.

"All right, Armstrong," Jonathan said after taking a second long draft. "Explain to me why you were kissing my fiancée."

Knowing Regent had every reason to be outraged, Trace decided to disregard the man's rudeness. If Trace had walked in and found some stranger perched on *his* fiancée's bed, all but nuzzling her neck, hell, he'd be ticked off, too.

Fighting the surge of guilt that was chewing at his gut, Trace combed back his thick, black hair with his fingertips and chose his words carefully. "I'm afraid you've misread the entire situation, Mr. Regent. I wasn't kissing Ms. Wilder." *But I might have been in another second if you hadn't walked in.*

Jonathan slammed the tumbler on the chrome and glass coffee table. Amber liquid sloshed over the edge of the glass, and the air was instantly redolent of expensive cognac. "I've got eyes, man!" he shouted. "Do you take me for a fool?"

"No." Trace shook his head emphatically. "Not at all. And I can see where you might have gotten the mistaken impression that I was . . . kissing Ms. Wilder."

"Then just what in hell *were* you doing?"

How could he explain something to Jonathan Regent that he didn't understand, himself? Trace had never been the kind of man who got involved with married, or even engaged, women. Some kind of macho honor, maybe. But his growing attraction to Mary Wilder drained his nobler instincts. If Regent fired him, Trace knew he'd probably never see Mary again. That possibility left him feeling shaken and somehow forlorn. Knowing that he was guilty as charged, Trace nevertheless tried to smooth over the situation. "She was asleep. I didn't want to wake her, but I wanted to make sure she was breathing evenly." That was lame, but the best he could come up with on short notice.

"And I'm supposed to believe that?"

Suddenly, the guilt Trace had been feeling shifted and metamorphosed into irritation. If the man had punched him in the jaw, he'd have taken it. But Regent seemed determined to talk him to death. Worse, Jonathan hadn't even asked about Mary. After taking a slow ten-count, Trace tucked his fingertips into his back pockets and stared with deliberate challenge into Regent's startled gaze. "Quite frankly, I don't give a damn what you believe. *Sir.* But if I were you, I think I might be a little more concerned about my fiancée's health than my injured ego."

"What the hell are you talking about, Armstrong? What's wrong with Mary's health?"

"You mean you don't know? Bob Newland was supposed to give you a message." In spite of Mary's decision not to call Jonathan herself, Trace had felt it necessary to report the incident.

With a toss of his silver-flecked head, Jonathan snarled, "Well, as it happens, I haven't talked with Newland since lunch. I've been unavailable. Suppose *you* tell me what's going on, Armstrong."

Amazed that Bob Newland hadn't tracked down his boss, Trace launched into a detailed explanation of the tainted candy. When he finished, he was startled to see the tortured expression on the older man's face.

"Why?" Regent asked rhetorically. "Why would anyone want to hurt my sweet Mary? She's so...pure...so angelic."

Trace wasn't sure he agreed with the angelic part. He'd seen that lush streak of sensuality that bubbled just beneath her demure surface. He didn't think this was the optimum time to discuss Mary's latent sexuality with her incensed future husband.

In fact, Jonathan had taken to pacing, his spit-polished black Vitadelli loafers almost disappearing in the plush ivory carpet. Jonathan paused and shook a finger at Trace. "This is monstrous! I won't have my fiancée stalked and annoyed like . . . like one of those pitiful women on television talk shows.''

For the first time, Trace wondered if Regent's over-the-top agitation was fear for Mary's safety or fear of public scandal. Cursing himself for being so cynical, and not wanting to examine his own motivation too closely, Trace hastened to reassure the distraught man. "Try not to worry too much, Mr. Regent. Nine times out of ten, these kinds of things turn out to be the actions of a spurned lover.''

"Mary doesn't have lovers!" Jonathan snapped. "I told you, she's pure. Innocent. She merely went out with this Mark Lester character a few times. Nothing more.''

Suddenly, Trace recalled Bob Newland's description of Mary as a "brass-plated gold digger.'' How could one woman present three different faces—three different images—to as many different men? Newland had all but called her a deceptive tramp; Regent apparently thought she was only a step away from sainthood, while *he* found her…intriguing, even seductive. But which one was the real Mary Wilder?

Looking up, he saw Regent staring at him with an expectant expression on his face. It was clear he was waiting for Trace to apologize for besmirching Mary's pristine name. "No disrespect intended, Mr. Regent,'' he murmured in a mollifying tone.

"None taken.'' Jonathan nodded sharply. "Now. Last week I had Newland send Lester a warning, but apparently the man has decided not to heed my advice. I want you to find hard evidence that Lester has been harassing my fiancée. Once I know for certain that he's behind all of this trouble, I swear I'll use every ounce of influence I have to see that he's locked up and the key tossed into the Potomac!''

MARY SURPRISED TRACE by being out of bed and dressed when he arrived at her apartment the next morning. Apparently fully recovered from the ipecac mishap, she was bright and cheery. And looking entirely too beautiful standing in the rays of the morning sun as it filtered through the open patio door.

She was wearing a silky outfit that was the color of winter wheat. Almost the identical shade as those paler streaks in her blond hair. When she walked away from him to pick up her coffee cup from the dining room table, her flowing skirt swirled around her knees, offering a tantalizing glimpse of smooth, tanned thigh. It should be illegal for a woman who was already promised to another man to walk around looking like a golden goddess come to life. Jonathan Regent's goddess, Trace reminded himself.

"I thought I told you to keep the patio door locked," Trace growled. "And keep the blinds closed." With one powerful tug, he pulled the drapes across the broad expanse of glass.

Mary clamped her fists on her hips and glared at him. "And I said I wasn't going to live in a dungeon!" She stormed past him and yanked the curtains wide open. Turning to face him again, she demanded, "How do you manage to wake up on the wrong side of the bed every morning?"

"Not the wrong side, just the wrong bed," he grumbled under his breath. Any bed that didn't have Mary curled in it would be the wrong one.

In a deliberate effort to wrest his mind from the disturbing image of Mary snuggled in *his* bed, Trace strolled into the kitchen and poured himself a steaming mug of coffee. Caffeine. That's what he needed. Either that or a cold shower.

He lifted the cup and took a long quick drink. "Dammit!" Trace exclaimed as the scalding hot liquid took the first layer of hide off the roof of his mouth.

"Drink some cold water. It'll help stop the burning." Mary's voice was soft behind him. She stepped into the kitchen and held a glass under the nozzle on the refrigerator door.

She handed Trace the glass and stood leaning against the counter while he downed the soothing water.

When he finished, he set the glass on the counter and looked at Mary, a sheepish grin on his face. "Let's start over. Hello, Mary Sunshine. And how are you this fine spring morning?"

She grinned in return. "Fine. In fact, truly fine. Thanks to you."

"Me?"

"Yes. I never did get the chance yesterday to thank you properly for all you did."

Trace turned away. He didn't deserve her thanks. He hadn't done anything except show up in time to take her to the hospital. Not exactly a stellar recommendation for a man who was supposed to be protecting her. Realizing she was waiting for a comment, he muttered, "It was nothing."

"I'd hardly call saving my life nothing," Mary insisted in that quiet tone Trace was already starting to think of as her forged-steel voice. When she used that tone, he knew she wasn't about to change her mind, or be dissuaded. Mary had made a decision about him, and she was going to cling to that decision with steely determination.

"I didn't save your life," he insisted, even though he knew it was pointless to argue. "You heard the doctor, it was only a prank. You never were in any real danger." Picking up his mug, Trace took a cautious sip.

"You couldn't have convinced me of that yesterday. I felt like I'd have to die to feel better." Mary finished off her own coffee and rinsed out the mug. "Anyway, whether you like it or not, I *am* grateful."

"Hmmph. So what's up for today? Are you being presented to royalty?" He nodded at Mary's silk dress.

"What—this old rag?" She waggled an eyebrow in ersatz disparagement. "Actually, I have an appointment with Madame Guillarge at nine this morning."

"Is she bringing a crystal ball or does she read tea leaves?"

"Peasant! I'll have you know that Madame Guillarge is the foremost wedding consultant in the capital."

Trace lifted a pinky and raised his mug in a mock salute.

"Actually, Jonathan set up the appointment," Mary continued as she twisted her engagement ring around and around on her finger. "She's due at nine. Any minute." She looked up suddenly, the expression on her face one of pure bewilderment. "Do you know exactly what it is that a wedding consultant does?"

Trace shrugged. "Wedding consultants are out of my league."

Mary lowered her gaze. "Mine too, I'm afraid," she murmured.

"Tell you what. While you're meeting with Madame LaFarge—"

"Guillarge," Mary corrected automatically.

"Sorry. Anyway, according to the phone book, there are only a half-dozen outlets for Splendora Chocolates in the metro area. I thought I'd visit them and see if we can get a line on who might have purchased a two-pound box of liqueur centers in the last day or so. With any luck, some clerk might remember."

"I still can't believe it was Mark," Mary said.

"Yeah. Well, scorned love is a pretty strong motive."

"Maybe. But for one thing, Mark could barely afford to take me for pizza once a week. How's he going to buy a two-pound box of expensive candy?"

"Why don't we ask him? After Madame Tussaud leaves, why don't you see if you can find out when Marky-boy will be home this afternoon. I think it's high time we paid that young man a visit."

A long, shuddering sigh escaped Mary's lips. "I suppose you're right. It's just that... I hate to believe Mark could be behind all of this stuff. And I guess that I'm afraid to find out the truth."

Trace reached out and chucked Mary under the chin with his knuckle curved. An electric charge sizzled up his arm and he quickly pulled his hand back. But he couldn't still the muscles in his stomach that were twitching in response to Mary's high-voltage magnetism. Hoping she didn't hear the sudden wobble in his voice, he picked up the thread of their conversation. "I can understand your not wanting your friend to be the guilty party, but hiding your head in the sand like an ostrich isn't going to make this problem go away."

The bleating of the doorbell saved her from further reply.

She trailed behind Trace as he went into the foyer to answer the door.

Madame Guillarge swept into the room, totally ignoring Trace. Although on closer examination, Madame Guillarge was surely approaching seventy, she gave a first impression of being much younger. Maybe, Trace thought, it was the extremely dramatic dress she affected, a Technicolor vision of flowing lavender scarves and layered mauve clothing. Behind her, a frazzled assistant struggled with a stack of photo albums.

Spying Mary, the older woman put her hands to her bosom and sighed eloquently. "Ah! You must be zee bride. Monsieur Regent said you were chez lovely."

"Thank you, Madame. Won't you come in?"

"But of course! Come, Mitzi," Madame Guillarge called over her shoulder to the overburdened young woman. "Don't dally, mon pet."

"I think I'll be going now," Trace said as he stared after the flamboyant woman who was now ensconced on the sofa, picking out the cashews from a silver dish of mixed nuts on the coffee table.

"Coward," Mary mumbled as she stepped forward to lock the door behind him.

THREE HOURS of Madame Guillarge's flamboyance and on-and-off accent were more than any person should have to tolerate, Mary thought when she closed the door behind the woman, her assistant and all their accoutrements.

She was going to hurt Trace Armstrong for ducking out and leaving her to endure this ordeal alone.

Feeling rebellious, Mary stormed over to the patio door and yanked open the vertical blinds. To her surprise, the morning's sunshine had disappeared, replaced by a dull, gray drizzle. At least the weather matched her mood now.

Actually, Mary didn't mind the soft spring rain. She only wished she could go out walking in it. Raise her face to the sky and feel the mist penetrating her pores. Pretend she was someplace marvelous, like Paris or London. Although Georgetown was a wonderful substitute. The old-world ambience suited her nature, Mary decided, as she watched the passersby scurry to escape the rain.

Then, she saw him.

He was standing under a tree in the park across the street, his arms folded over his chest. That purple ball cap pulled low over his eyes.

She ducked back and quickly pulled the blinds closed. Dear Lord, she thought, grasping the cord with shaking fingers, was she never going to have a moment's peace again? Why was this man tormenting her?

When she got up the courage to peek through an opening in the blinds again, the watcher was gone.

Although she tried to convince herself he'd been a figment of her imagination, or a father waiting to escort his child to school, Mary knew better. It was him. That same unknown man who dogged her night and day.

She looked out the window several more times during the next hour, but she never saw him again. Nonetheless, a thrill of relief raced through her when she heard Trace's distinctive banging on the door.

Hurrying to meet him, she obediently looked through the peephole to make sure it was him, then left the chain engaged until she was certain Trace was alone.

"Don't say a word, not one word," Mary warned as he stepped inside. "That woman has given me zee migraine terrible," she added in a mock French accent.

"That woman would give me a pain in the—"

"Never mind," Mary interrupted. For some reason, she found herself unwilling to tell him about her having spotted the man on the street below. After all, what could Trace do now? He'd just become even more paranoid and chew her out for having the drapes open in the first place. Quelling the small prick to her conscience, she asked, "Did you find out who bought the candy?"

Trace shook his head. "No, not really. Although one clerk who works at the store that sells Splendora Chocolates in the Crystal City Mall wasn't in today. So I still may get something from her tomorrow. What about you? I don't suppose you had the chance to check on Mark Lester's whereabouts?"

"Not yet. But why don't you fix us a sandwich while I change clothes. After we eat, I'll see what I can find out."

An hour later, Mary hung up the phone. "Bingo! Mark goes into work at five today, so it's a safe bet that he's over at the American University library studying, if you still want to track him down this afternoon."

Trace leaned back against the soft cushion and stared at the Dali painting over the fireplace. "No, that's too public. Does he usually go home and change clothes before going to work?"

"Usually."

"Good." He stood up. "I think we should be waiting for Mr. Lester when he gets home. He's so full of surprises lately. Let's give him one for a change."

Mary rose to her feet. "Then we'd better get going or we'll get caught in the afternoon traffic."

When Trace's car pulled out onto the slick street, the brief misting of rain had stopped, having done its job of washing the air and leaving the city smelling cleaner. Mary loved the fresh earthy scent immediately after a downpour and rolled down the passenger-side window to inhale the sweetness. For just a moment, if she closed her eyes, she could imagine herself back at her parents' summer camp on the shores of Lake Superior.

But when Trace pulled up in front of the ratty-looking apartment building just off Columbia Pike in nearby Arlington, Mary's illusion was shattered. They were back in the city.

"You wait here and I'll go see if he's home," Trace said, getting out of the car.

"I'm going with you," she said, opening the door and joining him on the sidewalk.

"But if he sees you—"

"I said I'm going with you."

Recognizing her forged-steel tone, Trace decided there was nothing to do but give in gracefully. "All right, but let me do the talking."

"Sure. As long as you say everything I want you to say."

"You know, there are times when I almost feel sorry for Jonathan Regent." Taking her by the elbow, Trace steered Mary up the sidewalk.

There was no doorman or security buzzer, so he pushed open a plate-glass door and they stepped inside. Typical of thousands of similar cheap apartment buildings, the foyer consisted of a wide space in the hall that held a bank of mailboxes and a steep flight of stairs. There was no elevator.

Mary peeked into a mailbox marked Lester, M., Apartment 3-C. "His mailbox is still full. I don't think he's home yet."

"Then we'll wait. Let's go sit in the car."

"Let me say hi to Mrs. Martino, the manager," Mary said.

Without waiting for Trace to agree, she slipped around the staircase. He could hear her knocking on a door. A moment later, a booming female voice echoed through the quiet corridor. "Mary! What a pleasant surprise. Come in, dear."

"Trace? Are you coming?"

"I'll wait in the car," he called back. "I don't want to take a chance on missing . . . our friend."

He didn't have long to wait, however. He had just pushed open the entry door leading outside, when a lean young man with shaggy hair and black-framed eyeglasses bounded into the lobby. One of the arms of his glasses was mended with adhesive tape, and a large purple and yellow bruise was blooming on his right cheek.

He didn't even glance at Trace, but stopped and inserted a small brass key into one of the mailboxes. The one labeled Lester, M.

Lester had scooped out a handful of mail and started up the narrow staircase, when Trace said, "Mr. Lester? I'd like to have a word with you."

The man stopped and slowly turned around. He was clutching his bundle of mail against his chest in a protective manner. "Wh-who are you?"

Trace reached into his pocket and pulled out the ID card the secret service had issued when he "retired."

Lester merely glanced at the laminated card before returning his complete attention to Trace. He'd inched farther up the staircase and had his back firmly against the wall as if he expected Trace to assault him. "Wh-what do you want with me?'' His high-pitched voice was an irritating whine.

"I'm here to talk to you about Mary Wilder. Jonathan Regent asked me to stop by.''

Lester's face whitened. Then, without warning, he pitched the handful of envelopes toward Trace and fled up the staircase. Running as if demons from hell were nipping at his heels.

Chapter Six

In the split second it took for Trace to recover from his surprise, Mark Lester had disappeared up the staircase.

"Damn!" Trace kicked the flurry of envelopes aside and bolted after his quarry.

No sign of Lester on the second floor. Trace trotted up the next flight of steps. As he rounded the third-floor landing, he heard Lester's feet thumping down the hallway away from him.

Trace reached the top of the staircase and sprinted down the hall after the shadowy figure. Mark Lester was in front of his apartment door, his shaky hands trying to insert his key into the lock.

"Hey, wait a minute!" Trace called.

Lester glanced over his shoulder and renewed his hurried efforts to open the door. In his haste and nervousness, he dropped the keys onto the threadbare carpet. Seeing Trace's advancing figure, Lester took another searching look around the narrow passageway and ran.

But there was nowhere to go.

Faced with the dead end of the corridor, he backed against the wall and shook his fist threateningly. "Don't touch me! Stay away!"

Trace slowed down and paused ten feet from the agitated man. He was like a wild creature caught in a trap—

frightened and desperate. Lester's gaunt features were strained. The acrid scent of his nervous perspiration rankled the air between them. His head jerked constantly from side to side as he searched for an escape route. Mark Lester was the picture of a certified paranoid.

Not wanting to further provoke him, Trace held up his hands, palms forward, and advanced slowly. "Hey, man, don't freak out. I'm not going to hurt you. I just want to talk to you."

Lester shook his head forcefully. "I don't want to talk to you. Go away. Why can't you people leave me alone?"

Perplexed, Trace studied the frenzied man who was huddled against the wall, his fingers scrabbling at the faded plaster. Despite Bob Newland's assertion that Mark Lester and Mary had once been lovers, it was hard—no, impossible—to believe Mary had ever been involved with this bundle of neuroses. In fact, the more Trace became entangled in this situation, the more he was certain that Bob Newland had totally misjudged Mary Wilder.

The problem now, however, was to try to figure out what had Lester so spooked. First he had to get him calmed down enough to converse with him.

"Come on, buddy. Take it easy. I just want to talk to you. Can't we go inside for a minute?"

Lester's eyes were wild, as if he had just been zapped by a stun gun. "No! Go away, I told you. Just leave me—" He broke off suddenly, and stared over Trace's shoulder. "Mary! Wh-what are you doing here?"

Trace swiveled his head and saw Mary slowly coming toward them. Her eyes were moist and filled with compassion. When she reached them, she said only, "Trace."

The single word reverberated with meaning. With one syllable, she'd managed to convey her empathy for Mark Lester and her disappointment in Trace. Clearly, she thought that Trace had already physically intimidated her friend.

Trace blew out a long, frustrated breath. Now wasn't the time to correct Mary's misinterpretation. The best thing he could do to minimize the tension was to let Mary try and smooth things over. Wordlessly, he stepped aside and allowed her to approach the other man.

Mary stepped between them and laid a hand on Lester's shoulder. For an instant, Trace felt a flare of jealousy at the tenderness in her voice.

Suddenly, Mary gasped. "Mark? My God, what happened to your face?" With infinite gentleness, her fingertips brushed his pale skin, lightly touching the largest bruise at the base of his cheekbone.

Mark jerked away, as if her touch burned. Trace could sympathize with the man; he, too, had been seared by her touch.

"I'm okay," Lester muttered in an obvious attempt to regain some of his composure.

Mary shoved her hands into her jeans pockets. "Please, Mark. Come inside and talk to us."

He shot a nervous glance at Trace. "Not him. I don't want to talk to him."

Mary's forehead wrinkled in confusion. "Do you two know each other?"

"No," Lester said. "But I've met his kind before. They're all alike. I don't want to talk to him."

Mary shook her head. "No, it's all right. He's with me."

"With you?"

"Yes. I promise, no one's going to hurt you. Can we go inside now?"

Looking at Mary with the blind trust of a puppy, Lester hesitated for a long moment, then nodded.

Trace stood back and allowed them to precede him down the hall. He watched with an odd, gnawing sensation in the pit of his stomach as Mary draped a protective arm around the man's thin waist. Lester's gait was still uneasy and Trace could see the muscles twitching in his neck.

This guy was a real fruitcake. Mary was wrong about him, really wrong. Mark Lester was a walking time bomb. Trace only hoped they could defuse him before Mary was injured in the explosion when he finally went off.

Trace deliberately trailed behind as they trooped into Lester's stuffy apartment. It was a small efficiency unit, dark and Spartan. The utilitarian furniture was cheap rental quality.

Mary went over to the single window in the living room, pulled open the blinds and raised the sash. The late-afternoon sunlight did little to ease the gloom in the depressing studio, but the fresh air helped dispel the mustiness that pervaded the tiny apartment. Trace looked around at the thick layer of dust that coated every surface. Housekeeping wasn't Lester's strong suit.

In fact, judging by his home, it didn't appear that Mark Lester had any kind of life at all. There were no throw pillows on the sofa, no mementos topped the table or bookcase. The only item of a personal nature in the entire apartment was a framed candid photograph of Mary on the stand beside the rumpled single bed.

A sign of Lester's obsession or merely a reminder of what might have been?

While Trace was deciding the best way to approach Lester, Mary surprised him by taking control. She sat down on the sofa and patted the spot beside her. "Here, Mark. Let's you and I talk."

Trace leaned against the wall next to the refrigerator and smiled in appreciation. Mary was instinctively handling the situation just right, turning an interrogation into a friendly chat. Trace slid into the shadow of the fridge, knowing her efforts would be more productive if he stayed in the background.

After Lester had lowered himself onto the edge of the couch, Mary said, "Now tell me what happened to your face."

"I fell. Down the stairs."

Trace didn't buy the feeble explanation. Lester had taken one glance at his official-looking identification card and bolted. Obviously, the man had run afoul of the law in the not too distant past.

Mary, however, seemed to accept Lester's story at face value. "You poor thing. Did you go to the hospital? You might have broken your cheekbone. It looks pretty swollen."

"I went to the health office at school. The nurse said it was just bruised."

"Still, it must really hurt."

He seemed to bask in her sympathy for a moment. "A little. What really burns me up, though, is that they won't let me wait on tables till the bruising's gone. I have to work in the kitchen."

"That's too bad." Mary paused as if to marshal her strategy. In a more thoughtful tone, she started, "Mark, we have to talk to you about...about some things that have been happening to me lately."

"It wasn't me! I didn't do it."

"Do what?" Trace asked mildly.

The other man's head snapped up. It was clear from his startled expression that he'd forgotten Trace was in the room. "I didn't follow her around," he muttered.

Mary drew in a sharp breath. She looked up, exchanging a quick, knowing glance with Trace. Her eyes were so expressive, he could read her hurt and disappointment from across the room. Obviously, her faith in Lester's innocence was being sorely tested.

Reflexively, she eased a few inches away from Lester and returned her thoughtful gaze to the man's haunted features. "No one mentioned I've been followed, Mark. How did you know?"

"I, uh, guessed."

That did it. Trace had held back as long as he could. Not only was this jerk a liar, he was really lousy at it. With a few long resolute strides, Trace crossed the distance between them. He reached down and grabbed a handful of Lester's shirt and pulled the man to his feet.

"Listen, you slime-bag. I don't have the time or the patience for any more of your garbage. You didn't *guess* anything."

"Trace!" Mary jumped to her feet and glared at him. "Stop it! You're hurting him."

Shaking his head, Trace did his best to ignore the stricken look on her face. "Not yet I'm not. But I'll gladly rearrange the other side of his face if he doesn't start telling us the truth."

"I won't let you touch him," she insisted.

"Mary, this guy's just pulling your chain. But he's going to talk to me, aren't you, buddy? And he's going to tell me the truth."

"If you hit him, there's no difference between you and the fiend who's been stalking me."

Her glacial tone poured over Trace like a bucket of ice water. Never had the differences between the advantaged world Mary had so recently come to inhabit and his own been more obvious. In the genteel world of state dinners and symphonies at Kennedy Center, people didn't resolve their problems with their fists. But in Trace's world, talking rarely accomplished a damned thing.

Not that he wished Mary a life of coping with Washington's mean streets, but he was a little disappointed that she'd been so easily absorbed into the realm of the privileged.

As she continued to challenge him with her accusing eyes, Trace felt more and more like the human gutter-trash that was usually his quarry. Trace suddenly saw how Mary and her friends viewed people like him. He was nothing more than an exterminator hired to eliminate the filthy pests and vermin that swarmed in their garbage. But they didn't want to actually *see* him do the dirty work.

His new awareness boiled inside him and erupted in a spasm of rage. Opening his fist, Trace used the flat of his hand to push Lester back down onto the sofa. Slowly shifting his gaze to Mary, he said, "If you don't want to see this, then maybe you'd better wait outside. Otherwise, sit down and keep quiet."

Mary blanched at the harshness of his words. Folding her arms across her chest in a determined manner, she lowered herself onto the sofa beside Lester. "You'll have to hit me first."

Trace's eyes blinked in disbelief. This weirdo had been following her and plaguing her for days, and she still sided with him. Either Trace had been wrong and she was still carrying a torch for this guy, or... or he just didn't understand women.

What did it matter, anyway? When Mark Lester confessed and was safely behind bars, Mary wouldn't be Trace's problem any longer. Let Regent have her; they deserved each other. Deliberately shifting his attention to Lester, he continued, "All right, playtime's over. Now start talking. What the hell do you think you're doing following Mary around?"

Mark jerked his head up. "I told you! I've never followed her. Never."

"So that was just a lucky guess?"

Mark lowered his eyes and picked at the nubby weave of the sofa. "No. That's what...they said before. Why won't anybody believe me?"

Mary reached over and cupped his hand. "I believe you, Mark." She looked up at Trace's snarl of disgust. "Well, I *do.*"

Lester yanked his hand from beneath Mary's grasp. "Sure you believe me, Mary. Sure you do! That's why you had your boyfriend pay those—those two hired thugs to come over here and threaten to kill me unless I stayed away from you. Now that you're all high-and-mighty, you don't want to be bothered with the little peons from your past."

Mary's hand flew to her throat. "That's not true! Why, I would never—I mean, Jonathan wouldn't—" She broke off and looked up at Trace, her cocoa brown eyes even darker with pain.

Trace took a slow ten-count under his breath. Despite his own frustration with Mary, every fiber of his being wanted to throttle this skinny creep for taking his twisted rage out on her. But the guy had raised an interesting point. "Did either of these men actually tell you they were sent by Jonathan Regent?"

Lester thought for a long moment then slowly shook his head. "No, not in so many words. But who else would want me to stay away from Mary? I would never do anything to hurt her. I... I loved her."

Loved. As in the past tense. In the course of his job, Trace had all too often witnessed the destruction that sometimes ensued when love deteriorated into hate.

He shot a quick, compassionate glance at Mary. Her shoulders drooped and her head was bowed in response to Lester's pronouncement. She looked shell-shocked. Once again Trace wondered what her true relationship had been with Mark Lester. More important, why did it matter to Trace so much?

Not wanting to deal with his own confused feelings, Trace once again addressed Lester. "All right, let's start again. You're as innocent as a sacrificial lamb. So how did you know Mary was being followed?"

"I already explained that. *They* told me."

"Who?" Mary and Trace chorused.

"The two men who were here before."

"Oh, yeah, the mysterious thugs," Trace sneered. "When were they here? What did they want?"

"Last week. I don't remember which day. They said they had a warning for me." Mark rubbed his bruised face with quaking fingers.

"Did they do that to you?" Mary asked softly.

He didn't respond but the quick ducking of his head was answer enough. His fingers went back to their anxious plucking of fibers from the couch.

Trace paced in front of the cheap coffee table for a full minute as he tried to make sense of Lester's story. Despite the man's distraught mental condition, Trace could almost accept that Mark Lester believed his own tale. Almost.

Trace paused in his pacing and looked down at the agitated man. "Okay, let's give it one more shot. I'll make it real simple this time. Last week, two men came to see you, is that right?"

Lester nodded.

"And they accused you of following Mary?"

He nodded again.

"Then what? They just beat the stuffing out of you and left?"

Lester's dry, brittle laugh contained no humor. "I guess you could say that."

Mary reached out as if to pat his hand again but stopped herself at the last minute. Catching Trace's warning frown, she thrust out her chin in defiance and asked quietly, "What did those men look like?"

Lester shot her a dark glance. "Big. Real big. Like gangsters."

Trace leaned over until his face was only inches from Lester's. "Come on, Lester. Do you really expect us to believe that two Mafia types showed up out of the blue and beat you up on Mary's behalf?"

"I didn't say they were Mafia types. They were just big...thugs."

"Do you think you could identify these 'thugs'?" Trace asked as he straightened up again.

"No! They said they'd kill me if I told anyone."

"Kill you!" Mary exclaimed. "Because of me? But...but that doesn't make any sense."

She turned to Trace, her eyes glinting with confusion.

Trace shrugged. She was right. None of this made any sense. Was the man completely delusional or was his bizarre story the truth?

They continued to question Lester for a few more minutes, but it soon became apparent that he had already told them all he could—or would. He denied any knowledge of the threatening note Mary had received. And when asked about the tampered-with chocolates, his bewilderment was so convincing that Trace figured the man deserved an Oscar for best actor if he wasn't telling the truth.

Catching Mary's eye, Trace signaled her that it was time to leave. They wouldn't get any more out of Lester today.

She rose slowly to her feet. Turning her back to Trace, she gazed down at the man who had sunk into the corner of the sofa, blatantly ignoring her. "Mark? We're leaving now."

"Good," he mumbled into his chest.

Her shoulders heaved and a soft sob escaped into the still atmosphere. "Why are you so angry at me, Mark? We were friends. Good friends."

"Sure," he said bitterly, at last looking up. His facial expression was blank, his eyes strangely empty. "Have your people call mine. We'll do lunch." He immediately dropped his gaze, focusing once again on picking at the upholstery fabric.

With a slow, sorrowful shake of her head, she whispered "goodbye" and moved to stand beside Trace. He cupped her elbow and led the way to the apartment door, where he paused.

Mark Lester continued to stare sullenly into nothingness. Trace waited until the man looked up. Speaking quietly, but with authority, Trace said, "One last thing. If you *have* been hanging around Ms. Wilder, I'd strongly advise you to stop. Now. Do you understand me?''

Lester said nothing. Yet Trace knew he'd never forget the bitter eyes of the man who nodded mutely in response. Eyes filled with pure hatred. Was Lester's animosity directed against Mary or his assailants? If they even existed.

One thing was certain: it didn't really matter whether Lester had had a run-in with the local cops, been roughed up by a pair of wise guys or if he'd in fact fallen down a flight of stairs. Mark Lester was a man on the edge. The most dangerous kind of all.

MARY KEPT her troubled thoughts to herself while Trace cut a swath through the congested traffic clogging Route 50. Showing his intimate knowledge of area back streets, he bypassed the more heavily traveled bridge nearby, and made a circuitous loop around the city, crossing the Potomac on the Francis Scott Key Memorial Bridge in a more direct route to Georgetown.

Normally, Mary was enthralled by the beauty and grandeur of the centuries-old architecture, but today her interest sagged beneath the weight of the afternoon's disconcerting events.

She'd never seen Mark so...so peculiar before. True, he'd always been a sensitive man, given to mood swings and bouts of depression. But this manic animosity was a side of him she'd never suspected he possessed. Mark was the first friend Mary had made after moving to the capitol area. And though she rarely saw him anymore, he'd remained her best friend. Until today.

Then there was Trace.

She'd been totally unprepared for that streak of violence he'd exhibited with Mark. The raw, almost savage way he'd grabbed Mark by the shirt, and his brusque unrelenting questions had left her awed and almost frightened.

Mary realized anew that her small-town childhood had left her ill-prepared for the reality of city life. Since leaving her parents' peaceful and isolated home on the shores of Lake Superior in northern Michigan, she'd felt as if she'd fallen into a caldron of brutality and harshness. Her first few weeks of working in the District had introduced Mary to poverty, drugs, homelessness and street crime.

Then Jonathan had walked into the small bookstore where she worked, and Mary's life had changed overnight. It had been so easy to be swept up by Jonathan. Not only was he wealthy, handsome and powerful, he'd treated Mary with a gentle courtliness that had made her feel cherished and protected from the violent world around her.

Jonathan had introduced her to a life-style she'd only read about. Skiing trips to Aspen, glamorous embassy parties, weekends on Nantucket. Once, they'd even dined at the White House.

Suddenly, almost from the moment their engagement was announced, everything had started to change. He'd wanted her to revamp her hairstyle and wardrobe, drop her old friends, completely divorce herself from the woman she had been. At first, Mary had resented Jonathan's insistence that she curtail her relationship with Mark; although now it looked as though Jonathan had been a better judge of Mark's character than she. Then had come her vague misgivings and the sense of being pursued by a shadowy figure. And lately, even Jonathan had changed. For the past few days, he'd been stiff and irritable, and she'd found herself eagerly looking forward to Trace's laid-back manner.

But now she had this new, frightening dimension of Trace to contend with. For a brief moment, Mary considered throwing it all away and running home to Michigan. Back to safety. Back to the soft comfort of a life-style she knew and loved.

"Butte, Montana, is where I'd go," Trace said suddenly.

"What?"

"If I was going to run away, that's where I'd go. Butte, Montana."

Mary chuckled despite herself. "We're going to have to talk about this mind-reading skill of yours."

Trace tossed her a quick grin before returning his attention to the traffic. "Hey, I don't have to be Kreskin to be able to read your face. And just a moment ago, you were at least a thousand miles away."

"Not a bad guess, Armstrong," she conceded. "Why Butte, Montana?"

He shrugged. "When we were kids—I have three brothers—I guess we were quite a handful. Usually my mom kept her cool pretty well, but once in a while..." He paused as if reliving a fond memory. "Once in a while, she'd line us all up and tell us that she'd had all she could take and she was leaving. Nobody would ever find her in Butte, Montana, she always said." He chuckled. "Of course, she never left. We knew she didn't mean it, anyway. But we'd pretend to be scared and toe the line for a few days."

"Your mother was right," Mary said thoughtfully. "Sometimes the reality is that we just have to stick it out. I can see where fantasizing about chucking it all and fleeing to a faraway place would somehow make reality more bearable."

He gave her a long, appraising glance. "And is that what you want to do, Mary? Chuck it all and run away?"

She turned her head and stared unseeingly at the traffic outside the passenger window. "Sometimes. Times like today."

"Mmm. Mark Lester."

She shifted on the seat and faced Trace once again. "It didn't take psychic ability to figure that one out, Armstrong."

"No, it didn't. But I'll admit I'm baffled by one thing."

"What's that?"

They stopped for a traffic light and Trace drummed his fingertips on the steering wheel for a long moment before answering. Finally, he seemed to make up his mind to continue. "Your relationship with Lester. Both Regent and Bob Newland told me that Mark Lester was an old flame of yours that you threw over for Regent."

"And?"

"And you've never confirmed or denied it." After the light turned green, Trace kept his eyes on the road as he drove. "But to be frank, I can't quite bring myself to believe that you were ever involved with that character."

"Mark's a very nice person," she said, knowing she sounded as though she was reciting a dull but often-repeated argument. She was dismayed to hear her own doubts filter through her upbeat declaration.

"I heard Regent was thinking of getting into politics," Trace said in an apparent non sequitur. "You'd make a great politician's wife."

"What's that supposed to mean?" she asked sharply.

"It means that your Mark's-a-very-nice-person answer was no answer at all."

Mary felt her agitation growing. Sometimes, Trace's investigative instincts dueled mightily with her own sense of privacy. "Why is my relationship—or lack of one—with Mark Lester any of your business?"

Trace stopped the car at a stop sign and twisted in the seat to face her. "Because I'm trying to keep you alive and it would make my job a hell of a lot easier if I knew what was really going on."

He stepped on the accelerator and made a sharp right turn.

Mary sighed aloud. How could she explain to Trace when she wasn't sure she even understood, herself? Right now, all she wanted was to escape from her problems, and Trace's troublesome questions, for a few hours.

They had reached Georgetown proper by now and the streets were less crowded. Mary truly loved the old Georgian and colonial buildings, with their aged brick exteriors and brightly painted doors and shutters. They were only a few blocks from the Georgetown Regent and she found she was looking forward to the sanctity of her own apartment.

In fact, she wished there was some way she could cancel her dinner with Jonathan because, suddenly, she wanted nothing more than a quiet evening to sort out her disquieting emotions.

As Trace steered the ancient Mercedes into the Georgetown Regent's parking garage, Mary said quietly, "Mark and I were never 'involved,' I think was the word you used. We were friends. Close friends. But nothing more. Although... although there were times when I felt Mark wanted a more intimate relationship. But he never pushed me. Never."

"That seems to come easily for the men in your life, doesn't it?"

"What do you mean?"

"I've been your shadow for three days now and I sure haven't seen any signs of overwhelming passion when it comes to your relationship with Jonathan Regent, either."

"How dare you!" Mary couldn't believe her ears. The nerve of the man! Her physical relationship with her fiancé was none of Trace Armstrong's business. Even, a tiny voice whispered in her ear, even when he was right.

"How dare I what—point out the obvious? Most people who are on the verge of marriage usually can't keep their hands off each other. That's clearly not a problem with you and Regent."

"Mr. Armstrong, to some people, marriage is more than a license to copulate. For some people—*civilized* people—

marriage is also a sharing of commitment, companionship and respect.''

He nodded sagely. "Yeah, those are important. But without that hot, almost frenzied desire two people feel for each other to see them through the tough times, a marriage doesn't stand a chance.''

She tried to banish the sudden, and completely unbidden, image of she and Trace fumbling for each other's clothes in that "frenzied desire" he referred to. She shook her head, momentarily dispelling the forbidden thought. "The hotter the fire, the faster it burns out," she said primly.

"Maybe so, but I'll be damned if I'd want to miss the blaze.''

Mary had had enough of his probing. Worse, he was causing her to dissect issues that she feared wouldn't withstand too fine an examination. "Look, Trace, I really don't care about your opinion of my love life. Quite frankly, I'd appreciate it if you'd just stick to your job and keep your nose out of my personal life!''

"As you wish, princess.'' He reached down and turned up the car radio, drowning the silence between them in the hot, sultry jazz of Kenny G.

Mary stared out the window, trying to erase Trace's pronouncement from her memory. *I'll be damned if I'd want to miss the blaze.*

Was that what she was doing—selling herself short, because she and Jonathan didn't have the kind of relationship where they were constantly fumbling with each other's clothes in frenzied rushes of desire? Wouldn't that come later?

Trace just didn't understand; he came from a world where people were more direct, wore their emotions on their sleeve. She and Jonathan didn't need to make that kind of public avowal.

Once they were married and their love had the chance to grow and blossom, surely the heart-thumping passion would follow. And despite Trace's unflattering portrayal of her relationship with her fiancé, Mary and Jonathan did love each other. It was just a different, easier, more genteel kind of love.

Suddenly, Trace reached over and flipped off the radio. "I apologize for dipping into your business, Mary. What I said was crude and crass and...and I don't know what in hell caused me to spout off like that."

She knew. Trace had only been picking up on the erratic hormonal impulses she'd been emitting since he'd first walked in her door. Pheromones, the scientists called them. Sexual signals. Well, Trace Armstrong was setting off a pheromone bonfire! "No problem," she murmured. "It's already forgotten." But deep inside, she knew the impact of his telling words would linger in her mind well into the night.

In an obvious attempt to move their conversation onto safer ground, Trace asked, "You never did tell me why Regent believes your relationship with Mark Lester was more...intimate...than it actually was."

Mary sighed. How could she explain? There was no single moment when the confusion had cleared in her mind. At first, she had thought Jonathan understood her friendship with Mark. Then when it became clear he believed they'd been dating, she'd assured him that she and Mark had never shared a sexual relationship. That seemed to satisfy Jonathan, and Mary saw no reason to disillusion him. While Mary knew she was reasonably attractive, she had no fantasies about being a *femme fatale*. Only Jonathan believed every man in the country was lined up at her door.

Jonathan always treated her as though she was so special, proclaiming her beautiful and desirable. She hadn't wanted him to change his mind, to see her as the wallflower she'd always known herself to be. A woman who'd lived in an area populated predominantly by men and hadn't had a single real date in nearly six months.

Besides, Mark seemed to relish his role as her spurned lover.

Trace parked and came around to open Mary's door.

She slipped out of the car and looked up at him in the dim lighting of the garage, her heart thumping unexpectedly in response to his strongly defined, exceedingly masculine profile. Trace's physical appeal was so very unlike Jonathan's. Jonathan was mannerly, refined. Safe.

But Trace... Trace appealed to the wild, wanton side of her nature that Mary kept deeply hidden. Even from herself.

He was so different from most people. So straight-ahead. To Trace Armstrong, everything was always either right or wrong. Black or white. He had no gray in his world.

Taking advantage of the murkiness hiding her face and her emotions, Mary finally found the strength to answer his question. "I didn't push the issue with Jonathan because I wanted very much to be the gorgeous, coveted woman he thought I was."

Thoroughly embarrassed by her humiliating confession, Mary turned away and started walking swiftly toward the hotel entrance.

Trace caught up with her and grabbed her by the upper arm, spinning her around to face him. A trembling weakness overtook her at his touch and she felt herself sagging against him. Using every ounce of her self-control, Mary straightened her shoulders and raised her gaze to meet his.

A strange quaver in his deep voice, he held her by her shoulders and looked deeply into her eyes. "Mary Wilder, you're ten times the woman Jonathan Regent thinks you are. Don't ever doubt it."

Chapter Seven

Jonathan was particularly attentive when he arrived at Mary's shortly after eight.

"Ah! Delightful, absolutely delightful," he said in frank admiration of her new dress. "Who is the designer?"

"I think Camille said it was Arnold Scasi."

"I should have known. The man is inspired."

Mary looked down at the deceptively simple lines of the satiny garment. "But horribly expensive."

"I don't care. It's worth every penny. You ought to wear red every day, darling, the color's great on you."

Wrapping a protective arm around her shoulders, he asked, "And how are you feeling? You *look* wonderful, but... but I keep thinking about that candy. The consequences could have been far more serious. Who could do such a thing?"

Slipping out of his grasp, she patted his soothing hand. "Now, Jonathan, it's over and done with. It was a prank. Someone's sick idea of a joke."

"You're right, of course." He gave her a wide and thoroughly charming grin. "Let's not spoil our evening."

Mary gratefully returned his smile. It looked as though the "old" Jonathan was back. While he mixed cocktails, he recounted one anecdote after another about his afternoon golfing with three of the power players from the senate nominating committee.

He was the most focused person she'd ever met, Mary mused. Once Jonathan had decided to run for office, he'd immediately set out to make every possible contact in his political party. He'd shown the same zeal when he'd decided to court her, she recalled in a sudden burst of insight.

After finishing their drinks, he wrapped her satin shawl around her shoulders and kissed her lightly on the cheek. "I'm so delighted that you haven't let that unfortunate incident with the spoiled candy upset you. You're a real trooper, Mary."

She didn't know whether to be gratified or disappointed. While she was indeed glad that she had suffered no long-lasting consequences from having eaten the tainted chocolates, she mildly wished Jonathan hadn't been so quick to accept her explanation of the incident. Somehow, his blithely dismissing the candy episode made her feel as if he was just as blithely dismissing the entire string of frightful events that preceded it.

When they settled into the rear seat of the limo, Jonathan leaned back into the leather seat and said, "So, tell me about your day. I've prattled on long enough."

In halting tones, she told him about the visit she and Trace had paid to Mark Lester. The scowl on Jonathan's face expressed his opinion of their foray.

"I wish Armstrong hadn't taken you along. He's supposed to be protecting you, not exposing you to more danger."

"Jonathan, you can't put me in a glass case and set me on the mantel! He had no choice. I would have followed him if he hadn't taken me."

Jonathan laughed. "Ah, Mary, my darling, you're such a delight. But, seriously, pet, I do wish you would learn to curb your more...shall we say, impetuous nature. After all, it was your involvement with Lester that started all of this in the first place.''

She exhaled a long, slow sigh. They'd had this fight at least a half-dozen times and she was truly in no mood for a rematch. In an effort to change the subject before both their tempers flared, she asked, ''Before you hired Trace, did you send anyone else to talk to Mark?''

Jonathan's frown was clearly visible even in the muted light. ''Of course not. Why do you ask?''

''Because Mark told us that two men came to visit him last week. He had the impression that you had sent them.''

''I can't imagine what gave him that idea. What did these men supposedly say?''

Mary chewed a knuckle as she remembered the painful-looking bruises discoloring Mark's face. ''They told him to stay away from me. Then they... they beat him up.''

''What! And you thought I had something to do with that?''

''No, of course not. I was only repeating what Mark told us.''

''Well, if you ask me, Mark Lester is obviously suffering from some extreme mental affliction.''

Mary couldn't argue with that. Everything she had seen of Mark that afternoon seemed to prove Jonathan's theory. Mark had been agitated almost to the point of panic, and he'd exhibited several sharp mood swings in the brief time she and Trace had been with him.

Still, she felt a strong bond of loyalty with Mark and didn't want to belittle him to Jonathan. Fortunately, while she was still searching for a rebuttal, the car came to a halt in front of the fabled Jean-Claude restaurant on DuPont Circle. A uniformed doorman appeared to help them alight, and a moment later they were walking into the opulent building.

"Ah, Mr. Regent, it is our pleasure to have you with us this evening," the maître d' crooned. "May I take your wrap, Ms. Wilder?"

After the man handed her shawl to a red-jacketed assistant, he led the way across the dining room to a secluded table set for four. Plucking an intricately folded linen napkin from the tabletop, he draped it across Mary's lap. "The Senator and Mrs. Castnor phoned a moment ago to say they have been delayed but should be arriving shortly. May I have Armand bring you something from the bar?"

"Mary?" Jonathan asked, "Would you like a cocktail?"

"Just some wine, please."

"Excellent. The sommelier will be with you momentarily. *Bon appetit.*" Ducking his head obsequiously, the maître d' departed, clicking his fingers for the wine steward, who appeared a second later.

While Jonathan and the man conferred, Mary gazed around at the five-star restaurant. Jean-Claude's was one of Jonathan's favorite haunts. They'd come here several times previously but Mary still felt a flush of awe at the elegant surroundings. High, mirrored ceilings were softened by recessed lighting and silk wall hangings. Huge displays of exotic flowers brightened the tastefully muted decor.

It was a far cry from the woodsy atmosphere of the Wildwood Country Club where her family had always gone for special occasions. Suddenly, Mary felt a rush of longing for the simpler, more familiar life she'd forsaken. *Stop it,* she chided herself, feeling like a spoiled ingrate. It was silly to yearn for fresh-caught lake trout when a sublime lobster banquet was hers for the asking.

By the time she'd convinced herself that she was only suffering from a natural bout of homesickness, Jonathan had concluded his business with the wine steward and had turned to face her.

"Frankly, Mary, I'm just as glad that Brad and Camille have been delayed. It gives me a chance to talk to you."

She couldn't suppress the sense of foreboding that his casual words provoked. Tonight she wanted only light-hearted banter. No serious topics. But she could tell from his tone that Jonathan wouldn't be swayed.

Forcing a smile, she asked, "Did you want to talk about something in particular?"

"Yes." He leaned back in his chair and thrummed his fingers on the damask tablecloth. "I've made a decision."

"About?"

"Our wedding." He held up a hand, forestalling her quick response. "Before your feminist hackles are raised, let me rephrase that. I've changed my mind about something, come around to your way of thinking on one issue."

Mary twiddled with her engagement ring, still unaccountably nervous about what Jonathan was trying to impart. "What issue is that?"

He laid his palm on the tabletop with a sharp slap. "I've decided you're right—we don't need a huge wedding with a thousand guests. A small intimate affair would be more in keeping with the mood of the nineties. No conspicuous consumption . . . getting back to the basics, that sort of thing."

"I see." Relief flooded through her. She hadn't been looking forward to the media circus that would have accompanied the extravaganza Jonathan had originally outlined.

"You don't sound too thrilled."

"No, truly. I'm very pleased." She didn't know what else to say. A week ago she would have been thrilled at his capitulation, now she found herself questioning his motives. Had he deferred to her wishes to please her or to please his future constituents?

"In fact," he continued, "there's no sense in delaying our wedding for several months. If we're going to have the small private ceremony that you wanted, we can move the date up accordingly."

"When . . . when were you thinking of?"

Jonathan stared up at the mirrored ceiling in deliberation. "How about sometime in June?"

"June! That doesn't give us much time." June was only two months away. Suddenly, Mary felt as if her air supply had been severed. Was this an attack of the infamous premarital jitters?

"What's happening in June?" Camille Castnor's husky voice reverberated at Mary's shoulder.

She hadn't seen Camille and Brad approaching but, for once, she was grateful for their appearance. "Brad! Camille! How nice to see you both," she gushed a little too forcefully.

Camille looked somewhat taken aback by Mary's sudden burst of enthusiasm but Brad was his usual nonplussed self.

He leaned down and bestowed a friendly kiss on Mary's cheek before pulling out Camille's chair. After shaking Jonathan's hand, the corpulent senator demanded, "What's this about June?"

Jonathan covered Mary's hand with his own. "We've decided to get married sometime in June. I'll leave the actual date to my bride."

"But, Jonathan," Camille protested, "surely you're joking. Even Madame Guillarge would be hard-pressed to put on a wedding of any substance in such a short period of time."

He waved a hand in the air, dismissing any objections. "The wedding will be small and intimate—just as Mary wanted."

Further conversation was delayed by the arrival of the sommelier with the bottle of Romanee-Conti Montrachet that Jonathan had ordered. Despite her own personal opinion that all the hoopla in opening a bottle of wine was a bit overdone, Mary nevertheless watched in fascination as Jonathan and the steward went through the elaborate procedure of uncorking, sniffing and tasting that preceded the consumption of a bottle of expensive wine.

After all four glasses had been filled, Jonathan called for a toast. "To a June wedding!"

"Here, here!" the Castnors chimed in unison, Camille having apparently overcome her earlier reservations.

In the jocularity of the moment, Mary hoped no one took notice of her own silence. Jonathan was right. She *had* wanted a small wedding. And she'd argued against a long, drawn-out engagement. But now, when actually faced with the prospect of setting a date, she found herself wanting to pull back. Everything was moving too fast. She was still too... too what? Too unsure of her feelings?

She sipped her wine in an effort to dispel the disconcerting thought.

"I have a wonderful idea," Camille said suddenly. "Why don't you have the ceremony at our place in Middleburg? An outdoor wedding, wouldn't that be lovely? We could put up canopies and trellises with climbing roses and—"

"Why, that's an outstanding idea," Jonathan cut in. "Don't you think so, Mary? It would be played up in the media as a down-home, folksy kind of wedding. Just the sort of thing voters love."

Mary shot him an irritated glance. "I'm not planning my wedding around the media, Jonathan. That's precisely why I wanted a smaller ceremony, in the first place—to avoid a media circus."

"Of course, of course." He patted her hand in a soothing gesture. "But if you get the kind of wedding you've always wanted, and it still plays well in the press, what have we got to lose?"

Plans for the upcoming nuptials continued while the waiter served their salads. Mary took little part in the discussion. Instead, she sat back, her annoyance growing with each passing moment as Camille and Jonathan plotted out the details.

It was decided that Madame Guillarge would be retained first thing in the morning—Jonathan would delegate that task to Bob Newland. Madame Guillarge could work directly with Mary and Camille to arrange the catering and seating for the five hundred guests Jonathan considered a small gathering.

The conspirators continued to map out every detail while the main course was served. Jonathan had called ahead and ordered Jean-Claude's specialty, magret duck with dates and honey, for the foursome. To Mary, the normally excellent dish tasted like rubber.

Worse, she wasn't even sure why she was so upset. She knew absolutely nothing about planning a wedding. She should be glad of Camille's help. And yet…and yet, Mary felt somehow removed from what should have been the most exciting event in her life.

At first she tried to convince herself she was feeling a natural resentment toward Jonathan and Camille for taking over what should be her role, but in her heart, Mary knew it was a lie. What was bothering her was clear. A haunting mirage that had suddenly taken over her mind. No matter how hard she tried, she couldn't dispel the disturbing and impossible image of herself dancing in the moonlight. Feeling the warm, thrilling embrace of strong hands on her bare arms. Basking beneath the caress of eyes that were steamy with desire.

Eyes that didn't belong to Jonathan.

Eyes that were catlike and predatory. Trace Armstrong's eyes.

Mary sipped her wine, nibbled at her meal and pretended to pay attention to the conversation swirling around her. Normally, she found their discourse witty and urbane; tonight, the table talk seemed forced and superficial. Who had changed? she wondered. Jonathan and the Castnors?

Or was it her own attitude that had somehow been trans-figured?

When Jonathan announced they would have to cut the evening short, Mary stifled a sigh of immense relief.

"It'll be quite a shock to the old system, getting up at 4:00 a.m.," Jonathan said, pushing aside his half-empty wineglass.

Mary mentally forced herself back into the conversation. "Why do you have to get up so early?"

"Didn't I tell you? I'm flying to Nome in the morning."

"Nome? As in Alaska?" When he nodded, Mary continued, "No, you didn't say a word. How long will you be gone?"

Jonathan shrugged. "A week. Maybe ten days. You know we're planning a resort out on the Alaskan tundra and we've run into a snag with the damned environmentalists. Looks like I'll have to handle this one personally."

Camille leaned forward and patted Jonathan's hand. "That doesn't surprise me. Your business acumen is truly amazing."

So fervent was her declaration that Mary's gaze was immediately drawn to the senator to see if he, too, had noticed. The dark, hovering glare that he shot back and forth between his wife and Jonathan was answer enough. Mary could see that Brad was well aware that his wife was still carrying some sort of torch for Jonathan Regent. She could also see that Brad Castnor didn't like it one bit.

THE NEXT MORNING, Trace deliberately waited for a "decent" hour before he called Mary. Still, he could hear the foggy remnants of interrupted slumber in her voice as she snarled into the receiver, "What?"

"And top o' the morning to you, too, Mary. Such a delight to hear your cheerful voice."

"Armstrong, don't you *ever* sleep? The sun isn't even up yet."

"Hey, it's after six. Long past time you hauled your lazy, but lovely, rear out of the sack."

"Leave my rear end out of this. What do you want?"

He leaned back in his empty bed and imagined Mary, fresh and cuddly from her night's slumber. Probably wearing a satin gown, cool and soft to the touch. It would have a deep vee in the front, exposing just enough cleavage to tantalize. Her soft blond hair would be tumbling in careless abandon around her face. Yep, no doubt, Mary Wilder curled up in her bed was a winsome and alluring vision. And definitely off limits to the hired help.

Bringing himself back to reality with a frustrated groan, Trace rubbed his knuckles across his stubbled chin to rid his mind of the taunting image. "I wanted to tell you I'd be late this morning."

"Good."

"Jeez, you're a grouch. Don't you even want to know why I'll be late?"

"No." She yawned loudly. "Okay, why?"

He hesitated, wondering just how much to tell her. A niggling suspicion had been growing in his mind for the past couple days, and he wanted to put it to rest—or prove its validity. "I thought I'd be waiting for Bob Newland when he gets to work this morning. I've got some questions for him."

Mary snorted. "Well, wish him a bad day for me."

"Hmm. That's really an interesting hostility you two have for each other. Want to tell me what's behind it?"

"Why don't you ask Bob, excuse me, Robert, Newland?" she snapped. "He's been a real jerk since the day I met him."

"Okay, I will. I should be at your place by ten. Oh, and Mary?"

"I know, I know, keep the door locked."

Trace replaced the receiver and allowed a grin to capture the lower half of his face. Sleepy, grumpy and incredibly intriguing, Mary Wilder grew more interesting by the minute.

TRUE TO HIS WORD, Trace was waiting in Newland's anteroom when Jonathan's assistant opened the door.

"Armstrong! What brings you here so early in the morning? Nothing else has happened, has it?"

Trace tossed aside the newspaper he'd been skimming and uncrossed his long legs. "I don't know. Why don't you tell me?"

Newland's eyebrows rose. "Is that supposed to be some kind of a joke?"

Trace unfurled himself from the leather and chrome chair and stood looking down at the smaller man. "I never joke about attempts on a woman's life, Newland. Never."

"Has something else happened?" Newland asked again. "Come inside." He fumbled with the lock on his private office door. "Let's talk about this."

Following the assistant into his cubbyhole of an office, Trace remained standing, maintaining a subtle advantage. As if sensing his ploy, Newland, too, stayed standing and paced behind his neatly organized desk. Rubbing his hands together in an apparent attempt to calm his nerves, he finally asked, "So what's happened?"

Trace rested a hip on the edge of Newland's desk. "Nothing. At least, nothing I haven't already reported. But what about you, Bobby? Aren't there some things you kind of forgot to mention?"

Wincing at Trace's choice of nicknames, Newland wiped a sudden sheen of perspiration from his forehead. The confident man of Trace's previous visit was gone. "I . . . I don't know what you're talking about."

"Sure you do, Bobby."

"Don't call me that! My name's Robert. Please, grant me that courtesy."

Leaning over the desk, Trace braced himself on one elbow. "All right...Robert. Suppose we start by talking about Mark Lester."

Newland shrugged. "What about him? I told you from the beginning, the man's low class. I'm sure he's behind all of Ms. Wilder's problems."

"Maybe. But one thing's certain. Mark Lester didn't give himself that shiner he's sporting."

"Shiner?"

"You know, mouse, black eye. Mr. Lester claims he was roughed up. And he thinks you might have hired his assailants."

"Th-that's preposterous!"

"Is it?" Trace eased off the edge of the desk and walked around the corner until he stood toe-to-toe with Robert Newland. "I don't think it's so preposterous. I think it makes perfect sense. You sent a couple of roughnecks over to give Mark Lester a warning, didn't you?"

"I did not!"

"My only question is, were you acting for Jonathan Regent or were those thugs protecting *your* interests?"

Taking two halting steps away from Trace, the harried assistant continued to wring his hands. As if realizing a lie was futile, he apparently decided on bravado. "All right, so what if I did hire those men? Mr. Regent only had his fiancée's welfare in mind. He knew Lester had to be behind all of Mary's problems, so I—we—thought the easiest solution would be to scare him off."

He frowned, and added, "Clearly, it didn't work."

Trace shook his head in disgust. Regent might be a world-class businessman, but he was nothing more than a punk in an Armani suit. At any rate, at least one mystery was solved.

Heading for the door, Trace waited until he was in the doorway before he slammed Newland with his second shot.

"Oh, by the way, what have you got against Mary Wilder?"

"Why...why, nothing, of course! She's engaged to my employer."

"Is that why you told me she was a brass-plated gold digger?"

Fresh droplets of shiny perspiration appeared on Newland's face. Obviously, they were treading on very dangerous territory. "I'm afraid you might have misunderstood what I said—"

"Oh, no," Trace cut in. "I recall your exact words. Would you like me to repeat them for Mr. Regent?"

"Please! It...it's not like you're thinking."

"Why don't you tell me what it's like, then?"

"I don't have anything against Ms. Wilder. Not really. It's just that...well, Mr. Regent has such great political aspirations and...surely even you can see that she's completely unsuitable for him."

"Mmm," Trace muttered noncommittally. The truth was, that on this single point, he *did* agree with Newland. The luscious Mary Wilder deserved a better man than Regent. His hand still on the doorknob, Trace assumed a pleasant, conversational tone of voice. "So, just because you decided she was 'unsuitable' marriage material for your boss, you set about to break up the relationship?"

"No! I mean, I didn't actually try to break it up. I just thought if Ms. Wilder was exposed to the kind of attitude and...opinion that was sure to follow her marriage, that she might be dissuaded."

"But what does it matter to you? I mean, Regent's political aspirations are his affair. What harm or gain can come to you if he marries Ms. Wilder?"

For the first time since their interview began, Robert Newland straightened his shoulders. Smoothing his rumpled hair, he said stiffly, "My entire career is attached to Mr. Regent's. If he fails, so do I. But if he realizes his political potential . . . well, he'll need a chief of staff in the White House.''

Trace whistled. Talk about a man who planned ahead. Jonathan Regent hadn't yet officially tossed his hat in any political ring, but his assistant was already picking out his office in the White House. Robert Newland was a pitiful creature, surely. But despite his better judgment, Trace was almost convinced the man was telling the truth.

As CAMILLE had forecast, Madame Guillarge was at first adamant that no wedding with any degree of gentility could possibly be pulled together in such a short time.

But when Mary handed her the sizable retainer check from Jonathan, Madame Guillarge's interest heightened immediately.

She folded the check in half and stuffed it down her neckline, into the recesses of her formidable bosom. "*C'est difficult*," she cooed, "but not impossible, *mon petite*. Not impossible."

At noon, when Madame Guillarge suggested they send out for room service to save time, Trace threw aside the newspaper he'd been reading and rose from the easy chair in the corner, an annoyed expression on his face. "How much longer do you think this will last—this picking posies, and whatever?"

Madame Guillarge waved a ring-bedecked hand. "Oh, hours, I am afraid. Zees planning of zee wedding is very complicated, no?"

"Hmmph. Very tiring, I'm sure," he said grimly.

Needing a moment's respite from Madame Guillarge's robust personality, Mary went into the bedroom to use the telephone. While she was ordering salads from the hotel restaurant, Trace tapped on the doorframe and poked his head into the room. Pointing to his chest and shaking his head, he signaled that he didn't want lunch. Ignoring

Mary's curious gaze, he left the room and returned a moment later, his worn leather jacket slung over his shoulder.

She hung up the telephone and brushed a lock of hair out of her eyes. "Going out for lunch?"

"Since you're going to be tied up here all afternoon, I thought I'd head back over to the Crystal City Mall to see if that candy-store clerk is working today. I'll grab a burger or something at the mall."

Mary frowned. "Do you really expect a salesclerk in a busy mall to remember who bought a box of candy two or three days ago?"

He patted his jacket pocket. "Bob Newland gave me some photos this morning. Maybe seeing a picture will jog her memory."

"Photos of who?"

"Mark Lester, the Castnors, a couple of Jonathan's more vocal opponents. Just about anybody I could think of who knows you or maybe has a grudge against your fiancé."

Mary wrapped her arms around herself, as if claimed by a sudden chill. "I still keep hoping the culprit is a stranger. Someone we don't know."

Trace cocked his head. "I'm not sure that I wouldn't rather be dealing with someone we know, rather than an unknown stalker." He'd no sooner said the words than he wanted to bite his own tongue. For the past few hours, she'd been happily planning her wedding, and now he'd gone and put that shadow of fear back onto her face. What was the matter with him?

Jealousy.

The simple answer came to him in a lightning bolt of insight. He was plainly and perfectly jealous because Mary Wilder was so contentedly planning her wedding day to that pompous ass Jonathan Regent.

It wasn't that Trace had any designs on the woman himself, he mentally insisted. It was just that he hated to see her settle for a man who was so obviously unsuitable for her.

Regent's wealth was shining so brightly in her eyes that Mary couldn't see the truth. But Trace could see what was going on. Mary was one of the plain people, like himself. She'd soon tire of this glittery whirl of cocktail parties and staid embassy receptions. And then where would she be? Married to a workaholic and spending her afternoons shopping for yet another expensive dress that she didn't need or want.

And if this was so clear to him, why couldn't Mary see the truth for herself?

Still, it was none of his business, and unless he wanted to lose this easy and lucrative job, Trace knew he'd do well to keep his opinions to himself. But if Mary gave him any inkling that she wasn't deliriously happy with her upcoming nuptials...

Then, in that case, he might just have to point out a few facts to her.

Mumbling for her to stay in the apartment until he returned, Trace disappeared down the hallway.

When she heard the door click shut behind him, Mary sighed and returned to the living room. She tried to give her attention to the wedding consultant, but her enthusiasm had left with Trace. Suddenly, the last thing on earth she wanted to do was pore over pages of invitations, flower arrangements and bridesmaid's gowns. She wanted nothing more than to forget the entire thing. At least for a few hours.

A knock at the door announced the arrival of their noon meal. After making sure that she recognized the room-service attendant who was pushing the stainless-steel cart, Mary stood aside while he set up the salmon salad and iced tea luncheon.

Madame Guillarge, as Mary suspected she would, devoured her meal with gusto. Mary had taken only a few bites of a hot, crusty roll, when the flamboyant woman shoved aside her own empty plate.

"So! Vee are ready to get back to work, no?"

No. Silently, Mary acknowledged ruefully that she'd rather be mall-walking with Trace than concentrating on picking her color scheme.

Nonetheless, she admonished herself to display at least a semblance of interest when Madame Guillarge hefted a photo album filled with pictures of wedding cakes onto the dining room table.

By the time they had gone through the entire album and Mary had selected a cake and buffet menu, her eyes were burning and her head felt as if it would explode at any moment.

"Enough for today," she declared, rising to her feet.

"But, my child, we still need to talk about zee flowers, no?"

"No," Mary insisted firmly. "Not today. I'm exhausted."

Madame Guillarge rose ponderously. "Zen you must call zee front desk for a strong man."

The flamboyant wedding consultant had arrived *sans* her able-bodied assistant that morning, but a bellman had carried up her cargo. Obviously, the woman would need help getting all of her gear back downstairs.

When Mary telephoned the bell captain, she was dismayed to be told that the delegates of a medical convention had just arrived and it would be nearly an hour before a bellman was available. Mary knew she'd scream out loud if she had to endure Madame Guillarge that much longer.

Picking up her keys, she said, "Come on, I'll help carry this stuff down to a taxi."

"Oh, if you're sure." Madame Guillarge hefted her handbag onto her shoulder, picked up a silk pouch filled with fabric samples and sailed to the entry, leaving Mary to wrestle with the remaining pair of canvas tote bags.

When they reached the lobby, Mary gladly handed her burden to a bellman and asked him to see the tiring bridal consultant into a taxi.

As she handed a tip to the young bellman, Mary felt a moment's loss when she realized she didn't know his name. Until a few days ago, she'd spent five or ten minutes in the lobby every morning. Under the pretense of fetching her mail, she'd chatted with everyone from the desk manager to the custodian.

Now she felt a virtual prisoner in her luxurious apartment. And a stranger was now someone to be distrusted, instead of a potential friend.

She knew Trace was justified in insisting on these stringent precautions. Yet . . . yet sometimes Mary yearned for a return to the peaceful anonymity of being a bookstore clerk.

With a wave to Rick, the desk manager, she crossed the sparkling lobby and waited for the next elevator. During the slow, soothing ascent, Mary tried to forget the stalker and the concessions in her personal freedom he'd forced upon her, concentrating instead on the positive changes in her life.

She was mentally reliving the lazy afternoons she used to spend poring over exhibits in the Smithsonian, when the elevator pinged, announcing she'd arrived at her floor.

Stepping off, she was still smiling at the wonders of the Smithsonian while she made her way down the hall toward her apartment. The faint whir of the elevator cab returning to the lobby was the only sound in the echoing silence.

Suddenly, she sensed a movement ahead of her and looked up.

A strange man was bending over in front of her door. She was certain he was trying to jimmy the lock.

Chapter Eight

With a quirk snap of her head, Mary scanned the empty hall for an escape route. The emergency stairwell was on the other side of her apartment, effectively cut off by the stranger at her door.

The elevator had already returned to the lobby. Even if she could get another in a few seconds, it was unlikely she would continue to be unnoticed by the intruder while she awaited its return.

She thought about screaming, but knew no one would hear her through the soundproof walls. Besides, her mouth was so dry she doubted she could utter a sound.

The man was still bending over her doorknob, so intent on what he was doing that he hadn't yet noticed her. But it was only a matter of time.

Tiptoeing backward toward the elevator, Mary kept a wary eye on the man. As she watched, he moved slightly and lifted his head. For the first time, she caught a glimpse of his profile.

He was wearing a bright purple baseball cap.

She no longer could deny the truth. He was the stalker, the man who had been following and watching her for days. Now, he was here. A hard, cold knot of fear settled in her stomach. She leaned back against the wall, as if she could somehow disappear into the pale gold wallpaper.

Suddenly, Mary heard the distinct click of a door being unlocked somewhere behind her. She swung her head toward the welcome sound. Someone was in one of the other suites! If she could just get inside before the stranger noticed her . . .

It was already too late.

He, too, had heard the door catch being unlocked and had straightened up. Mary's heart thudded in her chest as icy fear stalked her spine. The man was staring straight at her with a cold, penetrating gaze that bored through her.

They were so close she could easily make out the gold insignia on the front of his cap. It was the profile of a howling wolf. Horrifyingly appropriate.

A cool rush of refrigerated air poured over her already icy flesh as the apartment door directly behind her swung open. She sensed rather than heard another presence in the hall.

"Help!" Mary squeaked, finding her voice at last.

The intruder took one step in her direction, then turned and bolted toward the emergency stairwell. The metallic clang of the heavy steel door slamming behind him reverberated in the stillness of the empty corridor.

In an instant, the stalker had vanished as though he'd never existed.

"What's going on out here?" a querulous voice called out behind her.

Mary twisted around, weak with relief at the sight of the old man who was the only other full-time tenant on her floor. "Oh, Mr. Waltham, I'm so glad you were home. Someone was trying to get into my apartment!"

He hobbled into the hallway, leaning heavily on his cane. "Damnable hooligans! This used to be a nice city, but these young punks think they own the world. No respect. That's the root of all this crime, you know. No respect. Come on inside, girl, and we'll call hotel security and the police. Not that they'll be able to do a blessed thing. Punks have taken over everything."

Mary sagged against the wall, allowing his familiar tirade to wash over her like a soothing balm. Ever since the elderly man had been mugged by a group of young roughnecks a few weeks earlier, the irresponsibility of modern youth had been his favorite topic of conversation. Mary was afraid this incident would only incite her neighbor to redouble his harangue, but she couldn't bring herself to confess that her intruder hadn't been a kid from a street gang.

The man at her apartment door had been older, in his early forties, perhaps. His features had been shaded but she vividly recalled the defeated slump of his shoulders and the slight bulge of his belly hanging over his belt. His hands had been knobby and rough.

No, the man who'd tried breaking into Mary's apartment hadn't been a street kid looking for trinkets to hock. There had been obvious purpose to his movements, a sense of urgency. She shuddered, thinking what his purpose might have been.

"You're right," she said suddenly, pushing herself away from the stabilizing wall. "I should call the police. I'll go do that right away."

Mr. Waltham shook his head. "Come inside, girl. The rest of his gang might be waiting for you."

"No, he was alone. I'll be all right once I lock the door. But I'd appreciate if you'd watch until I'm safely inside. And I do thank you for coming to my rescue."

The contentious senior paused, his drooping shoulders straightening just a fraction. "Hey, I guess I did rescue you, huh?"

Mary patted his arm, feeling his frailness beneath the heavy flannel shirt. "That's right, Mr. Waltham," she said softly. "If you hadn't been here, there's no telling what that man might have done."

His shoulders straightened a bit more as he hitched up his trousers. "Glad to do what I could. You need anything else, you just holler. Even though I haven't got the speed I used to have, my hearing's still right keen and I can sure dial a telephone. Not that the cops or hotel security would get here anytime soon. Damn shame what's happening in this city."

Giving the older man a weak smile, Mary walked swiftly down the hall to her own apartment, anxious to get away before Mr. Waltham picked up any more steam. She held up her key ring and reached for the dead bolt.

To her surprise, the brass plate around the knob was shiny and unscratched. Almost as if the man *hadn't* been trying to jimmy the lock. Curious.

Then she noticed a white, crumpled envelope was jammed between the door and the frame. The stalker had left her another note.

Nausea burbled in her stomach and her fingers shook as she reached for the cursed white envelope. It was as if, by leaving his venom in the form of another hate letter, the stalker had left a part of himself behind. Once again, she'd been bested, defeated, by this unknown man who hated her relentlessly and without apparent cause.

Biting her lip, she forced herself to remain calm, to concentrate on one thing at a time. She'd think about the note later. Right now, she had to open this lock.

Mr. Waltham was still standing in the hallway, watching her fumble with the door latch. Mary felt inordinately comforted by the dubious safety his vigilance offered. Bolstered by his concern, she forced herself to forget the envelope and concentrate on the lock. At last, the tumblers in the dead bolt disengaged and she slipped inside her apartment.

Once she reached the sanctuary of her home, Mary bolted the door behind her and raced for the telephone. Now that she was safe, her body gave in to the delayed reaction of the harrowing experience. Her fingertips trembled as she dialed Jonathan's number.

"Mr. Regent's off—"

"Bob! This is Mary. Is Jonathan in?"

"No, I'm afraid Mr. Regent is out of town at the moment. May I take a message?"

Mary felt his disapproval zinging over the telephone lines. She had never figured out exactly what she had done to make her fiancé's assistant dislike her with such intensity, but the man took very few pains to keep his animosity from showing. Only in front of Jonathan did he put on a smooth performance of amiable servitude.

"No," she said at last. "No message. Just tell him I phoned, please."

"Certainly," Newland said before replacing the receiver without the courtesy of saying goodbye.

Refusing to dwell on the man's boorish attitude, Mary punched in Trace's beeper number. While she waited for him to return her call, she carried the portable phone into the living room and sank into the corner of the sofa. Only then did she notice the white envelope was still clutched in her left hand.

She sat quietly, staring at it with the same mesmerized intensity with which a snake charmer watches a trained cobra. Mary knew the stinging bite of the hate letter could be every bit as fatal as the bite of a cobra.

The phone rang and Mary jumped, her heart thumping wildly.

"He-hello," she breathed into the receiver.

"Mary? What's happened? Are you all right?" Trace's deep voice poured over her shattered nerves like a soothing lotion.

"I'm fine, I guess. Just a little shaken."

"What happened?" he repeated.

"Someone . . . was trying to break in. He left another note."

Trace's outrage rippled over the phone lines. "Son of a—I thought our visit might have dissuaded our Mr. Lester."

"It wasn't Mark," she said quickly.

"How do you know?"

"I saw him."

There was a long pause during which Mary could imagine Trace fitting the pieces together. "Does he know you saw him?"

"Yes."

"Call Regent. Tell him I need to speak to him right away. I'll be at your place in—" he broke off, and her mind's eye saw him looking at his watch "—fifteen minutes. Don't answer the door for any reason before I get there. Understand?"

"Yes," she whispered.

There was another long pause. This time, Mary couldn't guess what Trace was thinking. When he spoke again, his voice was lower-pitched, somehow gentler. "Mary, are you sure you're okay?"

"Other than having had a good scare, I'm fine."

"Don't worry, sweetheart, I won't leave you alone again."

Trace hung up the phone and Mary sat staring at the receiver. He'd called her sweetheart. An innocuous enough endearment, yet she knew that they'd moved onto another plane in their relationship.

She and Trace were tied together by more than a mad stalker. There was some cosmic connection that they'd both been trying to deny since the moment they'd met. And with his utterance of that one word—sweetheart—they'd both somehow acknowledged the connection.

MARY WAS STILL NESTLED on the sofa, when she heard Trace's key in the lock a short time later. Her subconscious registered the comforting heft of his footfall in the apartment, but her conscious thoughts were still taken up by the startling and overwhelming emotions engulfing her. Her mind was filled to overflowing. Fractured images of the malevolent stalker were mixed in a disquieting montage of Trace and Jonathan hovering over her. Protecting her. Wanting her.

Suddenly, Trace was in front of her. He dropped to his knees and took her hands in his. "Mary? Are you all right? Tell me exactly what happened."

The white envelope fluttered, unnoticed, onto the carpeting.

Taking a deep breath, Mary collected her thoughts and tried to keep the events in sequence as she described her trip to the lobby to help Madame Guillarge. And the man waiting on her doorstep when she returned.

To Trace's credit, he didn't waste a moment in recriminations. He didn't remind her of her broken promise not to leave the apartment without him. Not a single I-told-you-so passed his lips.

When she finished her story, Mary looked up at Trace. "So I locked myself in and called you." *And Jonathan.* Mary couldn't help making the mental comparison. Trace had come running to her aid immediately, while Jonathan hadn't yet found the time to return her phone call.

Trace rocked back on his heels and rubbed his chin thoughtfully. Mary noticed the persistent dark wreath of razor stubble along his chin. It was somehow endearing. Her fingers itched to skim the rough surface, but she held her hands tightly entwined until the urge dissipated.

She closed her eyes and forced her mind into a soothing void. She had to stop thinking like this. Obviously, her highly charged emotional state was coloring her logic. Trace had come running because that was his job. Jonathan, on the other hand, was a powerful, busy man who—

"Did you get a good look at him?" Trace asked suddenly.

Glad he'd interrupted her thoughts, Mary shook her head. "Only enough of an impression to know that he's the same person who's been following me."

"What did the note say?"

The note! "I don't know. I...I haven't opened it yet. In fact, I'd forgotten all about it. Now, where did I put that..." Mary dug in between the sofa cushions until she spotted the pale envelope on the floor.

Following her gaze, Trace scooped the envelope off the floor and held it up to the light. "No sense having it dusted for prints. Our boy is too smart to leave traceable evidence."

Slipping his fingernail under the flap, Trace slit the edge of the envelope. As before, a single sheet of heavy bond white paper was all that the envelope contained.

He turned the paper over so that Mary could read along with him. Also as before, the words were cut from magazines and newsprint and glued to the single sheet. It read:

THIS IS YOUR FINAL WARNING.
CALL OFF YOUR WEDDING OR DEATH WILL
BE YOUR HONEYMOON COMPANION.

Trace read the words a second time, then a third. Slowly, he raised his gaze to meet Mary's and saw the color fade from her face. The poor kid was devastated. Who wouldn't be? Out of the corner of his eye, Trace watched as Mary valiantly fought to stem the flow of tears, but a telltale sheen of silver brightened her eyes.

"Wh-who?" she asked. "Who could hate me so much?"

A red tide of anger started low in Trace's gut and rose higher and higher until he thought he would drown in rage. He was going to find this sicko if it was the last thing he ever did. Rising from the floor, he eased next to her on the sofa and gathered her into his arms.

Most women would have fallen apart under such severe provocation, but Mary Wilder had a core of forged steel, Trace discovered anew. After a single teardrop slipped down her cheek, she pulled away from him and knuckled off the drop of moisture. "I think the man I've been seeing was hired by someone else. I don't think he's the real stalker—the person who wants to harm me."

Trace gave her an appraising look. "Why do you say that?"

Mary tossed her head, dislodging a strand of glimmering golden hair. She pushed the hair from her cheek with careless ease. "I don't know exactly. Except, doesn't it make sense that the culprit is someone I know? I mean, why would someone I don't even know want to...to kill me?"

The idea of anyone wanting to harm Mary was inconceivable to Trace. In the past few days, he'd grown to see her not as the greedy, ambitious gold digger that Bob Newland had described, but as a gentle, affectionate and courageous woman. A woman he was growing to care for, maybe too much.

Trace had to keep reminding himself that Mary was already committed, engaged to another man. It was only their constant proximity that was making him feel protective and tender. Not to mention that the long hours he'd been keeping since he'd taken this assignment were fogging his thinking. He'd never been involved with a client before and he wouldn't let sweet Mary be the first.

Moving a safe distance away from her, Trace swiped the fatigue from his face. "Let's go over this again. Other than Mark Lester, you can't think of anyone else who might be carrying a grudge?"

Mary hesitated. "Only one name comes to mind. But he wouldn't...no, no. There's no one."

"Only who?"

"It's silly. A name popped into my head, that's all. Someone I don't think likes me very much, but he wouldn't have any reason to hate me."

"Who?" Trace insisted, a hint of exasperation sneaking into his voice. If she kept absolving every possible suspect, they'd never find the person behind these threatening notes.

Mary paused again and nibbled her upper lip. "Well, like I said, I don't have any reason to suspect him, but Jonathan's assistant doesn't seem to like me very much."

Newland's actions that morning hadn't absolved the man in Trace's eyes. But until there was proof of the assistant's involvement with the stalker, Trace would keep his continued suspicions to himself.

"You mentioned the possibility of the man you saw being a hired messenger," Trace said noncommittally. "If Bob Newland is behind all of this, he would have to hire someone to do his dirty work."

"Robert Newland is a pompous stuffed shirt, but he's not a stupid man," Mary admitted, "why would he have pushed Jonathan to hire you if he's the one masterminding this?"

"Doesn't make much sense, does it?"

"So we're right back where we started," Mary said. "Square one. Not a single viable suspect."

"Well, maybe one," Trace hedged.

"Who? Did you find something out at the candy shop?"

Trace's forehead furrowed in a thoughtful frown. Raking his fingertips through his dark hair, he said hesitantly, "The clerk *did* recognize one person."

Mary's heart thumped in dreadful anticipation. "Who?"

"Camille Castnor."

The name hung on the air between them for a long moment. Finally, Mary asked, "What did the clerk remember about her?"

Trace shrugged. "Only that she'd been in the store earlier this week and bought a box of chocolates. She couldn't remember what kind or what size box. She wasn't even certain which day, but she sure remembered that fur coat."

"Oh, the clerk must have been mistaken. Plenty of women wear fancy furs around here. Didn't the store have records?"

"She paid cash."

Mary rubbed her fingertips across her suddenly throbbing forehead. Camille? But...why? No, it had to be a simple coincidence. "Just because Camille bought a box of candy doesn't mean she's the culprit."

"That's right. But, quite frankly, it seems a little peculiar to me that she'd never mention the purchase to you. Especially since she was the one who delivered the tainted chocolates to you in the first place."

The telephone rang, interrupting their disturbing conversation. Mary reached for the receiver, and a flush stole up her cheeks when she recognized the caller. "Jonathan, I've been waiting for your call."

Trace rose and crossed to the patio door, allowing a discreet distance so Mary could talk with her fiancé with some degree of privacy. With his fingertip, Trace pushed aside the vertical blinds and stared, unseeing, down onto the bustling street below.

That blush of excitement on her face had been a dead giveaway. His fanciful daydreams had been just that—fantasies. Why had he imagined for a single moment that Mary would consider tossing over her rich boyfriend for a bodyguard? At least, Trace thought with a hint of rueful satisfaction, he hadn't made a complete jackass of himself by exposing his snowballing feelings to her. No doubt she'd have gotten a good chuckle out of the idea.

"Trace?" Mary's voice called out behind him.

He dropped the blinds back into place and turned around, forcing a nonchalant tone into his voice. "Yeah?"

She raised the telephone toward him. "Jonathan wants to talk with you."

A feeling of dread settled in the pit of Trace's stomach as he crossed the room and took the receiver from her. "Armstrong here."

Trace listened with an expanding sense of foreboding as Jonathan Regent told him of the business trip that was going to keep him out of D.C. for the next couple of weeks. "I'm very concerned about Mary's well-being, Armstrong."

"So am I."

"This fiend is getting too close."

"I agree," Trace said. "I'd like you to authorize me to put some more operatives on this case. I think Mary should have round-the-clock protection."

"Hmm. More operatives? No, no, I don't think so."

"But, Mr. Regent, I'm only with Mary eight or ten hours a day. She's still unprotected better than half of the time."

"That's a good point, but the way I see it, the more people involved, the more chance of something going wrong. No, the only person I want on this case is you, Armstrong."

"But—"

"It's not a matter of money. Charge whatever you think is fair. But until this business trip is over, I don't want you to leave Mary's side. I want you to move into the spare room and stay with her. Right away."

Move in here? Live with Mary? Didn't Regent see what he was doing, throwing them together like this? It was too dangerous. "Mr. Regent, I don't think that's such a good idea."

"Why?" Jonathan asked sharply. "Is there something you're not telling me?"

Plenty. But nothing Regent would want to hear. "No, nothing like that. It's just that... I think there's safety in numbers." *For himself as well as Mary.*

Jonathan didn't answer right away, but when he did, there was a razor-sharp edge in his tone. "I don't agree.

Too many people involved and someone gets sloppy. Just you, Armstrong. That's my final decision.''

Trace took a deep breath and considered his options. He could resign. The financial well-being of his company wasn't dependent on the Regent account. But if he quit, who would protect Mary from the stalker?

And if he moved into her apartment, who was going to protect her from her bodyguard?

Chapter Nine

That night, Mary lay awake well into the small, dark hours after midnight. At first she'd resisted the idea of Trace moving in. Granted, she felt physically secure when he was with her, but emotionally...well, emotionally, Mary knew she was treading in very dangerous territory.

Lately, Trace Armstrong occupied almost as much of her thoughts as the stalker.

She punched the pillow and rolled onto her side but sleep still eluded her. Lying in the darkness, curiously disturbed by Trace's presence in the next room, Mary stared at the dancing shadows on the wall and thought about the strange twists her life had taken.

Just a few short months ago, she'd left her parents' home in northern Michigan and moved to Washington. Armed with an almost useless degree in cultural anthropology, her aim had been to acquire a position at the Smithsonian Institution. Unfortunately, the single opening had been filled before her arrival, forcing Mary to take the low-paying clerical job at the bookstore.

Undaunted, she'd kept a close watch on the job openings at the Smithsonian, moved into the studio apartment across the hall from Mark Lester and took those first baby steps into the life-style she'd always yearned for. At the bookstore, she'd been privy to thought-provoking lectures by visiting authors, and she and Mark had spent many evenings sharing pizza and arguing opposing sides of a legion of issues.

Mary was caught in the memory of Jonathan Regent walking into the bookstore one morning last fall. Her life had been a breathtaking roller-coaster ride ever since.

First had come the multitudinous baskets of flowers, delivered by a uniformed chauffeur. Catered picnics beside the reflecting pool near the Lincoln Memorial. Then, that first huge box of Splendora Chocolates. But when he invited her to a private gala at the Smithsonian and she had been immersed in conversation with a host of Jonathan's entertaining and cosmopolitan associates, Mary knew she was hooked. Jonathan was simply the most generous and sophisticated man she'd ever known.

Even when, like Pygmalion, he'd set about "refining" her image, she knew he had only her best interests at heart. True, sometimes his insistence on always being socially correct annoyed her, but Mary had to admit Jonathan's world was of her own choosing, and, for the most part, she'd been content.

At least, she'd been content before the stalker had crept into her life, tainting her world with his vicious presence. Closing her eyes and grasping the extra pillow to her chest, Mary again questioned the identity of this unseen person who'd rather see her dead than married to Jonathan.

Trace felt Camille Castnor was responsible. Jealous, perhaps, that Mary had succeeding in "luring" Jonathan to the altar, where she, herself, had failed. Could Camille's cool exterior be hiding an inner rage? Mary wondered.

Or was Bob Newland the guilty party?

From the first day, Jonathan's assistant seemed to find Mary an odious presence, well beneath Jonathan's exalted station. But was that motive enough to threaten murder?

And, of course, there was still Mark Lester. Despite his denials, Mary felt her old friend was hiding something from her. Because of her relationship with Jonathan, Mark's pain was an open, festering sore in his soul. Had Mark decided to ease his own anguish by causing Mary to suffer as he had?

As sleep finally captured her, Mary's last thought was of the man she'd found apparently trying to break into her apartment. Although his face had been somewhat hidden by the brim of his cap, she'd seen enough to know one thing: the would-be intruder wasn't Bob or Mark or Camille.

He was a stranger.

THE NEXT MORNING, following a leisurely, but somehow tense, breakfast of granola-topped yogurt and fresh fruit, Trace poured the remaining dregs of coffee into his cup and sat back in his chair. "So what's on the agenda today?"

Mary glanced at the kitchen clock. "I have a fitting on my wedding gown this morning. After that, I don't have any specific plans."

Trace grimaced. "Wedding gown, huh? Sounds like fun."

From the tone of his voice, Trace obviously thought shopping for a wedding dress would be about as much fun as shoving bamboo shoots under his fingernails. His crabby manner was really starting to annoy her. "I *am* in the final stages of planning my wedding, you know."

"How could I forget?"

"What's that supposed to mean?" Mary's brown eyes flashed dangerously.

"Nothing. Peace." He smiled. "Anyway, after the fitting, I think we ought to pay your friend Camille a visit. If you ask me, I think the senator's wife is one guilty lady."

"Well, I think you're wrong."

"Why?"

Mary shrugged and poked a section of cantaloupe with her fork. "You just are."

"Now that's logic you can't argue with!" Trace threw up his hands in a dramatic gesture.

"Look, I'll grant you that Camille still has an emotional attachment to Jonathan—they're old friends," Mary said. "But she's a happily married woman. Why would she want to stop his marriage?"

Trace shrugged. "Camille might not want him, but that doesn't mean she doesn't want someone else to have him, either."

He looked up suddenly and caught Mary's gaze. For a long moment, they held the look, both of them taunted by the irony in the situation. Jonathan Regent, it appeared, was the key that could open—or bolt—the bonds that held all of them prisoners.

Camille Castnor might very well be in love with Jonathan, but she was bound by her ties to her husband. Just as Trace and Mary were constrained by her engagement to Jonathan.

Funny, Mary mused. Those very ties to Jonathan she'd once wanted so badly, were now confining her. And her guilt was suffocating her.

As if reading the torment in her soul, Trace dropped his gaze abruptly. Pushing his empty mug aside, he picked up a plump strawberry and made a production of hulling the berry and popping it into his mouth. After licking a drop of juice from his lower lip, he leaned forward, cupping his chin in his hands. Eyes focused on the tabletop, he asked, "What makes you think Camille Castnor's happily married?"

"Oh, for crying out loud!" Mary stood and pushed her chair in. She'd been having the same, ugly thought and was embarrassed that Trace had seemed to pick up on it. "Now you're a psychoanalyst. Camille and Brad are as happy as most couples." She raised a hand to forestall a protest from

Trace. "*I've* spent a lot of time with them—you haven't. Even if they were on the verge of divorce, Camille would still have no reason to harm me. She and Jonathan called it quits long before I came into the picture."

"Maybe. But Regent didn't have another serious relationship between Camille and you, did he? Deep inside, Camille might have believed she still had a chance. Until you came along. You know what they say—'Hell hath no fury,' et cetera."

Mary rammed her fists onto her hips. "My God, Armstrong, I seriously underestimated your truly amazing skills. Bodyguard, psychiatrist and now, expert on the female psyche. I am truly blessed by your presence!"

Trace's head popped up at the intensity of her pique. "I've heard of waking up on the wrong side of the bed, but you must have slept on a bed of nails last night. What's eating you this morning, Princess Mary?"

She opened her mouth to offer a stinging retort but the words hung in her throat. Trace was right; she was edgy to the point of bitchiness. What *was* bothering her? It wasn't just the stalker, something else was treading on her nerves.

The truth poured over her like a tidal wave. Trace's nearness was making her jittery.

She'd barely closed her eyes last night. She'd kept imagining him in the next room, with only a plasterboard wall separating them. When the night had been very still, Mary thought she detected the steady drone of his breathing. Occasionally, he'd shifted in the bed, and her fertile imagination had conjured up a disturbing picture of him curled in slumber, with only a thin sheet covering his unclothed body. An involuntary shiver raced down her back as the mental image came into focus.

"Mary?" Trace's fingertip brushed the top of her hand. His touch smoldered against her skin, and singed her frenetic nerve endings.

Mary flinched but didn't respond. Nor could she ignore the heavy shaft of guilt piercing her heart. She was engaged to another man. What kind of woman could be weeks away from marrying one man and having carnal thoughts about another?

Trace walked around the table and stepped close to her, invading the sanctuary of her personal territory. "Are you still here? You look like you've drifted off to la-la land."

Inching away from him, Mary blurted out the first thing that crossed her mind. "You want to know why I'm grumpy? Because you're smothering me! When I wake up in the morning, you're at my door. And, now, you don't even go away at night. I don't want you for a roommate. I need my life back!"

His easy grin faded and his jaw clenched. His tawny eyes narrowed like those of a stalking cougar. In a steely voice, heavy with sarcasm, he said, "Gee, Mary, I didn't mean to invade your space. I was only trying to save your spoiled, ungrateful little rear end."

Realizing his bitter tone was a cover-up for his wounded feelings, Mary pushed away the guilt that was gnawing at her like a hungry rat. She reached out a tentative hand and placed it on his arm. "I'm sorry. I didn't mean that the way it came out. Of course I'm grateful for all you've done. It's just that…my whole life feels upside down and I'm just not handling it well."

Trace breathed deeply as he studied her face. "There are no guarantees, Mary. No matter how carefully we plan things, no matter how secure our nests are, sometimes people intrude and…screw up our orderly little lives."

She gulped and dropped her gaze. Trace couldn't know how true his words were. His coming into her life *had* shaken her existence, but not in the way he meant. He thought he'd interfered in the order, the routine of her life. Far, far worse, his presence had caused her to question the direction of her future.

When she said nothing, he continued, "Anyway, your wedding is only a few weeks away now. You won't have to put up with me much longer. But this creep is getting more and more daring, and I'm not going to leave you alone. So, like it or not, Mary-Mary, until you exchange wedding vows with Jonathan Regent, I'm going to be your shadow every minute of the day."

The determined edge in his voice told her that further argument was useless. In silent, mutual accord, they slowly turned from each other and ambled into the living room. Mary collected her sweater and handbag while Trace strapped on his shoulder harness.

Wordlessly, they walked to the foyer. Arm held straight out, Trace kept her from view while he checked out the peephole, then cautiously opened the door and scanned the empty hall. Still irritated by his cavalier attitude, Mary pushed past him and started into the corridor.

Her passage was halted, however, by the latest "surprise" waiting on her doorstep.

A huge funeral wreath was standing on a wire frame on the doormat. The blossoms, once fragrant and lovely, were all dead, giving off a sickly sweet odor of decay. The foliage was the gray of a graveyard on a rainy day, and forlorn brown petals littered the hallway. Only the wide black ribbon that ran across the wreath looked new. In bright gold script, the message on the black sash read, "In Loving Memory."

Her hands rose involuntarily to cover her mouth, smothering the scream she felt rising to the surface. She felt weak and cold. Horribly cold. Wordlessly, she sagged against Trace's chest.

"What's—" Looking over her shoulder, Trace spat an epithet when he saw the sick "gift."

"Damn it!" he shouted as he aimed a high kick that sent the funeral spray flying down the corridor. "Double-damn the bastard to hell!"

THE BRIDAL BOUTIQUE in old town Alexandria wasn't like any store Trace had ever been in before. It was more like one of the mirrored and gilded drawing rooms he'd seen on a PBS special about the palace at Versailles. Obviously an establishment frequented primarily by women, the owner was nonetheless prepared for a male visitor.

A clerk handed him a china cup of herbal tea, and a magazine filled with pictures of honeymooning couples splashing in heart-shaped bathtubs, then relegated him to an uncomfortable chair in the waiting area.

Not that he minded being excluded from the festivities. Mary's upcoming wedding was none of his concern; and he'd do well to remember that. He was her bodyguard, her hired hand. Nothing more.

Sipping the bland tea, he tried to balance the cup and saucer on his knee for a few minutes, before he gave up and set them on the floor. The damn cup didn't hold more than a thimbleful of liquid in the first place.

But Trace knew it wasn't the ritzy surroundings or the fragile china that was frustrating him. It was his inability to get a handle on who was stalking Mary.

It had been over an hour since they'd called the front desk to have the funeral spray removed, and yet Trace's fury had barely abated. He shifted on the dainty Louis Quatorze-style chair and in his mind replayed the events of the past few days. What was he missing? There had to be some clue, some tiny detail that he'd overlooked that would give him the key to nail the perpetrator.

He was inclined to agree with Mary that the man she'd spotted several times—the one who'd been waiting on her doorstep—was a hired gun. Someone else, some unseen hand, was orchestrating the attacks. But who?

Camille Castnor was his first choice. Sending "poisoned" candy was the kind of stunt that women pulled. Anonymous letters were also thought by criminologists to be a female-dominated crime. Yeah, the senator's wife was a pretty likely suspect. No doubt she had the money to hire a thug to act on her behalf.

A gabble of excited voices from the dressing room interrupted Trace's thoughts. He raised his head, expecting Mary to emerge from the draperied cubicle, but the murmur of voices faded and he was left alone with his thoughts again.

Earlier, Mary had mentioned Bob Newland as a possible suspect. Trace had to admit that Bob had spoken of Mary quite harshly. Still, disliking a person seemed a puny reason for sending death threats.

Nor was Trace convinced of Mark Lester's innocence. The man was a nut case, that much was certain, but he'd seemed devoid of the cold-blooded malice that you'd expect in a stalker. Trace bit his lip in frustration. He didn't feel any closer to the truth now than the day he'd agreed to take the case.

He fidgeted on the uncomfortable chair and glanced at his watch. *How long could it take to try on a dress? What was keeping Mary?*

As if in tune with his thoughts, the hum of voices suddenly grew louder, the dressing room curtains parted and Mary stepped into view. No, Trace thought, his breath caught somewhere under his rib cage, Mary hadn't stepped into the room, she'd floated in. With a long, sibilant sigh, his pent-up breath escaped, leaving a furious pounding in his chest.

Mary, a dream, a vision in white glided magically over the wine-colored carpeting, the store owner and two salesclerks following in her wake.

All brides are beautiful. The old adage drifted into his consciousness. Maybe so, but Mary opened a whole new meaning for the word *beautiful*. Shimmering. Mesmerizing. Sultry, sensual, yet heartbreakingly innocent.

Mary and her entourage of store clerks stopped in front of a three-way mirror. With regal serenity, Mary stood still while the two attendants draped a filmy veil over her hair.

She looked up, catching his eye in the mirror.

Struck mute by the impact of his confused emotions, he simply stared back until, finally, she broke the visual connection and turned away.

Mary reached up to adjust the veil and realized that her hand was trembling. No matter how she tried to deny it, she couldn't forget that look in Trace's eyes in the mirror. For once, she'd caught him in an unguarded moment, and there was no mistaking the pure enchantment in his reflected gaze.

Nor could she ignore the sudden pounding in her breast; a primal response to the predatory and hotly demanding look in his eyes.

A shrill ringing of the telephone took the store owner away, and she left her two assistants to attend to Mary. Both were young women, full of giggles and whispers. Now that their boss was gone for a moment, they broke into excited chatter. While they fluffed the satin skirts and adjusted the lengthy train, Mary allowed her thoughts to drift away. Allowed herself to wallow in the dangerous fantasy that had been nibbling at the edge of her awareness for the past few days.

She was in the back of a small church. White baskets bursting with fragrant pale pink flowers banked the altar. Tall white tapers cast a golden glow on the covey of people standing nearby. In her mind, Mary could see her mother in the front pew, a weepy smile on her face.

Then, the organist shifted in her seat and the first distinctive notes of Lohengrin's bridal accompaniment filled the air. Mary's father appeared beside her, offering his arm and, together, they started down the long aisle.

All around her, the people crowding the church rose to their feet, all eyes following Mary's slow progress to the altar.

That's where *he* waited.

Tall, darkly handsome. His black suit emphasizing the breadth of his shoulders, his face still turned from hers.

It was Mary's wedding day, the happiest day of her life. The man she loved, the man whose ring glittered on her finger was slowly turning to face her.

As they approached the altar, her father disengaged her hand from his arm and stepped back, making way for the man who would now come first in her life.

In her fantasy, that man bent and gently lifted the filmy veil from Mary's face. With the gauzy material no longer obstructing her vision, when Mary opened her eyes again, the face she would see was that of her betrothed. The man whose bed she would share for the first time that night, and every night for the rest of her life.

As she lifted her head in preparation for Jonathan's kiss, her eyes opened and Mary blinked in stunned disbelief.

It wasn't Jonathan waiting for her in his black tuxedo; it was Trace Armstrong.

"Miss Wilder? Are you all right, dear?" The store owner had returned, and her brisk, businesslike voice had the same effect as a bucket of cold water.

Mary whirled, her face a mask of confusion. "I'm sorry. What did you say?"

One of the clerks, the short, plump one named Gerda, patted Mary's arm. "That must have been some daydream, honey. You sure looked like you were enjoying it. Not that I can say as I blame you." She nudged her companion and they both cast a knowing glance at Trace.

The other clerk raised an eyebrow and said slyly, "Mmm-mmm. Honey, if that were *my* fiancé, I guarantee we'd be eloping. Right now!"

Mary started to protest, but the store owner was already chastising the girls roundly and she didn't want to add to their troubles. After all, they had no way of knowing that Trace wasn't her fiancé.

But *she* knew better.

Had she no shame? The ring on her finger had been placed there by Jonathan, not Trace. Jonathan loved her, trusted her. And how did she repay his faith? By fantasizing about another man. She was sickened by her own disloyalty.

"How do you like the gown, dear?" the store owner asked, a concerned frown on her face.

"Fine. Just fine." Her cheeks stinging with embarrassment, Mary turned around to retreat to the dressing room, when an image out of the corner of her eye halted her.

Slowly twisting her head, she stared at the plate-glass window at the front of the boutique.

As her eyes adjusted to the brilliant light flooding in the storefront window, she made out the image that had intruded into her subconscious.

A figure was standing just outside the shop, looking in.

As the blood chilled in her veins, Mary raised a wobbly hand and pointed at the shadowy figure. It was the man in the baseball cap. The man who'd been waiting on her doorstep yesterday.

The man whose note said he was going to kill her.

Chapter Ten

His eyes following Mary's accusing finger, Trace threw down the magazine and leapt to his feet.

That bastard had followed them!

Acting with the quick, sure instinct honed by years of experience, Trace bolted from his seat and flew out the front door.

The quaint brick sidewalks were filled with passersby, tourists mainly, judging from the cameras strapped around their necks, but there was no sign of a fleeing figure in a purple ball cap. Trace was unwilling to admit that the creep had gotten away clean. Dodging the milling tourists, he picked a direction at random and raced to the nearest corner. Seeing nothing, he crossed the street and reversed his direction.

But after several fruitless minutes of popping his head in storefronts and scanning the passing throng, he had to admit defeat.

The stalker had vanished into the crowd.

More frustrated than ever, Trace reluctantly made his way back to the bridal boutique. As he neared the door, his pace slowed. He was in no hurry to see the look of disappointment in Mary's eyes.

By the time he trudged into the salon, Mary was waiting just inside the door, dressed in the simple linen sheath she'd worn from home. "Thank heavens, you're all right! You were gone so long that... that I was getting worried."

Trace mopped his sticky forehead with his sleeve. His recent exertion barely discernible, he shook his head. "Sorry, but he got away from me. No luck."

Her expression was strained and anxious, but there was no hint of the reproach or disappointment he expected. Instead, she hesitantly asked, "But you did see him, didn't you? I mean, it wasn't my imagination. Was it?"

Despite his earlier declaration to keep a firm emotional distance between them, her forlorn manner melted Trace's resolve. Placing both hands on her shoulders, he pulled her to him. "I only had a glimpse of the filthy snake, but he was for real, all right. So help me, Mary, I'll get him next time. I swear it."

She raised her head and looked up at him. "It's not your fault. I just wish we had some idea who he is, or who's behind all this. And why."

Hearing the wobbly catch in her voice, Trace knew she'd almost reached the end of her rope. She'd been through a lot these past few days. More than she should have to endure in a lifetime. "Are you finished here?" he asked.

When she nodded her reply, he wrapped an arm around her shoulder and opened the plate-glass door. "Let's get you home then, kiddo. It's been a long morning."

WHEN THEY RETURNED to the hotel, Trace ordered lunch from room service while Mary took a long, reviving shower. Walking over to the glass patio door, he looked down on the peaceful-looking street below. Mary had finally won the battle they'd been waging over whether or not to keep the vertical blinds drawn. They'd struck a bargain wherein she'd reluctantly agreed not to stand near the window, and he'd just as reluctantly agreed to keep the blinds open during the day.

Now, he was regretting that bargain. Somewhere down there was an obsessed weirdo watching Mary's every move. Trace could almost feel the man's presence. Even now, he could imagine the man in the purple ball cap in that tall building across the way, spying on him with high-powered binoculars.

Over his long and sometimes violent career, Trace had become immune to fear. When he was still working on the presidential detail for the secret service, he'd finally reached the point where he didn't flinch at every strange noise. Didn't wake up every morning and wonder if this was the day he'd take a bullet meant for the president.

For years now, Trace's life had been so empty that the specter of death was no longer frightening. Suddenly, everything had changed. Now, fear was his constant companion. Fear not for his own safety, but for Mary's. The all-too-real dread that Trace wouldn't be able to stop the stalker in time to save her life.

That very concern for Mary was causing him to lose his edge. Because of this incredibly primal urge to protect her, Trace found himself jumping at every shadow. A nervous bodyguard made mistakes. Mistakes he couldn't afford. Not with Mary's life hanging in the balance.

Hearing the shower stop abruptly, he pulled his mind to the present and strode into the kitchen. He had already placed the covered plates delivered by room service onto a pair of linen place mats. Carrying two tumblers of root beer, Trace was in the kitchen doorway when Mary came down the hall.

She was barefoot, dressed in scruffy jeans and a red T-shirt. A thick towel was wrapped around her head, and her face was devoid of makeup. She looked as young and carefree as a teenager. Trace grinned; Mary was so fresh and shining, the entire room was illuminated with her glow.

It was the first time in days that her face was free from tension. He instantly made it his goal to keep her that way.

At least for a while. To keep the mood light, he set the
glasses on the table and said, "Luncheon is served,
m'lady." He bowed and pulled her chair out with an exag-
gerated flourish.

Falling into his playful mood, Mary curtsied and slid into
her seat. She sniffed the air appreciatively. "Smells heav-
enly. What are we having?"

He lifted the stainless-steel lid from her plate. "Chili dogs
à la Regent."

As if relieved by the silly distraction, Mary laughed
aloud. "They don't have chili dogs on the menu."

"I know." Trace pulled out his own chair with his foot.
"I had to bribe the chef an extra ten bucks to go buy some
from that guy who has a cart on the corner."

"So, you're a true gourmand. I'm impressed. Not every
man has an appreciation for nitrates, unspeakable pig parts
and preservatives." She picked up her hot dog and bit into
it with obvious gusto.

Conversation became limited to a few moans of pure
pleasure while they munched on their junk food. Mary was
still wiping the greasy residue from her fingers, when the
telephone rang. She was so enjoying the break in tension
that her first impulse was to let the phone ring. But the
thought that it might be Jonathan calling from Alaska
brought her up with a guilty start.

Jumping back from the table, she rushed to grab the
phone before the recorder could kick in on the fifth ring.
"Hello?"

"Mary, what's going on? You sound out of breath."

"Oh, Jonathan, I thought it might be you. Where are
you?"

He sighed and replied slowly, "Don't you remember? I
told you that I had to go away on business—"

"I know," Mary interrupted. "Alaska. It's just that this
connection is so good, you could be in the next room. How
was the trip?"

"Fine. Fine," he answered in a distracted manner. "I'm leaving for Anchorage tomorrow. But I'm more interested in hearing about you. I tried to phone earlier. Where were you?"

Wrapping the cord around her fingertip, Mary related her trip to the bridal salon. Not wanting to worry him, she gushed at length over the gown she'd chosen, then lightly skimmed over the incident of the man's watching her through the window.

When she finished, Jonathan held his silence for a long, tension-filled moment. In an accusing, judgmental tone, he continued, "So Armstrong wasn't able to nab him?"

That was unfair—the stalker had had a big head start. And the streets had been extremely crowded. Mary shook her head in vigorous denial of his inference. Then, realizing he couldn't see the gesture, she forced a light, confident tone into her voice as she added details of the chase. "Of course," she finished, "Trace had to break off his search because he didn't want to leave me alone so long."

"Hmm. I see. I guess that makes sense. So you think the bodyguard is able to handle the situation? You feel secure with him?"

Did she feel secure with Trace? No, no, no! She felt vulnerable and frightened of her own crazy emotions. But was she afraid for her physical safety? Again, no. When Trace was with her, Mary felt cosseted and protected.

She thought about the hard determined heft to Trace's jaw when he'd taken off after the man who'd been watching her. She thought about the careful way Trace's eyes scanned every room before she entered it. The way he sensed her moods before she did and placed a protective arm around her shoulders whenever she was feeling exposed and vulnerable.

Realizing Jonathan was still waiting for an answer, she whispered, "You don't need to worry about me. Worry about your business meeting. If anyone can handle this situation, Trace Armstrong can."

Mary hung up the telephone, feeling strangely reassured. She'd told Jonathan the truth—she was safe from the stalker as long as she was with Trace. But who would protect her from her own confused emotions?

By the time she returned to the dining room, Trace was clearing the table. "Regent?"

She nodded. "He's in Seattle. Leaving for Anchorage in the morning."

Trace nodded. "Listen, I need to go over to my apartment and pack a few clothes. Another day and this shirt's going to be able to stand on its own."

Mary laughed. "I was going to mention that," she said jokingly. "How long will you be gone?"

He shook his head. "I want you to come with me."

Mary hesitated. She wasn't at all sure that it would be wise to go to Trace's apartment. She was having a hard enough time keeping their relationship on a professional level. Going into his home, taking a peek into his private life would only make it more difficult. Still, she *was* curious about the way he lived. . . .

"While you were in the shower, I called Camille Castnor and made an appointment for us to see her this afternoon."

Obviously, he'd already made the assumption that Mary would be accompanying him. Glad for the chance to shift her thoughts in a less personal direction, she said flatly, "You want to talk to her about that box of candy."

"We can't ignore her possible role in this just because she's rich and married to a powerful man."

Mary shrugged. "I still think you're wrong about Camille. You won't be too...aggressive when you question her, will you?"

Trace rolled his eyes and pushed away from the table. When he looked at her again, his cat eyes burned bright with anger. "No, Mary, despite the fact that I'm only a lowly bodyguard, I'm not going to embarrass you in front of the senator's wife."

"That's not what I meant!"

He waved a dismissive hand toward the bedrooms. "Okay, fine. Just go get dressed, will you?"

She wanted to argue more. As a matter of fact, it seemed every conversation she'd had with the prickly and stubborn Trace Armstrong degenerated into verbal combat. Either that or he made these inflammatory statements then refused to discuss them. If he wanted to think she'd belittled him—fine. Let him keep on thinking it.

Turning on her heel, Mary stalked into the bathroom to blow-dry her hair.

MARY HADN'T SAID a word since they'd left her apartment. Getting more irked by the moment, Trace missed his turnoff and had to drive through the city. He was so annoyed, he forgot to change gears. His car stalled in a busy intersection, eliciting colorful comments from drivers forced to go around him. After that, they caught every red traffic light and Trace could feel his irritation building into a full-blown storm.

He glanced beside him where Mary was staring out the window, still obviously enjoying giving him the silent treatment.

With a frustrated snarl, he made an abrupt turn down Fifteenth Street. The tranquil beauty of the Tidal Basin always soothed him when he was in a funk, and his temper could sure use some soothing right now.

Spring had finally erupted with a lush, glorious profusion. The cherry trees, late to bloom this year, had burst into flower and the air was redolent of the sweetness of their breathtaking blossoms. Trace felt his irritation evaporating with every whiff of the heady fragrance. By the time they'd circled behind the Jefferson Memorial, he had his temper back under control.

He wasn't mad at Mary or the traffic. He was furious with himself. He'd broken his cardinal rule and allowed himself to become personally attached to a client. A no-win situation under the best of circumstances, it was even worse now because Mary was only weeks from wedding another man. Like it or not, those were the facts. The best thing Trace could do for either one of them was to get his emotions back on track and keep his mind on the job.

Casting another glance at her, he was struck anew by her wholesome beauty, which flowed from an inner wellspring of gentleness and integrity. "Sorry I was such a jerk. Guess this case has me more worked up than I thought."

Mary turned her head and gave him an appraising look. Her blond hair was in a ponytail. A long strand had come loose and was snuggling against her cheek. Her eyes were guileless, yet at the same time, distrusting.

"No problem," she said carefully.

"Yes, it is a problem. I was worked up about this guy and took it out on you."

"I understand."

The sweet forgiving expression on her face echoed her words. Why did she have to be so damned understanding?

"So, how many presidents have you guarded?" she asked in an obvious attempt to shift to a safer subject. "I'll bet you could tell some wonderful stories."

The iciness between them quickly melted and they chatted all the way to Trace's apartment in Falls Church. They talked about the beauty of the Virginia countryside, the unseasonably balmy weather and even touched on a couple of entertaining episodes that had occurred while Trace had been working in the White House.

To discuss anything remotely personal would break an unspoken taboo.

Leaving Mary to look around his clean, but disheveled condo, Trace checked his messages, thumbed through a stack of accumulated mail and threw some clothes into a battered suitcase.

It was disconcerting, somehow, to watch Mary studying his home, touching mementos from his life in government service. She asked no questions, honoring their nonverbal agreement to avoid personal topics.

A half hour later, he tossed his suitcase into the trunk and they headed for the Castnor home in the rolling hillsides of Middleburg, Virginia.

Following Mary's directions, they turned onto a wide, tree-lined road edged by white wooden fences that seemed to go on for miles. Here and there, Thoroughbred horses foraged through the rich, green grass, looking haughty and regal on their slender legs.

Oak-shrouded driveways allowed occasional glimpses of huge colonial-style brick homes set well back off the road. Stables were visible through the trees, and training rings the size of football fields dotted the landscape. Although Mary's penthouse apartment in Georgetown was sumptuous by any standard, Trace knew that Middleburg was the big-money district. A former president he'd once been assigned to had retired only a few miles away.

Undoubtedly, when Mary became Mrs. Regent, she'd have a fine home on a few hundred prime acres in this area. Once again, Trace felt an unwelcome resentment of Regent's wealth and his ability to give Mary the kind of lifestyle Trace had never even dreamed of.

"Turn here," Mary directed suddenly, pointing to a barely visible driveway on the left.

An impressive wrought-iron gate was standing ajar, allowing them passage. Only a discreet brass plaque on the brick stanchion holding the mailbox gave any indication they'd reached the Castnor home.

When they pulled up the circular driveway in front of an imposing plantation-style house, complete with six pillars across the portico, the front door opened immediately and a formally attired butler greeted them.

Showing only slight disdain for their casual attire, the butler led them inside to a sitting room of comfortable dimensions, yet cold and unwelcoming in the perfection of its decor.

When they turned down refreshments, the butler withdrew. Almost immediately, Camille Castnor swept into the room in his wake.

"Mary, darling! How lovely to see you." Camille crossed the room and blew air kisses in Mary's direction. "I hope that nothing is wrong. Your man seemed quite insistent that I change my schedule and see you today."

She didn't speak to or acknowledge Trace in any way. He was Mary's "man," with no greater value than a piece of Louis Vuitton luggage.

Trace bristled at her deprecating manner, but said nothing, allowing Mary to take the lead.

When they'd all taken a seat, Mary leaned forward. "I do apologize for the short notice, Camille, but we both felt it was important to talk with you right away."

"Both? Is Jonathan involved in this?"

"No. I meant Trace and I."

Camille jerked her head in his direction and studied him closely. Trace had the distinct impression that this was the first time she'd ever noticed him.

Settling back against the ivory brocade wing chair she'd selected to sit in, Camille lit a cigarette and blew smoke rings into the air. Her tone as frigid as her demeanor, she again turned to address Mary. "What's this about?"

Trace had had enough of Camille's snooty manner. "It's about the two-pound box of chocolates you bought at the Crystal City Mall on Tuesday. And about the two-pound box of ipecac-laced chocolates you delivered to Mary on Wednesday morning."

"I resent your insinuation!"

Trace shook his head slowly. "I didn't make any insinuations, Mrs. Castnor. I merely said we'd come to talk about it. Any reason why you're so defensive?"

"Trace!" This time it was Mary who objected.

"Look, ladies, I'm really sorry to upset your sensibilities with all these sordid little details, but in case you've both forgotten, some sordid little weasel has threatened Mary's life. I don't intend to let him carry out his threats, so if I have to step on any delicate tootsies to do my job, so be it."

Camille rose to her feet. "I don't care for your manner, young man, and I don't have to stand for it."

Trace, too, stood up and looked her in the eye. "No, you don't have to stand up, you can sit back down. Or we can leave and the police will be your next visitors. Wouldn't that give your neighbors something to talk about—this being an election year, and all?"

Camille slowly dropped into her chair and puffed furiously on her cigarette. "I'll give you five minutes, then I'll phone the police myself."

Mary leaned forward, her hands clasped tightly on her knees. "Camille, this is getting out of hand. No one is going to call the authorities. Trace just needs to ask you a few questions."

Camille stubbed out her cigarette. "You have four minutes left."

Stilling Mary with a shake of his head, Trace asked, "Do you admit that you bought a two-pound box of Splendora Chocolates on Tuesday?"

"Yes."

"And did you inject ipecac syrup in those candies and deliver them to Mary the next morning?"

"No."

Trace had to admit that Mrs. Castnor was one tough cookie. She didn't fidget in her chair or shift her gaze; she kept her cold, unblinking stare focused on his eyes. "But you do admit that you delivered a box of chocolates to Ms. Wilder?"

"Yes. You have three minutes left."

"What did you do with the candy you purchased, Mrs. Castnor?"

"Gave them to the senator's secretary. It was her birthday."

That would be easy enough to check. Trace pulled out a small spiral notebook and wrote himself a reminder.

"Is there anything else?" Camille's tone was nonchalant, as if he were a census taker or encyclopedia salesman, not the man who was questioning her about her possible involvement in a felony.

Mary stood up. "I think that's all we need, Camille. I'm truly sorry."

Slowly, the older woman lifted her gaze to meet Mary's. "Sorry? I should think so. I've befriended you, taught you how to dress, how to behave at state receptions, even offered the use of my home for your wedding—"

"I said I was sorry," Mary cut in. "But surely you can understand that the coincidence had to be explained."

Camille uncoiled herself like a viper. "The only thing that needs to be explained is what Jonathan saw in a pitiful little country bumpkin like you in the first place! You have one minute left. Either use it or get the hell out of my house."

Trace stepped forward between the two women. "It won't take me a full minute, Mrs. Castnor. This was merely a courtesy visit. Mary didn't want to press charges without offering you the opportunity to explain. The truth is that we already know you tampered with those chocolates."

Camille turned as pale as the brocade chair she'd been sitting in, and Trace knew that his bluff had worked. She *was* involved in this—all the way up to her perfectly capped teeth.

While she was still off guard and rattled, he pressed his advantage. "You thought you were being clever by leaving that box on the counter in the lobby. That *was* clever. If you'd just walked away, nobody would have paid any attention. But you couldn't just let it be, could you? You had to see Mary's face when she got her 'surprise,' didn't you?"

When she didn't answer his charges, Trace felt his rage growing. His hunch had been right all along. Camille Castnor's nasty, jealous little mind was behind all of this.

Hoping that he could continue to guess the correct sequence of events and not raise Camille's suspicions, he continued, "The bell captain remembered you came in twice in a short period. He's willing to swear to that in court, Mrs. Castnor. Why don't you save us all some grief and just admit it?"

"All right, damn you! All right." Camille sank into the wing chair and buried her face in her hands.

Trace forced himself to ignore the stricken expression on Mary's face. This was no time to let up the pressure, no matter how pitiful Camille now seemed. "Who did you hire to follow Mary and leave those threatening letters?"

Camille's head bobbed up, humiliation and shock equally evident on her tear-streaked face. "But that wasn't me."

Mary still hadn't said a word. Her face was now a complete blank.

Taking her silence for assent to his continuing the questioning, Trace shook his head sadly. "Come on, Mrs. Castnor, you may as well get it all off your chest."

"But it's true! I didn't hire anyone to follow or harass Mary. In fact, her talking about it all the time gave me the idea."

"And you expect us to believe that?" Trace asked, skepticism dripping from his voice.

"It's the truth!"

Breaking away from his accusing stare, Camille turned and picked up her cigarettes. With trembling fingers, she pulled a filter tip from the cellophane package and held it in the air, like a fetish that would ward off more questions.

Trace knew he couldn't thrash the truth out of her, but the urge was strong. Very strong. This spoiled, sulking witch could have seriously harmed Mary. He'd have the truth or, by God, he *would* call the police.

"I don't believe you," he said coldly. "Are you implying that someone else is involved in this?"

"Whether or not you believe me doesn't change the truth. I don't know any more about Mary's stalker than she herself has told me."

For the first time since Camille's startling confession, Mary spoke. Her soft voice was saturated with deep unrelenting pain. "But why? I thought . . . I thought you were my friend."

"Friend!" Camille spat the word out of her mouth as though she'd tasted something vile. "I tried to be nice to you, I truly did. For Jonathan's sake. I took you around Washington as though you were my protégée. But how did you repay my kindness? By bragging about every gift Jonathan gave you. Flashing that pretentious diamond in my face. Rubbing my face in your happiness!"

Mary blanched at the horrible accusations. She swayed on her feet like an outmatched boxer, until Trace feared she would faint. He placed a steadying hand around her waist and felt gratified when she leaned against him, as if absorbing strength from him.

Facing Camille, Trace no longer had any pity for the woman. Her spiteful indictment of Mary had cleared his conscience of any compassion. "I don't want any more of your lousy excuses. Just tell me who you hired and where I can find him."

Without warning, Camille threw her unlit cigarette onto the oriental rug and charged at him. Trace grabbed her wrists, easily holding her off.

"Damn you!" she screeched. "Can't you understand English? I had nothing to do with the stalker. When Mary came to dinner that night and...and I saw Jonathan treating her like he never treated me, something just snapped. I never meant to really hurt her. I just wanted to make her feel sick inside...the way I felt watching her with Jonathan."

Her self-debasing tone finally cut through Trace's anger. There was a ring of truth to her pathetic story. He'd been right all along. Having long suppressed her feelings of rejection since Jonathan had broken up with her, Camille had finally assuaged her humiliation at Mary's expense.

They stayed another half hour pressing Camille for details, but she never wavered from her assertion: she'd doctored the candy but had no part in hiring someone to torment Mary.

The stalker was still out there.

Chapter Eleven

When Trace finally dropped into bed in Mary's spare room hours later, it was his turn to toss from side to side all night. Mentally going over the case again and again as though it were a sleep-inducing mantra, he found no answers in the ever-diminishing list of suspects.

Next he tried replaying the interview with Camille. Had he missed any subtle clue in their conversation? Had he been too deceived by the woman's histrionics to maintain his objectivity? No, he didn't think so. Camille Castnor was a lamentable and vengeful woman, but he believed her story. Yesterday, he'd been certain she had hired the stalker. Tonight, he was just as sure that she had no involvement beyond the tainted chocolates.

Still, it wasn't Camille's guilt or innocence that kept him from sleep. It was an image he'd been trying to put out of his mind all day. But there was no escaping the memory of Mary floating toward him in that wedding dress, her brown eyes sparkling with intelligence, wit and an incredible sensuality.

Nor could Trace forget her dreamy gaze watching him through the mirror, before the salesclerks dropped that nearly sheer veil over her eyes and blurred the hypnotic communion between Mary and Trace.

He sat up and punched the pillow. He turned on his left side and counted sheep. One, two, three white woolly lambs jumping over the pasture fence. Little lambs being led to slaughter. Mary had a little lamb. Mary. Mary...

What was he going to do about Mary?

When Trace's wife had left him—how many years ago had she been gone now? Five? Six? It didn't matter. He'd never seen her again. She'd left him a note saying she was tired of living from payday to payday on the paltry salary of a man who was rarely home. Trace couldn't really blame her. Diane, like any woman, needed more than a man who dropped in from time to time like a visiting relative.

Since Diane's defection, he'd managed to completely shut away his heart. After a while, he'd even learned to ignore the emptiness he felt in those rare nights alone in his condo. He'd told himself with the type of work he did, he didn't have time for a steady relationship, and certainly didn't have much chance at maintaining a successful one.

Back when he'd first realized the depths of Diane's unhappiness, it had never occurred to him to look into pursuing a different type of work. But for a woman like Mary...

Bloody hell! He flipped onto his back. He had to stop obsessing about Mary. His only connection with her was as her bodyguard. His job was to protect Mary Wilder, not fall in love with her. But Trace wondered if it wasn't already too late.

Fate had handed him a wonderful gift, but had wrapped it with barbed wire. Suddenly, he had the capacity to care again. To feel again. And, unless he was seriously mistaken, Mary was beginning to have feelings for him, as well.

But she was engaged to be married to one of the richest men in the state—maybe even in the entire country. A man who was rumored to be the favorite son in the Virginia congressional race next year.

Get real, Armstrong. Like you have a chance against a man like Jonathan Regent. The Mary of Trace's fantasy wouldn't judge the measure of a man by the size of his wallet. But in reality, he had to face the fact that Mary *was* betrothed to a multimillionaire. What woman would give up so much for so little? And if Trace truly cared about her, he'd have her best interests at heart and wouldn't ask her to.

THERE WERE NO further incidents over the next couple of days. Trace and Mary went over her background again and again, but she could dredge up no incident, no relationship gone sour that might have provoked this relentless campaign of terror.

They made lists of every person she'd met since she'd moved to the District; one by one, they'd eliminated the names on those lists. All but one.

Jonathan's assistant, Bob Newland.

Newland's antagonism wasn't a figment of Mary's overwrought imagination. Trace vividly recalled Newland's disparaging comments about Mary, and the fanatical light of ambition that shone in his eyes.

Was it jealousy that incurred such rancor in the assistant? Or simple disapproval?

Perhaps more important than determining the man's motivation was finding out if Newland had acted on his dislike, counting on the stalker to frighten Mary from going through with her wedding plans.

Rather than challenge Newland head-on as they'd done with Mark Lester and Camille, Mary and Trace decided to discover everything they could about Newland before they forced a confrontation. Maybe something in the man's background would provide hard evidence they could use.

After meeting with Madame Guillarge to approve the design of her attendants' dresses, Mary and Trace drove south to the quaint resort town of Occoquan, Virginia, for lunch.

Trace had made a luncheon date for them with an old friend of his, Harley Tobias, who was currently on assignment as an instructor at the FBI academy in nearby Quantico.

It was another glorious spring day, and the proprietor of the seafood restaurant slapped Trace on the back like an old friend and led them to a table on a deck overlooking the river. They ordered iced tea while they waited for Harley, and a moment later, a tall, exceedingly handsome man appeared at their table carrying two glasses of tea.

"Harley Tobias! You old sonofagun." Trace jumped to his feet to greet his friend and former colleague. After setting the glasses on the table, Trace clasped his arms around Harley's back. "So it's finally happened, huh? The bureau fired you, so you got a job waiting tables."

"There's any waitin' to be done, you can wait on me, Armstrong," Harley said laughingly as he extended his large hand to Mary. "And who's this lovely lady with such bad taste in lunch companions?"

Trace made the introductions and drew up a third chair. The two old buddies entertained Mary with outlandish war stories during an excellent meal of crab cake sandwiches and coleslaw. After the plates had been cleared away, Harley leaned back in his chair, apparently waiting for Trace to broach the real reason for their visit.

While the waitress refilled their glasses, Trace laid a credit card on the bill. When she'd left, he filled Harley in on the details of Mary's perilous past few weeks.

Trace had just finished recounting the story, when the waitress returned with the credit slip for his signature. Again, Harley said nothing while Trace completed the transaction, but when he spoke again, his thick black eyebrows dipped low in a thunderous scowl.

"Don't mean to scare you, ma'am, but sounds like you've got yourself a first-class psycho. What does the Metro PD say?"

Trace shook his head. "The usual. Until we have an actual crime, there isn't much they can do. Anonymous notes don't rank real high when the police are fighting a drug war that averages a shooting death each day."

Harley nodded knowingly. "So what can I do to help? I don't see how the bureau can get involved. Stalking isn't a federal offense. Hell, it isn't even a criminal offense in some states. If we could just find a way to claim federal jurisdiction..."

Mary leaned forward. "We *do* have one suspect."

Harley laughed, exposing gleaming white teeth. "You been hangin' around Armstrong so long, you're talkin' the talk. Who's your suspect?"

Reaching into her handbag, Mary extracted the thin file of information they'd been able to compile on Bob Newland. Although his life was apparently an open book, the lack of any kind of criminal past had limited the information they'd been able to glean from the newspapers and public records.

Harley glanced through the file. "Says here he served a hitch in the navy. Went to college on the G.I. Bill. There should've been some kind of B.I. done."

"What's a B.I.?" Mary asked.

"Background investigation," the men answered in unison.

"How long do you think it will take?" Trace knew he didn't have to ask Harley *if* he'd do it. In the unspoken rules of their friendship, Trace wouldn't have asked for his friend's help if it wasn't extremely important. And neither man would refuse the other if the need was great.

Harley stood up. "Give me a day or two. Your number in this file?" he asked Mary.

"No. Let me write it down for you." Taking a pen from her purse, she scribbled her name and phone number on the front of the manila folder.

After a few more moments of pleasantries, Harley left, taking the file with him.

As Trace and Mary drove back toward the city a short time later, she said, "I guess there's nothing else we can do until we hear from Harley. I hope it doesn't take him too long."

Trace switched lanes; one car had been behind them longer than he was comfortable with. The car didn't change lanes with them and he breathed a little easier. "Harley will give it priority, don't worry."

As he negotiated the heavy traffic around the Capitol, Mary pondered whether they were acting wisely to pin all their suspicions on Bob Newland. Surely, there must be something else they could do while they waited for Harley's report. Any action at all was better than sitting around doing nothing while the stalker planned his next assault.

Once in the parking garage of the Georgetown Regent, they followed a now-familiar routine. Mary stayed in the car while Trace pulled his weapon and carefully scrutinized the dark garage. Once he determined no one was lurking about, he escorted her from the car to the elevator, his drawn gun ready at his side.

Once the elevator doors whispered open, she remained hidden from view while Trace scanned the hallway. Only after they were safely locked in her apartment, did he usually reholster his weapon.

Today, they followed the usual procedure.

With one major difference. When they reached Mary's apartment, the door was wide open.

Holding her back with his hand, Trace murmured, "Stay here. Don't move out of the doorway. If you see anyone coming—and I mean anyone at all—scream as loud as you can."

He disappeared inside and Mary waited, her heart thumping like a jungle drum, until he returned. Finally, after what seemed like hours, she heard his footsteps on the tile foyer floor. "What happened? Did the maid just forget to close the door securely?"

Trace shook his head as he stepped out into the hall and started to lead her away.

"What are you doing?" Mary asked.

He draped his free hand around her shoulders. In the other hand, he still held his revolver. "Someone broke into your apartment. We're going down to the lobby and call the police."

Mary felt the blood drain from her cheeks. She felt incredibly cold, yet a fire was starting deep in her soul. Her voice dropped to a barely audible whisper. "Do you think he's still inside?"

Drawing her close, Trace responded, "No. I checked pretty thoroughly. He'd done his dirty work and gone already."

She looked up at Trace with a bewildered expression on her face. "Then why don't we just use my phone?"

Leaving the door ajar, he strode toward the elevators, the strength of his arm forcing her along.

"Trace! Answer me, what's going on? Why did you leave the door open?"

"In case of fingerprints."

Horror growing inside with each passing second, Mary pulled free and stared at his blank expression. "Tell me."

"Later. Right now we have to call the cops."

Furious at his treating her like a child who can't be told adult problems, Mary whirled and ran through the open doorway into her apartment.

She'd taken no more than a half-dozen steps, when she stopped, shocked immobile by the chaotic scene that greeted her. The lovely Chinese vase usually on the phone table now lay in broken shards on the tile floor. The walls were smeared with streaks of bloodred paint.

Mary gulped, swallowing her terror. At least, she *hoped* it was only paint.

Without consciously realizing she'd taken any action, she took a step forward. Then another. Nothing within range of her vision had escaped the brutal assault on her home. The canvas on the expensive paintings was slashed, their ornate plaster frames smashed. The glass dining-room table was cracked; a heavy hammer lay abandoned on its crazed surface.

Still, her feet propelled her farther into the horror.

Somehow, she was dimly aware of Trace behind her. His sustaining presence was the only barrier between Mary and complete collapse.

When she reached the living room, she reached the end of her emotional endurance. The scream she'd been stifling began somewhere in her middle and welled up, through her chest, into her throat and at last, with a painful burning sensation, past her vocal cords. Yet only a pitiful little squeak emerged from her lips.

As she'd walked through her home, Mary had been battered by the images that met her. Her eyes were assaulted by the destruction but she'd been able to hold on to her lucidity by telling herself these were only *things* the madman had destroyed. He hadn't really touched her. Things could be replaced. Things didn't define her.

But here, in her living room, the sense of violation was so real, so potent, Mary ached as though she'd been physically battered. That ugly, abominable red paint was everywhere; on the furniture, the walls, the carpeting. The room she'd loved this morning now looked like a charnel house.

The mirror, which had hung behind the sofa, had been pulled from the wall and broken. Tiny fragments of shiny glass crunched beneath her sneakered feet. On the wall where the mirror had hung, the frenzied vandal had added his coup de grace.

Like a huge, jagged wound dripping red blood, the words JEZEBEL BEWARE! screamed at her.

Mary's stomach curled in fear and revulsion. The biblical reference was only too clear. Jezebel had been known as the whore of Babylon, and was pitched off a rooftop to die on the street below. Mary's eyes trailed to the balcony outside her living room. She imagined the busy pavement eight stories beneath her apartment and wondered if that horrible death was what the stalker had in mind for her.

The very idea of falling, faster and faster to her sudden ghastly death caused a shudder to undulate through her body. She felt as though an earthquake were erupting beneath her very flesh, tearing up her body and breaking down her spirit. Mary's legs suddenly folded, and she dropped slowly onto the ragged and torn sofa, finding little solace in her favorite corner.

She didn't know how long she sat there, drifting in and out of awareness. Taking part in but not absorbing the activity that bustled around her. She had a vague awareness of Trace finding an unbroken bottle of some kind of liquor, and then a bitter taste in her mouth as the stinging contents slid down her throat. She recognized but didn't relate to the team of paramedics who showed up and checked her for symptoms of shock.

Later, she was told that she answered all the questions of the hotel security men, then the police; but Mary couldn't recall talking at all.

Then, finally, thankfully, the circus was over and she and Trace were alone in the debris that had been her home. As if she'd been asleep for a very long time, Mary felt herself slowly returning to conscious perception. She was aware of Trace hovering over her, speaking in muted tones. She realized the apartment was silent but for the echoes of the madman who had ravaged it. How much time had passed since she'd drifted off?

Blinking rapidly, she brought Trace's concerned face into focus. He was kneeling in front of her and was gazing up, his expression drawn and wary.

"Everyone's gone?" she asked shakily.

His fingertips gently tracked the faint worry lines etched along the side of her mouth. Trailing upward, his fingers skimmed the soft skin, and followed the endearing trail of the small scar at the edge of her lip. "Yeah, they're all gone. Are you okay? The paramedics said you weren't in shock, but you seemed out of it to me. Not that you don't have every right or reason to just check out."

Worry had etched fresh crinkled furrows along his forehead, and smudged charcoal circles beneath his eyes. In a distracted manner, he shoved his hand through his hair with such force it was a wonder he didn't withdraw a clump of black hair.

Oddly enough, the gesture brought a weak smile to her face and her hand reached out to smooth the rumpled silkiness back into place.

For the briefest moment, Mary allowed herself to wallow in his tenderness, his all-encompassing warmth. He was always there when she needed him. His slightly sarcastic wit hid a heart filled to overflowing with gentleness. Her own heart burbled with gratitude and...something more. Something much stronger. Some emotion Mary was afraid to identify.

Trace grabbed her hand, bringing her icy fingertips to the warmth of his cheek. "Please, answer me, Mary. Say something. You haven't said a dozen words since the police left."

Again, that faint tremulous smile. "That's the first time I've ever heard a man complain because a woman *wasn't* talking."

Trace rocked back on his heels and laughed. "You're some kind of woman, Mary Wilder. Now, if you're feeling up to it, let's get some clothes gathered up for you and get the hell out of Dodge."

Knowing that Trace was doing his best to ease the horror in this abhorrent and bizarre situation, Mary managed a shaky half smile in return. Rising slowly to her feet, she said in what she hoped was a conversational tone, "So what was the final word from the police? I think I . . . kind of faded out a little there at the end."

His relieved smile disappeared, replaced by a furrow of concern plowing across his forehead. "Maybe we should call your own physician."

She waved off his suggestion. "I'm fine. Truly. I was just a little wobbly there for a while, but I think I deserved it."

A relieved grin was her reward. "Yeah, Mary Mary Quite Extraordinary, I'd say you deserved it. Anyway, the cops made a report and brushed the apartment for fingerprints, but unless our perp has completely changed his MO, any prints that aren't ours will end up belonging to the maid."

"In other words, they aren't going to do anything," she said bitterly.

Wrapping his arm around her shoulders, he gently pulled her close. "In other words, until and unless he surfaces again, there isn't much they *can* do. The only description we were able to offer was pretty vague—white male, late thirties-early forties, medium height, medium build, unknown hair and eye color and wearing a purple cap with a gold insignia of a howling wolf. Except for the cap, that description would fit nearly half the men in the country."

Mary felt her spirits sagging with the news. "I just feel so darned helpless. There must be something we could be doing."

Keeping his arm firmly wrapped around her shoulders, Trace guided her down the hall toward the bedrooms. "There is. On the off-chance that our perp did this himself, instead of hiring someone to do it, we can check on the whereabouts of our suspects when your apartment was being trashed."

Mary nodded glumly. "We already know Camille didn't do it, since we're her alibi for the time of the break-in."

"Maybe. But let's find out where Newland and Lester spent their morning."

Locating Mary's suitcase wasn't much of a problem. It was already reposing in the middle of her bedroom floor, where the intruder had yanked it from the closet. He'd also thoughtfully pitched her clothing into a heap nearby. A few articles had been ripped or smeared with red paint, but for the most part, Mary's clothing was in better condition than most of her other belongings.

While she tossed odds and ends into the crimson-stained suitcase, she voiced a tentative plan for checking out the alibis of Mark Lester and Bob Newland.

Trace listened with only half his concentration. Mentally, he was wrestling with a concern of his own. The police had pointed out one very disconcerting fact—the front-door lock showed no signs of forced entry. The hinges hadn't been pried off nor was the doorframe forced. There were no scratches on the polished brass surround. No nicks on the edge of the lock itself.

It was almost as if the intruder had a key.

Chapter Twelve

Although Trace tried his level best to talk Mary into moving into his condo until the stalker was apprehended, she steadfastly refused. The hotel manager was easily able to provide them with another suite, and Mary knew Jonathan would be upset if he tried to call her and discovered she'd moved out.

Trace countered by telling her to contact Jonathan in Alaska, but Mary pointed out that in order to get his phone number, she'd have to go through Bob Newland. And, at this point, they were still waiting for the FBI report from Harley before approaching Newland.

Trace was forced to accept her rationale, so they moved their belongings into a cold and impersonal hotel suite on the concierge level one floor below Mary's penthouse suite.

The main shortcoming of living in one of the regular suites became immediately apparent; there was only one bedroom. True, it had two king-size beds, but they were separated only by a nightstand.

Nor was there a kitchen, so they were forced to either go out for every meal or rely on room service, a situation that made Trace extremely uncomfortable.

That evening, as if the specter of the single bedroom stood between them, Mary and Trace sat up playing gin rummy until late in the evening. Both of them stifling yawns, he glanced up to see her knuckling her eyes like a small child fighting sleep. His heart melted at the telling gesture. He'd have to make the first move, and somehow reassure her that he wasn't going to sneak into her bed in the middle of the night.

Then he had to keep himself from actually doing it.

Throwing his cards on the table, Trace stood up and stretched. "I've had it. You want the bathroom first?"

Mary refused to meet his eye. "No, you go ahead. I'll straighten up out here."

"Okay." He forced a huge yawn. "I'm beat."

"Mmm."

"I'll probably be snoring by the time you come in, so I'll say good night now." He stretched again, forcing his hands skyward until the bones in his back creaked and groaned. Actually, he *was* tired, but how was a man supposed to rest with Mary snuggled into bed a couple feet away?

"'Night. See you in the morning." She stood up and started picking up glasses and potato-chip bags.

Knowing she needed this time to herself, Trace ambled into the shower. He was already in bed, the sheet pulled demurely above his bare hips when Mary tiptoed into the bedroom. Keeping his eyes closed, he feigned sleep while she quietly gathered her things and slipped into the small, adjoining bathroom.

A few moments later, the air was filled with her soft, delicious fragrance and he heard the sheets rustle as she crawled into bed. For a long time, the room was perfectly still as they lay in the darkness, both pretending to sleep. Eventually, Trace was able to decoy his mind away from her disturbing nearness, and sometime after midnight, sleep finally took him.

It was still dark when something awoke him. He sat up in bed. Alert. Listening intently to the night sounds.

A soft moan broke the waiting stillness. Mary! He eased his body to the edge of the bed and listened. Again, her voice broke the quiet as she cried out. She was having a nightmare, and one that was growing in intensity, judging by the way she was twisting in the bed.

Unmindful of his own nudity, Trace eased from his bed and crossed the small space between them. Lowering himself beside her, he called softly, "Mary?" He leaned over and clasped her shoulders, gently rocking her awake. "Mary, sweetheart, wake up. You're having a bad dream."

She moaned again and turned into his arms. Her body was damp with perspiration, and she burrowed her head against his bare chest. "No! Please. Stop..." Her words trailed off as a sob broke loose from somewhere deep in her chest.

A protective instinct such as he'd never known surged through him. The bastard—whoever he was. Wasn't it enough that he filled her days with terror? Now he was infiltrating her nights.

Wrapping his arms around her, he pulled her against him as if he could cushion her from the evil and fear that seemed to rule her life. "Shh, honey. It's okay. I'm here now. No one's going to harm you. I promise."

He held her until the sobs subsided, until the trembling in her limbs ceased and her breathing at last evened out. "Trace?" her voice whispered in the darkness. "Please don't leave me."

His heart lurched in his chest at the poignant pleading in her tone. Smoothing the silky texture of her golden hair, he murmured, "I'm here, Mary. I won't leave you. I promise."

She snuggled deeper against him, her hip nesting between his thighs. A torrent of heat rushed through him and he gritted his teeth to keep from hauling her into his bed. She was driving him crazy. But she was his client; his job was to protect her. Shield her. Defend her.

But how could he defend himself against these feelings that threatened to drown him?

Squinching his eyes closed against the desire flooding his body, he lowered his head and dropped a soft kiss on the top of her head. As if she'd been waiting for a cue, Mary twisted in his arms and lifted her lips to his.

The moment he felt the sweet softness of her mouth, Trace knew he was lost. With a groan of his own, he crushed her to him and at long last, savored the promise of her lips.

Mary stirred. She was drowning. Falling into a pool of silky softness. Warm water swirled around her, stroking her, caressing her. Suddenly, that smooth sensation became hands, touching her. Causing tides of sensation rippling through her body. It was Trace Armstrong. In her dream and in her heart, she knew his touch. Knew his delicious scent. Languorously, she lifted her arms and burrowed her fingers in his rich, thick hair as her mouth sought his.

Oh, it was so good. So right. So different from the dry, tentative kisses Jonathan—

Jonathan! Reality swept through her like an icy wind. This forbidden, treacherous need for Trace was going to destroy her. Dear God, how far would she have gone?

"No! Trace, no." Struggling to sit up, she pulled herself from his beguiling arms and huddled against the headboard, the sheet yanked up protectively beneath her chin.

Afraid to look at him, she nevertheless sneaked a quick peek at his shadowed features. Even in the near darkness, she could read his confusion.

"Mary? What is it? What..." His voice was husky and tinged with bewilderment.

Clenching her teeth against the ebbing tide of emotion, she growled, "What did you think you were doing?"

He leaned back and stared at her. "I was kissing you. And you were kissing back."

"I was not! I was asleep." And she was, at least, at first.

"You were awake! No one could have that kind of...passion while they were asleep. You make it sound like I took advantage of you and—"

"And maybe you did. Okay, so there's this...this chemistry thing between us. Fine. But we're adults, we're supposed to be able to rise above it."

For a long moment, he said nothing. Then he stood and slowly stepped over to his own bed. Dragging the bedspread loose, he draped it around his shoulders and snagged a pillow.

Pausing inches from Mary's bed, he said quietly, "I may be a lot of things, Mary Wilder, but I'm not something you need to rise above. You flatter yourself."

Without another word, he turned and marched out of the bedroom, leaving Mary alone with her guilt. And with a nagging itch of desire.

THE NEXT TWO DAYS were filled with ominous tension. Mary kept the incident with Trace hidden at the back of her consciousness. Concern because she hadn't heard from Jonathan mixed with frustration caused by her inability to check in with Bob Newland. For his part, Trace felt as though they were sitting on a ticking bomb. And he didn't know which wire to pull to stop the impending explosion.

Every instinct he'd honed over the years told him that one of his operatives should be on "baby-sitting" duty with Mary while Trace was pounding the pavement looking for answers. But Jonathan Regent had specifically ordered Trace to stay by her side. Anyway, Trace knew he would worry about Mary every second they were apart. Even if he wanted to wring her high-handed neck about half the time.

Worse, she wouldn't listen to him and keep her activities confined to the hotel room.

Insisting that she continue with her wedding arrangements, she hauled him to florists, caterers, seamstresses and engravers. Although Mary said Madame Guillarge was attending to the lion's share of the mundane details, it seemed to him that Mary was personally overseeing every facet of the involved procedure.

And that kiss in the darkness hung in the air between them.

In their comings and goings from the hotel, Trace had been certain that he'd caught a glimpse of the stalker at least twice before the man darted from sight. Once, just once, Trace wished the wretch was close enough to catch. Saying nothing to Mary, Trace pretended to ignore the stalker, hoping the man would become frustrated and venture just a little too close.

But they'd seen no sign of the stalker when they'd left the hotel this morning. Their destination, a music studio, was within walking distance of the hotel, and Mary, in one of her stubborn moods, insisted they walk. Although Trace kept his antennae tuned for a medium-size man in a purple cap, the stalker didn't appear. Pacing back and forth, Trace wasted half the morning twiddling his thumbs while she listened to a half-dozen different bands audition to play the music at the reception.

When they talked at all, they kept the conversation strictly impersonal. Current affairs, movies, books, "Jeopardy!" categories.

They returned to the hotel without incident, but when they walked through the revolving glass doors into the lobby, the day manager called out, "Oh, Ms. Wilder! May I see you for a moment?"

"Hi, Rick. What can I do for you?"

The manager reached behind him and pulled out a shiny brass key. "I have a surprise for you. The workmen have finished in your apartment. It's completely restored, although I'm afraid the furniture isn't the same. Couldn't be duplicated, you know. Antiques."

"Already? That's quite a surprise. I thought it would take weeks to clean up that mess."

The manager's chest puffed out proudly. "We've had a crew working night and day just for you, Ms. Wilder. And, if I say so myself, they've done an excellent job. Excellent."

"So...so my apartment's ready for me to move back in?"

"Whenever you're ready." Rick beamed. "Of course, we had a new dead bolt put in, and Mr. Regent insisted we have a high-tech security system installed. The representative from the security company will come right over and show you how to work the alarm as soon as you call him." He handed Mary a business card from the Beltway Alarm Company.

With considerable trepidation, she took the key and business card from the manager's fingertips. "Thank you."

Turning to Trace, she said, "I guess we may as well go check it out."

She didn't catch his response, but the brooding look on his face spoke volumes. Trace wasn't any more anxious to move back in than she was.

Together, they took the elevator to the top floor and slowly walked down the long hallway to Mary's apartment. Allowing Trace to open the door and check out the empty rooms before she entered, Mary took a deep breath and followed him inside.

Bolstered by Trace's support, she went through the rooms one by one. Because the decor had been changed, she was surprised at how little she was affected by walking through the same rooms that had been destroyed only a few short days ago.

It was only when she returned to the living room that Mary's heart pounded suddenly. On the blank wall above the sofa, was an explosion of red.

"JEZEBEL BEWARE!" her mind screamed. Instinctively backing up until she could feel Trace's warmth behind her, Mary closed her eyes, blinking away the shocking crimson color.

"What is it?" Trace murmured in her ear. "What's wrong?"

She leaned back against him, drawing comfort from his presence, gaining strength from his arms. How could she have endured these past weeks without Trace at her side? Even harder to imagine was how she would survive the future without him.

Gathering all her courage, Mary forced her eyes open. The hateful message was gone. Replaced by an enormous painting of bright red poppies on a creamy background. Her mind had only been playing tricks on her, but the effect was as vivid as reality. She would never be free of the remembrance of that detestable scrawl. Maybe she even deserved it.

The stalker hadn't been that far off in labeling her Jezebel. In her mind, she was almost as guilty as that wanton queen had been. Except for that single kiss when she'd been half-asleep, she'd never been physically unfaithful to Jonathan. No, her betrayal of him went deeper. Much deeper.

She'd only been fooling herself when she'd gone through the motions of preparing for her wedding these past few days. Fruitless, senseless busywork to keep her from dwelling on the painful truth.

Now, in this room, with the memories still calling her name, Mary knew the time had come to face her own emotions.

Her feelings for Trace were too strong to be denied any longer. For days now, Mary had ignored her growing attraction for the laconic bodyguard, and she had no idea if his attraction to her was only physical. It didn't really matter; at least, not right now.

For Mary was faced with another truth. She couldn't marry one man when she loved another. It was as simple as that. But Jonathan loved her. Adored her. Trusted her. What was she going to tell him?

He would be returning soon and Mary knew she'd have to make him aware of the harsh reality when he arrived. It was a scene she knew would be ugly and painful for them both.

Whirling, she bumped her nose against Trace's hard chest and looked up, melting in his golden gaze. "I can't move back in here. I know Rick Carey had his people work overtime to get it ready for me, but I just can't."

"You don't have to," he said softly. Cupping her face in his hands, Trace smoothed the satiny skin along her jaw. Moved his fingers up until they were buried in her glossy blond hair. Giving her a long, searching look, he whispered, "No one can tell you what to do with your life, Mary, except you. Stop worrying about what the desk manager wants, what Jonathan wants, even what I want. What do *you* want, Mary-Mary? Tell me. Trust me."

What *did* she want? She wanted life to be unsophisticated again. Where her problems could be resolved by a bandage. But wasn't that what adulthood was all about? Problems too complicated to be easily solved? Trace made it sound as if all she had to do was make a simple choice. Marry Jonathan or not. But it wasn't that easy. Plans had been made. News of their engagement had been announced on television and radio, in magazines and in virtually every newspaper in the country. Jonathan would be hurt, mortified if she just dumped him. And he didn't deserve to be publicly humiliated.

As she was trying to think of a way to explain all of that to Trace, the doorbell rang.

"Who could that be?" she asked. "Nobody but the manager knows we're up here."

"Go into the kitchen and stay out of sight." Trace gave her a gentle nudge in the right direction and pulled his service revolver. Holding it above his head, he eased toward the entry.

Mary waited just inside the kitchen door so she could still hear what was happening.

"Who is it?" Trace's deep voice had a harsh, threatening edge to it.

She couldn't make out the muffled masculine reply, but she heard Trace's response. "What messenger service are you from? I want to see your ID."

Again, a man's voice, but the words were garbled.

Then, Trace spoke. "Step back away from the door."

For the next few moments, Mary could detect the hum of their voices, but she could only catch an occasional word. Then, the front door closed, the lock was engaged with a sharp click and heavy footsteps moved toward her.

"Trace?"

"Just me," he answered.

Mary stepped out of the kitchen to meet him in the dining room. He was holding a white envelope—a duplicate of the others—in his right hand.

"Wh-who was at the door?" Her eyes fastened on the envelope as if it were a predatory viper that might suddenly strike at her.

"Messenger service. The envelope and the correct fee was left on the counter at the messenger office during a busy time this morning. Our boy's taking no chances delivering his garbage in person."

Mary closed her eyes tightly and hugged herself. She just couldn't face another hate-filled missive. "Open it," she told Trace. "Don't tell me what it says."

He sliced open the paper edge with his pocketknife and extracted the sheet of heavy bond paper. After reading it, he folded it and tucked it into his jeans pocket.

Curiosity finally overcame her sense of repulsion. "I take it back. What did it say?"

Trace shook his head. "I don't know if that's a good idea. It...it's not like the others."

"My God, what could be worse than threatening to kill me!"

Wordlessly, he pulled the crumpled sheet out of his pocket and handed it to her.

Mary read the terse message once. Then again. And again.

Finally, she appealed to Trace. "This is too bizarre. It doesn't make sense."

He pulled the paper from her hands and read it aloud. "You have ignored my warnings. This is your last chance. If you want to live beyond your wedding, you must listen to me. Meet me tonight, at midnight, at the Lincoln Memorial. To ignore this warning is to accept death."

Like the others, the words were cut from magazines and the message was unsigned.

Mary grabbed Trace's wrist. "What do you think this means?"

"It means he thinks we're really stupid. Obviously, this is a trap. What we need to do now is call the Metro P.D. and let them show up in our place at midnight tonight."

"No," Mary said. "He's too smart to fall for that. If he sees a bunch of cops, he won't show himself."

"They'll find him, don't worry."

"But what if they don't? What if he gets away again? What will he do next time? This may be our only chance to get this guy, Trace. We have to go for it."

"Are you crazy? Hold a midnight assignation with a man who has made repeated threats against your life? No way, Mary. I can't go along with that."

Once again, that normally well-hidden inner core of steely resolve surfaced in Mary's voice. "Suit yourself. Whether you go with me or not doesn't change a thing. At midnight tonight, I'll be waiting at the Lincoln Memorial."

Proving only that he could be just as stubborn as she was, Trace slammed his lips closed and refused to utter another word. They rode in silence down to their temporary home on the seventh floor.

The red light was blinking on the telephone. The desk clerk told Trace that a Mr. Tobias had called and left the message that "the subject was clean." With a snarl of frustration, Trace dropped the receiver back onto the base. If the FBI couldn't dig up anything on Robert Newland, that meant there was nothing to be dug up.

Of course, the fact that Newland had no criminal background didn't necessarily mean he couldn't be the stalker. Plenty of criminals got a late start in life.

Still, the lack of any background material to support his theory only added to Trace's lousy mood. He parked himself in an easy chair in the sitting area while Mary busied herself in the bedroom, both of them intent on keeping their distance.

When the phone rang, she picked it up in the bedroom. Her voice rose excitedly as she spoke with Jonathan, intensifying Trace's already dark mood. Although he picked up the newspaper and made an elaborate pretense of ignoring Mary's conversation, his subconscious kept listening for the terms of endearment one might expect to hear when an engaged couple are separated.

With a self-directed curse, Trace snapped the paper closed and dropped it onto the floor. *What was he doing anyway, wasting his time worrying about another man's intended?* He'd been hired to accompany Mary when she left the hotel. That's what he'd do. If she was either crazy enough or suicidal enough to want to tangle with a would-be murderer on the mean streets of Washington at midnight, it wasn't his business to dissuade her.

His business was to keep her from harm, and by damn, that's what he'd do. They'd make that appointment, Trace vowed, and he'd be right by her side with his gun drawn.

With any luck whatsoever, this whole thing would be over, one way or another, shortly after midnight. Tomorrow, Trace would be shed of Mary Wilder and his own senseless emotional entanglement with her. He'd go back to his solitary, but uncomplicated life having relearned a valuable lesson: never get emotionally involved with a client.

A moment later, Mary wandered into the living room. She'd changed into a pair of black jeans and matching turtleneck jersey. Her shoulder-length blond hair was swept up in some kind of knot and she carried a dark knit cap. Without preamble, she said, "That was Jonathan on the phone."

"Uh-huh."

"He's coming home day after tomorrow."

"That's nice."

"He agreed with you, by the way."

"Oh?"

Mary nodded, seemingly undismayed by Trace's lack of interest. "He didn't think I should go tonight, either."

Trace cocked his head. "You two are a good match. At least one of you has some common sense."

"Sulking doesn't become you."

"And I doubt lying on a slab in the morgue will do much for your appearance, either."

Mary stalked across the room and stood before him, her fists thrust on her hips in that defiant stance Trace had once thought endearing. Tonight, she just looked obstinate.

She glared at him for a long moment. "Look. We're arguing over a dead issue."

"Interesting choice of words."

"Maybe. But true, nonetheless. I don't feel like bickering. It's giving me a headache."

"Me, too," Trace admitted glumly. "Either that or we're both starving to death. We forgot to eat lunch."

Holding out her hand, Mary said, "Then let's call it a truce, shall we? Come on, let's go have Chinese. I'll buy."

Trace stood and solemnly shook her hand. "Deal." He glanced at his watch. It was already after seven. "Give me a minute to change clothes."

Following Mary's lead, Trace also put on dark clothing. When he took her elbow and led the way to the elevator, she broke the tension that was still hovering between them. "We look like a couple of cat burglars. I hope *we* don't get arrested."

It was a wonderfully balmy evening, so they walked to a nearby Chinese restaurant for dinner. Although their initial conversation was still uptight and stilted, they managed to relax somewhat during the course of their meal. By the time they finished their last cup of green tea, Mary and Trace were back on wary but friendly terms.

He looked at his watch again. "It's just a little after nine. We have three hours to kill, but I'd rather go back to the hotel for the car and head over to the memorial."

Mary nodded. "Stake out the scene?"

"Sort of. If we can find a spot with good concealment, we can be waiting for him—instead of the other way around. I'd like to at least have the element of surprise on our side."

She tossed her napkin on the table and returned her fortune cookie to her plate. "Let's go."

"Aren't you going to read your fortune first?"

Biting her lower lip, she shook her head decisively. "What if it tells me this is a good night for me to curl up in bed with a good book?"

"I can see where that might spoil your fun."

Mary's eyes slitted in warning. "Don't start with me, Armstrong. This isn't a game to me, and you know it. It's my life. You can get off your cute butt and come help me, or not. But I'm going to see this through."

He rose to his feet with a sigh and broke open his own fortune cookie. "Can't blame me for trying," he said as he read the message on the scrap of paper and tossed the scrap on the table.

"Aren't you going to tell me what it says?"

"Sure. It said this would be a good night for me to curl up in bed with a good woman. I don't suppose you'd volunteer?"

"You wish, Armstrong."

"Never hurts to ask. So, you really think I have a cute butt?" he teased as he led the way from the restaurant.

They continued their good-natured banter as they walked back toward the hotel. Hardly aware of his actions, Trace wrapped a protective arm around her shoulders and drank in her intoxicating nearness. He was only fooling himself with her temporary proximity, but he didn't care. Just for tonight, he'd pretend Jonathan Regent didn't exist, and that Mary's wedding date wasn't looming on the horizon.

A sudden breeze blew a silky strand of her hair against his face and Trace gloried in its crisp, clean scent. When she reached up and casually smoothed her hair away, he felt bereft, as if she'd taken something precious from him.

Using more self-control than he'd ever imagined he possessed, Trace forced himself to return his attention to their surroundings.

Traffic was heavy on the busy thoroughfare. Friday night. The city was out en masse, seeking entertainment and release from the tensions of daily life. Sleek black limos cruised the boulevard, shielding their occupants from the curious eyes of the riffraff on the streets.

As they continued to walk, Trace gradually became aware that the weather had changed dramatically while they were dining. The atmosphere was tense, still. The temperature had risen dramatically, as had the humidity. A storm was coming and its electrical energy was already charging the air.

Trace moved closer to Mary. Danger was also crackling through the airwaves. He could feel its fingers pinching his flesh, crawling up his spine.

Someone was watching them.

Carefully, so as not to frighten Mary, Trace eased his arm from her shoulder. Using slow, deliberate movements, he scrutinized the surrounding area and the passersby, his eyes seeking someone who would be staring back.

Perhaps feeling the tension emanating from his body, Mary asked in a low voice, "What's wrong?"

"I'm not sure. Just a feeling. Keep walking and don't look around. We're only two blocks from the hotel. We'll make it."

Mary didn't answer, but increased her pace fractionally.

They were only a block from the hotel, when Trace saw him. Across the street, sitting on a wooden bench in the small park, ball cap thrust low over his face.

"Stay here!" Trace shouted to Mary as he pulled his gun and ran to the corner.

He had to wait for a break in the near-solid line of traffic before he could cross the street. As he dashed across the blacktop, dodging honking cars, Trace was amazed to see his quarry hadn't moved. Surely, with all the commotion, the man saw him coming.

Once he reached the sidewalk on the other side, Trace picked up speed. With only a dozen long strides, he approached the park bench. The man sat, hunched over, unmoving.

Thrusting his gun back into his shoulder holster, Trace grabbed the man by the shirtfront and yanked him to his feet.

Shaking the man with all the rage he'd been storing inside, Trace said between gritted teeth, "All right, you miserable SOB. Start talking, and don't stop or I swear I'll beat you to a bloody pulp. Why have you been following Mary Wilder?"

The man moved then, tilting his head upward. "Careful, bub, don't break my bottle. What're ya so worked up about? I'll let you have a drop—got plenty."

Suddenly, Trace smelled the liquor that permeated the man like a vile, alcoholic aura. Still holding him by the shirt, Trace dragged him out under the streetlight. The ball cap was the familiar bright purple with the gold insignia of a howling wolf. But the face...the man's face was seamed with the lines and wrinkles of a lifetime of pain and booze. He held a brown paper parcel protectively against his chest and looked at Trace with red-rimmed, watery blue eyes.

Trace had just busted a drunk. A derelict. The old guy was nothing but a street bum.

But...but the hat was the same.

Frowning in confusion, Trace gave the drunk another, but much gentler shake. "Where'd you get that cap, old-timer?"

Still clutching his paper-wrapped bottle against his chest, the wino slowly reached upward with his free hand. "You ain't gonna take my new hat, are ya? A fella just give it to me."

Releasing his grip on his shirt, Trace patted the old man on the shoulder. "No, pal, I'm not going to take your hat. Mind telling me who gave it to you?"

The drunk swiveled on wobbly legs and pointed to a stand of evergreens on the edge of the park. "Fella over there give it to me. And this bottle, too!" He held the paper-wrapped package aloft like a trophy.

Trace scanned the edge of the woods, but no movement broke the stillness in the bushes. A sudden flash of lightning zigzagged across the sky, followed seconds later by a lazy rumble of far-off thunder. The storm was moving in.

Forcing his attention back on the derelict, Trace pulled a five-dollar bill from his wallet and waved it in front of the old man. "What did this guy want you to do? What did he look like?"

The old man's eyes glittered at the sight of the bill. "Looked like everybody else. Give me this hat, though. And a bottle, see?"

The old man was quickly losing his focus. "You already showed me," Trace said. "Why was this guy so nice to you? What did you have to do for him to be so nice?"

The drunk shrugged, and nearly toppled over. Trace caught him and led him back to the bench. Once the man had settled in his seat, he uncapped the bottle and took a long draft. "Just told me to sit here with this here hat on until I'd finished my drinking. Never met a nicer fella."

Trace frowned. It didn't make sense. But then, nothing about this case had made sense.

He was still pondering the meaning of the old man's story, when a piercing shriek sounded over the roaring traffic, immediately followed by the terrifying sound of screeching brakes.

Mary! Dear God, he'd forgotten about Mary.

Chapter Thirteen

Although one scream tends to sound like any other, Trace knew deep in his soul that it was Mary's frightened voice that had shattered the night.

He was already darting through traffic, when another spear of lightning jabbed through the sky. For one brief, awful instant, the tableau on the sidewalk was lit up like a stage drama. A city bus was parked, cockeyed, near the curb where a small crowd had gathered beneath a light pole and was staring at something—or someone—on the ground.

The quaking roar of thunder echoed the shudder of fear that rippled down his spine.

Finally, he reached the opposite side of the street and ran toward the cluster of onlookers. Nearly a dozen people had gathered, including the uniformed bus driver. Several of his passengers were leaning out the window, silently watching the unfolding drama as though it were a television program.

After shouldering his way through the crowd, feeling all the while as though he'd been sucker-punched in the gut, Trace stared in shaken disbelief at Mary's prone figure huddled on the sidewalk.

"Mary? Honey? Stand back, everybody! Give her some air." He flailed the air with his arms, as he made his way through the throng to drop to his knees at Mary's side.

Her eyes were closed and she was pale, ghastly pale.

Knowing he was breaking every first-aid rule in the book, Trace nevertheless was powerless to stop himself from gently gathering her in his arms, tucking her head against his pounding chest. "Oh, Mary, talk to me," he murmured against the golden softness of her hair.

To his disbelieving delight, her eyes fluttered open and a gentle smile curved the sweetness of her lips. "Why should I talk to you?" she asked in a weak voice. "You never listen, anyway."

A sudden stinging sensation, followed by a glistening in his eyes reminded Trace of the intensity of his relief. And broke him free from the horrific emotional maelstrom he'd been battling since he'd heard her cry and that horrifying squeal of brakes.

Keeping his voice soft so as not to alarm her, Trace asked her where she hurt while his gentle fingers probed her body, searching for injury.

"I don't think anything's broken," she said, struggling to sit up.

"You'd better stay still until we're sure."

In the distance, the familiar wail of a siren whined. Someone, at least, had called an ambulance. "What happened?"

She shook her head, then stopped abruptly with a groan.

"I thought you said you were okay!" In his fear for her safety, his voice took on an accusatory tone.

"Apparently, I banged my head when I fell, and except for my injured dignity, I'm fine."

The ambulance pulled up to the curb, quickly followed by a police cruiser. While the paramedics saw to Mary, the patrolman questioned Trace. Unfortunately, other than her name and address, he couldn't tell them what had happened.

The uniformed policeman turned around and addressed the nearest person in the crowd, who was still watching the proceedings with morbid fascination. "You. What happened here?"

The man's eyes widened when he realized he'd captured the attention of the authorities. With an obvious hesitancy, the man inched forward. "You talkin' to me?"

"Yeah." The cop took out a notebook. "What's your name?"

"James. James Stephens."

"Okay, James. Why don't you tell me what went down here?"

The man scrunched his shoulders in the universal gesture that meant he didn't have a clue. "All I know is I heard this lady scream and that bus slammed on its brakes. Guess she almost fell in front of it."

The bus driver stepped forward and verified James's story. He'd been on his regular route uptown. The bus he was driving was an express, so this corner wasn't one of his scheduled stops. Intending to drive past, he saw a woman lurch forward from the sidewalk—right into his path. "I swear, Officer, I thought for sure she was trying to kill herself and was jumping in front of the bus. People do that, you know."

"So I've heard." Turning back to Trace, the policeman asked, "Know any reason why your lady friend might try to off herself?"

"Absolutely not! This was either an accident or...or somebody tried to kill her."

The patrolman's eyebrows shot upward. Carefully raising his hat with the tip of his thumb, he appraised Trace. "Seems you got to that conclusion pretty quick, son. Want to tell me about it?"

Trace shook his head. If he revealed the various assaults on Mary the past few weeks, he had no doubt he'd end up at the station making a statement. They didn't have time for that. If Mary's head injury wasn't serious and the paramedics released her, Trace intended to lock her in the hotel room while he went to make their appointment at the Lincoln Memorial.

He could have one of his men come over and pinch-hit keeping an eye on her until Trace returned.

Feeling the policeman's watchful gaze, Trace said, "Nothing to tell except that this woman isn't suicidal. If you knew her, you'd know what a ridiculous idea that is."

The patrolman mumbled noncommittally and snapped his notepad closed. "Let's see what kind of condition she's in."

After taking a couple moments to disperse the lingering crowd, the policeman stepped over to where the paramedic unit was still examining Mary. "How's the patient, boys?"

The two young medics glanced at the patrolman. While one continued to speak in muted tones to Mary, the other shrugged. "She refuses to be transported to the hospital. Couple abrasions from her fall. No overt signs of skull fracture but I suspect a mild concussion. She's got a nice goose egg on the back of her head."

The other paramedic was taking the blood pressure cuff off her arm when Trace and the policeman approached. "Ms. Wilder?"

"That's right."

"Want to tell me what happened here?"

Mary nibbled her upper lip before slowly answering. "I was standing on the curb, waiting for him." She indicated Trace with a nod of her head. "The bus was stopped at the signal light. When the light changed and traffic picked up speed, I started inching back from the curb. Then, I felt someone's hands on my back and he pushed me in front of the bus."

"He?" The cop picked up quickly on her gender qualifier.

"He, she, whoever. I didn't see anyone, if that's what you're asking."

"Mmm." The officer scribbled in his notebook. "You don't think you were just jostled by someone trying to catch the bus?"

Mary shook her head emphatically, then stopped abruptly as pain washed over her.

They were interrupted by the paramedics, who handed a clipboard to Mary for her signature on their "Refused Treatment" form.

After they'd departed, the patrolman continued where he'd left off. "So somebody shoved you. What then?"

"I was so shocked, I just fell forward and landed on my knees in the street. All I could see was that bus coming at me." She broke off, shuddering visibly. All she could remember was that bus looming, closer and closer. For an instant, Mary had been paralyzed by the headlights, like a doe caught on the highway. Then, thankfully, something had broken loose and she'd scrambled back onto the pavement.

"Must've been a close call," the policeman muttered as he scribbled in his notebook. "So the bus swerved and missed you?"

Mary slowly shook her head. "He swerved, but...but if I hadn't managed to get back on the curb, it wouldn't have mattered." With a nod, she pointed to the skid marks that were clearly visible under the street lamp.

Trace's eyes followed the invisible path of her fingertip. A cold sweat popped out on his forehead as he read the clear, undeniable story told by the skid marks. By the time the bus driver had seen her, it would have been too late.

The huge, multi-ton vehicle had driven right over the spot where Mary had been lying only seconds before. If she hadn't found the strength to move at the last second, she would be dead right now.

A rage, the like of which he'd never experienced, built up inside Trace. He wanted to bellow his fury, to beat his fist into the nearest brick wall. He wanted to find the madman who'd almost killed Mary and—

The patrolman cocked his head, and looked at Mary curiously. "Yeah, you'd have been a goner, all right. And you believe this was a random act of violence? Nobody's got a grudge against you."

Mary didn't reply. To avoid his probing query, she rubbed her arms and legs. "Can we go now?"

Trace wrapped a protective arm around her shoulders. "Don't you think she's had enough for this evening, Officer? Surely this can wait until morning."

"Just a couple more questions, folks. Then it's up to the detectives in the morning, if they think there's something to follow up on." With a deep sigh, the man went back to his routine questioning. "So after you got back to safety, the guy was gone?"

Tears glistened in Mary's eyes as she relived the horrible minute that had felt like a lifetime while it was happening. "No," she whispered, "he was still there. He pushed me again. Harder. But...but I was prepared this time. I grabbed hold of that light pole and tried to drop to the ground, while I screamed bloody murder."

"Quick thinking," Trace said, his eyes bright with pride.

Mary shrugged off the compliment. "I took a crime prevention course shortly after I moved here. That's what the instructor told us to do. Anyway, it worked. He—whoever—let go. By the time I turned around, several people had gathered around, but none of them looked...evil, or anything. Mostly curious."

The policeman asked a few more questions and then polled the remaining onlookers, but no one admitted to having seen the assailant. Apparently realizing there was no point in taking a formal statement, the officer told Mary that a detective might be contacting her in the morning. Tipping his cap, he got into his police cruiser and drove back into the traffic.

They were finally alone.

Somewhere during the proceedings, the bus driver had gathered together his passengers and departed. The remnants of the crowd had dissipated when the officer had started asking for identification. Clearly, no one wanted that much involvement.

By the time they got back to the hotel room, it was almost eleven. Only a little over an hour until they were supposed to meet with the would-be killer.

Trace carefully cleaned Mary's face and hands and swabbed the scraped skin on her cheek with antiseptic cream. Fortunately, her jeans and long-sleeved shirt had protected her pretty well.

Taking an appreciative look at his handiwork, and noting that her skin tone was regaining its bloom, Trace leaned back on his heels. "Now, while I'm gone, I want you to stay locked up in here. Don't even answer the phone. This may be a trap to lure me out of the hotel, so do what I say."

He'd already fallen for the wino decoy in the park. He didn't intend to be caught again.

Mary blinked in confusion. "What are you talking about?"

"I'm going to the Lincoln Memorial." He rummaged in his overnight bag until he found a penlight and stuck it in his back pocket.

"Not alone, you're not."

Trace grasped her firmly by the shoulders and gave her his best ferocious glare. "This is no time to argue. You've just been through a terrifying and grueling experience. The best thing for you to do right now is—"

Mary pushed his hands aside and rose to her feet. A tiny wince of pain was the only sign she gave of her discomfort. "The best thing for you to do, Armstrong, is stop treating me like a poor, weak female with the vapors!"

"Now, that's not fair, Mary!"

"Neither are you. I'm going. If you leave without me, I'll follow in a taxi. Take your choice."

FIFTEEN MINUTES LATER, they were in Trace's car making their way along the almost deserted Independence Avenue near the Lincoln Memorial. He had kept a sharp eye on the rearview mirror. No one had followed them. When they pulled into the empty parking area beside the reflecting pool, he took a moment to double-check his revolver and scan the area.

Mary pulled her dark knit cap out of her pocket and jammed it on her head, covering her glowing blond hair.

Hand in hand, they cautiously started toward the memorial, keeping in the shadow of the trees that lined the reflecting pool.

With the approach of the witching hour, an eerie stillness had descended over the night. Even earlier in the evening, the Lincoln Memorial, like the other national treasures that dotted the city, would have been lit with enormous floodlights. But after ten, the lights were turned off for energy conservation, and the area was now dark and foreboding. The very air reverberated with menace.

It was dark, very dark. The moon had escaped behind the concealing cover of a bank of storm clouds. A brief crackle of lightning illuminated the sky and cast them in an unearthly green glow.

Keeping his weapon by his side, Trace drew Mary closer as they came to the concrete apron that surrounded the huge memorial.

One more step, and they'd be out of the protective shadows that had been covering their approach. One more step and they'd be sitting ducks for a sniper at the top of the monument looking down at them.

A drop of rain slapped the ground in front of them. If it started to pour in earnest, Trace thought, it would provide at least a modicum of cover. He gave a silent prayer for rain.

Mary looked up at him. Her huge eyes were wide, but her step was sure, unfaltering. Trace squeezed her hand reassuringly and felt her warming smile. Her absolute trust in his ability to keep her safe was like a heavy coat that weighed down his shoulders.

He'd never felt his responsibility more strongly; not even when he'd been guarding the president.

But then, Mary was far more important to him than any politician. Than anyone.

Sniffing the air like a lithe jaguar seeking out danger, Trace took a cautious step forward. Then another. A sudden strong breeze whistled through the treetops, wailing like the cry of a banshee as death approaches.

Their sneakered feet were silent on the damp pavement as they approached the wide staircase leading up to the immense statue of Abraham Lincoln enthroned at the top of the memorial.

The moon suddenly poked out from behind a cloud, and the brief splatter of rain abruptly stopped. It was as if the sky was holding its breath, watching the drama unfolding below.

Trace's eyes made a continual sweep of the monument, the pillars above them, the vast emptiness below. But nothing moved in the moonlight.

They climbed the last few steps and found themselves beside a huge pillar. While their eyes adjusted to the dimness under the roofed structure, Trace stood as still as death, listening.

No sound, not even a cooing pigeon, broke the silence.

Then, he felt Mary's hand tugging at his arm.

Glancing down, he followed the track of her pointing finger. She was pointing at the enormous statue of Mr.

Lincoln. At first, Trace couldn't see anything, but then he thought he saw what Mary had noticed.

Motioning for her to stay behind the pillar, he eased forward.

After a few steps, he could more readily discern the outline of a male figure, propped against the base of the statue. A dark ball cap with a light insignia on the front sat on his head at a curious angle. Trace couldn't see the color, but he'd be willing to bet his pension that the cap was bright purple. They'd found the stalker.

Pointing his gun at the waiting man, Trace walked directly up to him.

The man didn't move.

Kicking the sole of the man's shoe with his own, Trace ordered, "Get up, you slug."

Still, no reaction from the stranger sprawled against the statue.

The first tingling sensation of something awry poked at Trace's backbone. Shifting his weapon to his left hand, he pulled his penlight out of his back pocket and aimed its thready light at the man's face.

The stranger's eyes were closed and his head lolled on his shoulders.

Was he injured or was this another game? Another trap?

"Mary, stay back!" Trace hissed as he felt her approach behind him. He wasn't surprised when she didn't heed his warning. In another second, she was directly behind him, her hand on his back.

"What's wrong?" she whispered.

In response, Trace redirected the light into the man's face. He appeared to be unconscious, but the purple cap glowed like an amethyst in the frail light.

"Recognize him?"

"I... I'm not sure," Mary said. "I can't really see his face."

Trace reached down and lifted the man's chin, and refocused the beam on his features.

Mary stared at the stranger for a long time. "I'm not sure," she finally said. "He looks vaguely familiar but I'm sure that I don't know him personally."

Trace released the man's chin and was mildly surprised when he jerked loose and moaned weakly. "Help...help me."

At the sound of his voice, Trace's hand jumped and the flashlight beam skittered to the ground. The reason for the man's lethargic reaction became readily apparent.

He was lying in a pool of bright red blood.

Trace's years of emergency training made his reaction swift and certain. Handing Mary the flashlight, he bent down to determine the extent of the man's injuries.

Feeling almost sickened by the vast quantity of blood that was creeping along the concrete floor, Mary swallowed hard and kept her gaze fastened to the man's face. His eyes were closed again and he looked almost peacefully asleep.

When Trace lifted him up, to look behind him, the man came fully to consciousness and cried, "God! Stop."

"Mary, shine the light back here."

Her hand trembled, but she shifted slightly and followed Trace's direction. The wooden handle of a kitchen butcher knife protruded from the stranger's back.

Trace looked up and caught her eye. With a small, sad shake of his head, he gently eased the man back against the base of the statue, taking care not to put more pressure on the knife.

Trace looked around. He had no idea where a telephone might be. He couldn't leave this man to die alone, nor could he allow Mary out of his sight. Not that it really mattered, he thought. Even if the knife wound hadn't ruptured any vital organs, the stalker had already lost too much blood.

The man was only moments—perhaps seconds—from death.

Mary redirected the beam and saw the man's complexion had paled to a frightful pallor. As she stared, his eyes drifted open and he looked directly into her face.

"Listen . . . to me," he croaked.

Mary dropped to her knees beside him. No matter what sickness had prompted him to torment her these past weeks, he was past her hatred now. She'd never experienced death up close before, but knew instinctively that the stranger's life was slowly draining from his body. They were too far from a phone; it was too late for help.

"Please," she whispered. "Don't talk. Save your strength."

"No." His hands clawed the air, seeking hers. His eyes drifted closed and she knew he was dying.

She dropped the flashlight and took his cold, shaking hand in her own. "Please, don't talk."

Using the very last of his breath, his life, he opened his eyes once again and whispered, "Martin . . . Watch out for Martin."

Chapter Fourteen

Mary slept straight through the morning into the middle of the afternoon. After they'd finally found a phone and reported the man's death, they had to wait for what seemed hours while the police secured the scene then tended to the forensic details. The homicide detective hadn't liked or believed their story so he had them brought to the station for further questioning. Only when Trace had finally been allowed to make a phone call and had convinced Harley Tobias to intervene on their behalf, had the police begun taking them seriously.

Eventually, a patrol car had been summoned to return them to where their own car had been left near the memorial. The early-morning traffic was already beginning to hum, and it was well past dawn before they trudged back into the Georgetown Regent, mentally and physically exhausted.

They'd talked very little. There was nothing left to say. Mary couldn't positively identify the dead man as her stalker, despite the meaningful purple cap. Was the dead man the same person who'd been persecuting her these past weeks? Had he tried to push her in front of that bus?

The biggest imponderable, of course, was why?

When she staggered into the sitting room, Trace was in a whispered conversation on the telephone. Gratefully spying the insulated carafe of coffee on the round table in front of the window, Mary poured herself a reviving cup and curled on the miniscule sofa and waited for Trace.

He hung up and swiveled to face her. "Hey, kiddo, how's it going this morning, er, afternoon?"

She sipped her coffee and shrugged eloquently. "So-so. Who was on the phone?"

"Harley Tobias. I asked him to see what the D.C. police learned about the man we found last night."

"And?"

Trace cupped his chin and rasped his fingers across the rather spectacular black stubble. "And nothing. He wasn't carrying any identification. His clothes were from a national chain and, other than the odd mole or freckle, no identifying marks. A complete blank."

"It's almost like...like he expected to be murdered and didn't want to be identified afterward."

"Or the killer didn't want him identified."

Mary nodded, agreeing that Trace's theory was more likely. "So that's it? We just wait and see if he's reported missing?"

Trace could hear the hopelessness in her voice and wished there was something he could say, some crumb of encouragement he could offer to spark the light back into her hollow eyes. "The only other hope is his fingerprints. Harley said he'd see what he could do to expedite the processing, but unless his prints were already on file somewhere..."

Mary knew what Trace didn't say. The odds were slim enough. But if the dead man didn't have some kind of record, they might never find out who he was. Or why he'd been stalking her.

Trace got up and stretched, his fingers entwined over his head. "I've been waiting for you to mention one thing."

"What's that?"

"Martin. The dead man said you were to watch out for Martin."

Mary carefully set her cup back into the china saucer and shoved her mussed hair from her eyes. "That's another problem. I've been wracking my brain and I don't know anyone named Martin."

"Hmmph. Makes it kind of hard to watch out for him then, doesn't it?"

When he saw Mary's shoulders slump in dejection, Trace decided she needed a change of pace. A complete mood lifter.

"Hungry?" he asked.

"A little."

"I've got an idea. Let's get cleaned up and go for a drive. There's this great seafood joint I know over on the bay in Maryland. They have an all-you-can-eat captain's platter that the fat lady in the circus couldn't finish."

"Gee, Trace, I'm still kind of tired. And grubby."

He knelt in front of her and dipped his fingers into the thick, blond tresses at the back of her head. "How's the old noggin? That's a pretty serious knot. Maybe we'd better have that x-rayed."

Mary grabbed his wrist and pulled his hand away. "Don't baby me. I'm fine. Really. It's just that I was thinking of staying in tonight."

He shook his head decisively. "And wallowing in your problems. No way. Dr. Armstrong has a surefire prescription for the blues. Now, are you going to take your shower, or do I have to help you?" He waggled his eyebrows in a comic exaggeration of a lecher.

Despite herself, Mary laughed at his antics. He was good for her soul. "Okay, okay. What's the dress code for this 'joint' you're taking me to?"

"Casual to mid-dressy."

Before she could head for the shower, the telephone rang. Mary, being closest, picked it up. "Hello? Jonathan. Are you back in town? Oh, tomorrow."

Trace watched surreptitiously while she spoke to her fiancé. He didn't get it. There was no love-talk, no dreamy expression on her face, nothing that would give truth to her claim of being in love with Jonathan Regent.

He unabashedly listened to her conversation while she glossed over last night's events, and wondered again why Regent didn't cancel his all-important business deals and come straight to his fiancée's side. How much more money did the man need, anyhow?

Trace knew one thing: if Mary Wilder was *his* woman, he'd have been at her side night and day until the stalker was apprehended.

"Trace!"

At Mary's stage whisper, he looked up. She had her palm over the receiver and was looking at him expectantly.

"Yeah?" he said.

"What's the name of that restaurant you're taking me to for dinner?"

"Cap'n Frank's. Why?"

"Jonathan wanted to know. Said he thought he'd been there."

Not likely, Trace thought as she returned to her murmured conversation. From what he'd learned of Regent, the man only frequented high-profile, ritzy restaurants where he stood a chance of having his photo snapped by the local paparazzi. Jonathan Regent had a penchant for the spotlight, and in Trace's mind, that was why he'd dumped Camille Castnor in the first place. Although Camille certainly was an attractive woman for her age, she didn't have the exquisite, soft beauty of Mary—nor the glamour of youth.

Again, Trace looked up as Mary's voice rose. "No, I *don't* think that's a good idea. We don't know for sure that it was him. This could be an elaborate setup by the stalker to make me think I'm safe."

She listened a moment longer, shaking her head in response to Jonathan's voice. "I just want to be sure before Trace leaves, that's all. We'll talk about it more tomorrow. All right. Good night."

Trace was standing beside her when she hung up the receiver.

"So Regent doesn't think my services are needed any longer?"

She shook her finger in his face. "Don't you know eavesdroppers never hear anything good about themselves?"

"That's part of my job." He grinned. "And you never answered my question. Your boyfriend wants to fire me?"

"Not fire," Mary hedged. "He thinks that since we can be reasonably certain the dead man was the one stalking me, I'll be okay on my own. He reminded me how much I argued against a bodyguard in the first place."

Trace tucked his fingertips in his jeans pockets and thrummed the carpeting with the toe of his sneaker. "So, what changed your mind?"

Patting his cheeks with her fingertips, she said, "The promise of an all-you-can-eat seafood dinner, what did you think? Now feed me, Armstrong. Feed me!"

THE DRIVE to the small beach community on the Chesapeake Bay was exactly what Mary needed to take her mind off her problems. The electrical storm that had threatened rain all last night had never really materialized, dropping only a light mist that cleared the air and colored the roadside a dazzling emerald green.

The sun was dipping low in the sky when Trace pulled into the gravel parking lot outside Cap'n Frank's. At first glance, the restaurant *did* resemble a dilapidated beer joint, but closer observation showed the silvery gray boards on the exterior had been deliberately weathered to enhance its nautical appearance.

When they started up a small ramp, it swayed beneath her feet and Mary discovered delightedly that the ramp was actually a short dock. Cap'n Frank's was a converted houseboat and sat directly on the water.

Inside, as they sipped icy margaritas and nibbled on crab-stuffed mushroom appetizers, Mary was glad she'd opted for "mid-dressy" attire. Although a quartet of rowdy young people in the corner were decked out in shorts and flip-flops, most of the patrons were slightly more formally dressed.

Like Trace. He looked absolutely gorgeous in white cotton trousers and a loose, aqua shirt made of fine linen. With his collar-length mane of thick black hair and the long, flowing sleeves of his open-neck shirt, Trace could have passed for one of the pirates that had prowled this area two hundred years before.

After a scrumptious, but far too abundant dinner, they adjourned to the cocktail lounge outside on the open deck. Mary patted her tummy. "That may have been the most wonderful meal I've ever eaten. It was certainly the largest!"

His appreciative gaze raked the length of her flower-sprigged sundress. "Glad you enjoyed it. Turn your chair around. Watch the sunset."

Mary frowned. "Trace, the Atlantic faces east. The sun sets on the other coast."

"Not from this side of the bay. See how this finger of land kind of curves around like a fishhook?"

Her enchanted gaze followed the path his finger directed and, suddenly, she gasped. The sun was, in fact, lowering itself to the opposite side of the shore. A fiery ball of color, it promised a spectacular finish to a glorious day. She twisted her chair closer to Trace's and sat beside him while they watched the sky shift through a prism of colors. Bright crimson, burning scarlet, into a softer pink and finally, a pale purple haze.

Somehow, Trace's hand slipped over hers. After a moment's hesitation, she let it linger. She'd never felt more secure, more restful, more...happy in her entire life. Just being here with Trace made her feel whole.

She didn't know how long they sat in silent communion, but when the waiter came to light the candles on each table, she was surprised to see that dusk had completely fallen.

When the waiter moved away, she lifted her glass of Kahlúa to her lips. As she tossed her head back to drain the delicious coffee-flavored dregs, Mary's gaze met Trace's. His eyes said all the words they'd both been avoiding for days. In those depths, Mary saw her own uncertainty and desire mirrored like a golden reflection. In that instant, she knew she was lost.

Trace shoved his half-empty glass aside. "Let's get out of here."

Wordlessly, she waited while he dropped several bills on the table, then taking her hand, led her out a side door and around to the little ramp.

Back on the shore, he passed by the parking lot, instead guiding them to the beach. Still saying nothing, they walked along the water's edge, listening to the gentle lapping of water. Since they were at the bay, and not the ocean, there was no heavy surf crashing with dramatic abandon. Only the lonely, haunting cry of an occasional gull foraging for its dinner and the soft slap of water whispering onto shore.

Darkness had fallen completely before they stopped and stared out at the moonlit bay. The wind had picked up; its whistling melody sounded like a love song. Trace found a fragment of seashell, examined it carefully, then tossed it out to sea.

Without warning, he turned to her and pulled her into his arms. "Mary-Mary, you're driving me crazy," he whispered, plunging his hands into her hair, just before he lowered his head and kissed her.

Mary felt herself melting in his arms. His pure, male fragrance was intoxicating, and she found herself returning his kiss. This time there was no fooling herself. She was fully, exquisitely awake. What she was feeling was no foggy remnant from a sensual dream. Her need for Trace was real. Now.

Raising her arms to grasp his neck, she feathered her fingertips through the ruffle of hair at his collar while her lips made demands of their own.

When at last he released her, Mary laid her head against his chest, and wrapped her arms around his waist. Her heart thudded violently in response to his nearness, while a shaft of shame pierced her flesh. She'd never responded to Jonathan like this. Never.

The stalker had been right all along. She *was* a Jezebel, a betrayer of men. A wanton woman who allowed herself to be ruled by her deceitful passions. The kind of woman who didn't deserve a man with Jonathan's goodness. Or a man who made her heart sing like Trace.

Pushing away from his chest with her palms, she murmured, "We'd better get back now."

"Mary, you can't keep kissing me and then pretending it never happened. We need to talk about this."

Guilt and embarrassment were consuming her, and in her pain she snapped at him. "We don't have anything to talk about! That kiss was nothing more than a reaction to the moonlight, the liquor."

"So it meant nothing to you?"

If she heard the cold warning edge of Trace's voice, she didn't heed its meaning. "Nothing! Except my shame."

"Shame!" He grabbed her by the shoulders and pulled her close, until their eyes were inches apart. "Don't be ashamed of me, Mary. Not now, not ever. I may not be in the same financial league as your boyfriend, but there's more to being a man than counting your money."

"That's not what I meant," she cried. Why couldn't she make Trace understand? It wasn't him—it was her. She couldn't betray Jonathan's trust. If she did, she wouldn't be able to live with herself. "Jonathan deserves better than this. And you deserve more than—" She broke off when a stinging sob caught in her throat.

His contempt leaking through his voice, Trace uttered coldly, "More than a quick toss in the hay with another man's woman? Is that what you're saying? Don't worry about me, Mary. I won't spoil it for you. I won't tell your precious Jonathan that your love for him is about as real as your concern for me."

Leaving her standing alone in the sand, with tears streaming down her face, Trace strode to the car.

At first, she wanted to call out to him, to make him understand. But, in the end, she decided his misunderstanding was for the best. Let him think the worst of her—she already thought poorly enough of herself. Besides, what did explanations matter? The hard truth was that Jonathan was a wonderful man and Mary wouldn't betray him. Period.

In time, she'd get over this infatuation for Trace Armstrong. In a few weeks, months or maybe years, he'd be a vague but pleasant memory.

After a moment, Mary wrapped her arms across her chest and followed him.

WHEN MARY CALLED Jonathan's office the next morning, Bob Newland told her gruffly that Jonathan wasn't available.

"Oh," Mary said, her disappointment heavy in her voice. "He told me he'd be back from Alaska, and in his office most of the morning."

"He's here," Newland acknowledged. "But he's in a meeting, and he left strict instructions that he didn't want to be interrupted. Shall I have him return your call?"

"Yes, please. Right away." She slowly replaced the receiver and leaned against the headboard. Bob's response to her had been chilly, as usual, but had she detected any real menace in his voice? Enough to wish her harm? She just didn't know.

She could hear Trace moving around in the sitting area. She didn't want to get up yet, to face him yet. What must he think of her? What did she think of herself?

Mary had been anxious to speak with Jonathan this morning. She wanted to feel his gentleness, remember what it was about him that had attracted her. They'd been spending entirely too much time apart. People on the brink of marriage were supposed to spend every possible second together; building up that hot point of sexual energy that would be released on their honeymoon, bonding their relationship. That was why she was so sexually responsive to Trace. Her hormones were already in overdrive.

Trace's cheery whistle penetrated the tissue-thin walls and Mary's confidence waned. He wasn't even in sight and her pulse leapt erratically.

The phone ringing beside her startled her. "Hello?"

"Mary?" Jonathan's voice was brusque, almost to the point of irritation. "What is so important?"

Their relationship. Her emotional infidelity. Couldn't he hear the crisis in her voice?

"I wanted to talk to you. See you," she told him.

There was a long hesitation. When he spoke again, his voice held a strange chilling remoteness. "Why?"

"I . . . I just miss you, Jonathan."

"I have a business dinner tonight with some of the boys."

The boys, Mary knew, was a euphemism for the political machine that was considering backing Jonathan's bid for election. "How about lunch?"

She heard him flipping through his calendar. "Sorry," he said. "I'm due in Richmond at one. Maybe tomorrow."

"Jonathan? Is something wrong? I mean, we're supposed to be getting married soon and you act like...like I'm a stranger off the street pestering you for a job."

"Sorry," he responded in that strangely clipped tone. He was silent for so long, Mary thought they might have been disconnected. Finally, he sighed deeply, sadly, and continued. "Mary, love, you'd better learn to be more cognizant of the stress I'm under. I make more momentous decisions before noon than you're apt to make in a lifetime. I have a living to earn—for both of us. Someone has to pay for your designer gowns and penthouse apartments."

"I've never asked for those things! For anything! Jonathan, I think we really need to have a serious discussion. Our relationship has gotten off track somewhere and—"

"You're absolutely right," he cut in. "That remark was uncalled for. I'm just...under a lot of pressure right now, darling." His voice softened dramatically, as he became almost supplicating in his tone. "Forgive me, sweetie-pie? Please?"

Mary didn't know which was more annoying, his occasional high-handedness or his silly baby talk when he was trying to regain her good graces. Still, knowing the telephone was no place to discuss the intricacies of their relationship, she forced a light tone into her own voice. "Of course, Jonathan. But I still want to talk with you."

"Tomorrow night. Promise. I'll take you someplace really special and we'll have a private leisurely dinner. You can give your watchdog the night off."

Unaccountably stung by his demeaning remark, she felt her hackles rising anew. "He's not a watchdog, Jonathan."

"My, we *are* touchy today, aren't we? Very well, give your man the night off tomorrow. Oh, by the way..."

"Yes?"

His nonchalant manner told her they'd at last gotten to the crux of Jonathan's annoyance. He was a consummate poker player, and the milder his tone, the more angry Jonathan was. "The desk clerk told me that you'd refused to move back into the apartment. Did the workmen leave something undone?"

Perhaps he felt her rejection of the apartment was in some way a rejection of him. How could she tell him that the luxurious penthouse suite now made her blood run cold? "The apartment looks fine, Jonathan. The workmen did a wonderful job restoring the place. It's just that I'm still uncomfortable there. I don't feel secure."

"I thought that's why we were paying your watch—your bodyguard such a handsome salary. To make you feel secure."

They haggled over Mary's living arrangements a few moments longer, before Jonathan abruptly ended the discussion, saying he was late for an appointment.

Mary strolled into the tiny bathroom for her morning shower, feeling strangely apprehensive. As the hot blast of water poured down on her like a fountain of knowledge, she suddenly realized she could no longer pretend otherwise: she didn't love Jonathan Regent. She'd been infatuated, surely. Overpowered by his charisma. But never really in love.

Whether anything ever developed between her and Trace wasn't the point any longer. She had to break up with Jonathan, and the sooner the better. To do anything else would be deceitful and cruel.

As she rinsed a film of sudsy lather from her hair, Mary felt a shudder of trepidation. Jonathan wasn't going to take this well, not at all.

She was still dressing, when she heard a heavy rap at the front door. Tucking a cotton T-shirt into her denim shorts, she poked her head out of the bedroom.

Trace was showing the FBI agent, Harley Tobias, into the sitting area.

Quickly twisting her damp hair into a short braid, Mary slipped on her sandals and hurried to join them.

Trace was straddling one of the chairs by the dinette table while the titanic agent was taking up most of the love seat. They both rose to their feet when she walked in.

"At ease." She smiled in greeting, carefully avoiding looking into Trace's eyes. Taking the other dining chair, she sat a careful distance away from him. "What's up, gentlemen?"

Not looking at her, Trace poured her a cup of coffee and pushed a bag of doughnuts her way. "Harley bought breakfast."

"Thanks." Mary reached into the grease-smeared white bag and found her favorite, a plain doughnut with a granulated sugar coating. After she washed down the first bite with a sip of the strong coffee, she and Trace both turned expectant faces toward Harley.

"We had a bit of luck in identifying your homicide victim." The agent reached inside his coat pocket and pulled out a sheet of paper covered with computer type. Handing the sheet to Trace, he continued, "He was a veteran, so his prints were on file. His name was King, Milo King. Mean anything to you?" He raised a sharp, black eyebrow in question.

Mary shook her head slowly. "No. I don't think I've ever heard that name before. Do we know where he was from?"

"Before his air force hitch, he was a factory worker in Kramer, a small town in the mountains in North Carolina."

Mary frowned. "I've never been to North Carolina in my life. How could this man know me?"

Harley stood up and dug around in the white bag for a doughnut, finally extracting a chocolate one. "Didn't say he still lives there, although maybe he does. No criminal record. But until we do a bit more nosing around, we don't know what he's been doing since his discharge."

"What about IRS records?" Trace asked as he handed the scant fact sheet to Mary.

Harley grinned. "Why, I'm surprised at you, Armstrong. You know we can't go digging into IRS computer records. This has to be done properly, through channels."

"Hmmph," Trace snorted. "By the time the 'proper channels' get around to passing on any information, we'll all be moldering in our graves."

"As it happens," Harley said after he licked the chocolate from his fingertips, "I know a little gal over in the IRS section. She might be able to do me a favor. Unofficially, of course."

"Of course."

Mary finished reading the computer-generated sheet Harley had brought on Milo King. Although a lot of the wording was in some cryptic government shorthand, she gleaned enough information to be more certain than ever that she'd had no previous connection with the man. Yet, she couldn't forget that jolt of recognition she'd felt when she'd first seen his face on the night he'd died. If only she could remember where she'd seen him before...

After Harley took his leave, Mary amazed herself by suggesting to Trace that they take a quick trip to Kramer, North Carolina.

"What do you expect to find?" Trace countered. "Like Harley said, the man may not have lived there since his discharge. Let's wait and see what else the bureau digs up."

She shook her head emphatically. "I'm tired of sitting around waiting for the ax to fall. I'm not going to be a victim and just wait for someone to come kill me."

"But this King person was the stalker and he's dead," Trace argued.

"Maybe, but somebody murdered him. I can't accept the coincidence that King was mugged, or something. His death was connected to me. Until we find out who wanted him dead, I can't believe I'm safe.''

Trace washed his weary face with his fingertips. He'd thought that if he could avoid the subject for a day or so, Mary might have some respite from the siege of terror she'd been under these past weeks. Sooner or later, though, she would have arrived at this conclusion. He was only sorry it was so soon.

"All right, let's throw some stuff into an overnight bag and hit the road."

Mary jumped to her feet and ran into the bedroom to pack before Trace changed his mind. She hadn't expected to convince him to travel to North Carolina quite so easily and wasn't going to give him time to reconsider. That he'd folded so quickly could only mean one thing: Trace had already reached the same conclusion.

She was still in danger.

Chapter Fifteen

It was already late afternoon by the time they pulled into Kramer, North Carolina. Because there was no airport in the small mountain community, they'd flown to Asheville and rented a car for the two-hour drive into Kramer.

A typical example of small-town America, Kramer was an orderly little town of white frame houses and tree-lined streets. They passed the library, an imposing structure of blue granite. An area apparently composed of fast-food restaurants. And, off on the left, the local high school. Mary and Trace exchanged a glance as they read the huge purple and gold banner spread over the front door: Kramer High School—Home of the Howling Wolves.

The profile of a wolf was embossed in gold on the edge of the banner. The same emblem was on Milo King's purple cap.

Kramer also had a weekly newspaper, the *Mountain Crier,* and they located it easily enough on the main thoroughfare.

Marvin Hechler, identified by his brass desk plate as the publisher/editor, was sitting at a battered metal desk, entering data into a desktop computer when they walked in. "Afternoon, folks. What can I do for you?"

Trace walked over and extended his hand. "Name's Armstrong and this is Ms. Wilder. We need to find out some information on one of your local residents."

Hechler shoved his glasses up on the top of his head, barely mussing the few strands of thinning hair. "Who'd that be?"

"A man named King. Milo King."

Hechler nodded. "King used to be a common enough name around these parts. Milo's the only one still lives around here. He's a decent old boy, lives out of town a ways. Married one of the Dulcie girls, if memory serves me right. What'd you say your business with Milo was?"

"We didn't say." Trace pulled out his federal identification. If anyone ever took the time to carefully examine his ID, they'd realize it only said he was retired from the secret service. Fortunately, Hechler, like most people, took a glance at the card and assumed he was still actively on duty. Trace didn't see any need to correct the man's assumption.

Hechler whistled through his teeth and returned Trace's card. "Feds, huh? Can't imagine Milo in trouble."

"We don't know that he is in any kind of trouble with the law, Mr. Hechler. His name came up in an investigation and we're just here to check it out. I'd appreciate any background you could give us."

Hechler scratched his balding scalp. "I was born and raised in these parts. Went to school with Milo's kin. The Kings were mountain people, through and through. 'Course, these days the mountains are loaded with over-achievers from the city trying to get away from it all, but back then, mountain people were different. More clan-nish, tended to stick together. The Kings were mountain people."

Mary leaned forward, placing her hand on the editor's desk. "Please, Mr. Hechler, I can understand that you don't want to say anything that might cause trouble for Mr. King, and I promise you, Mr. King won't be harmed." *Not any longer,* she thought as a shiver raced along her arms. "This is important. Truly a matter of life and death."

Hechler stared into her eyes for a long time then rose to his feet. Coming around his desk, he leaned one hip on the metal corner and crossed his arms. He gave Trace a cautious appraisal. "Don't suppose if there's a story in this, you'd give me an exclusive?"

Trace considered. "If there's anything I can release to the public, I'll call you first." He took a business card from a Plexiglas holder on Hechler's desk and stuck it in his pocket. "What can you tell us, sir?"

Again, Hechler shook his head thoughtfully. "Except for a hitch in the air force some years back, Milo's lived in these parts all his life. Works over at the Collins Sportswear plant. Good man. Matter of fact, he's the shop steward over there."

"What about family?" Mary asked.

"Milo's wife, Betty, died in childbirth some years back. Baby didn't make it, either. Like to broke Milo's heart. He never remarried."

"What about blood relations?" Trace knew the roots of some of the family trees in these isolated communities were deep and tangled. Surely King must have been related to half the people on this mountain.

Hechler scratched his head. "Not in these parts. Milo's parents are both long dead. His dad, Wilbur, was one of the more well-known moonshiners around here thirty or forty years ago. Bit of a local legend. The whole family kept to themselves pretty much. There was a passel of kids, as I recall. Four girls, it seems, and, of course, the two boys. The girls all left for the city and got married. Think Elda is down in Charlotte, don't know where the others ended up."

Trace raised an eyebrow. "But Milo has a brother? Maybe he can help us."

"Doubt that. Now if it was the *brother* you were looking for, I wouldn't be at all surprised. He was always peculiar. Hasn't been seen around here in years."

A strange premonition caused Mary to ask softly, "What was the brother's name?"

"Martin."

Trace and Mary exchanged a glance. Milo had warned her to watch out for Martin, had used his last breath to utter the warning, in fact.

Wrapping an arm around Mary's shoulder, Trace said, "Mr. Hechler, we need to find out all we can about these King brothers. Could we buy you dinner somewhere?"

Hechler regarded them for a long moment. "I suppose that would be all right."

Once they were seated in a cozy booth at the Kountry Kitchen Kafe, the newspaper editor gave them the rudimentary facts of the King "scandal."

Martin King had received quite a bit of publicity twenty years before when his wife was killed in a fire that destroyed their home shortly after their marriage. Martin had told the authorities that his wife had received threatening letters and telephone calls shortly before her death. No arrests were ever made.

"For a long time, folks were nervous. Figured if it could happen to Mrs. King, it could happen to their wives, as well. Those were sad times for the King boys, both of 'em losing their wives so close together. You'd think it might have made them closer. But, sad to say, the double tragedy seemed to drive them apart."

"What happened after that?" Mary bit into a fillet of fresh catfish, excellently prepared, but tasteless in her mouth. The feeling of impending devastation she'd experienced earlier kept growing in her stomach, like a cancer, spreading its evil throughout her body.

Hechler shrugged. "There was some kind of falling-out between the brothers, Milo and Martin. Never heard a breath of what it was all about, but they stopped speaking altogether. One morning, Martin up and quit his job over at the factory and left town. Far as I know, no one in these parts have seen or heard from him since.''

He paused as if coming to a difficult decision. Skimming his hand over his head, he apparently reached the decision to continue. ''Heard a rumor Martin had taken out a *very* large insurance policy on his bride. Caused considerable talk.''

''I imagine it would,'' Trace concurred.

When he asked about the possibility of getting a photograph of Martin King, Hechler nodded. ''Maybe. We might have run one during the scandal. Stop by in the morning and we'll see what we can dig up.''

''This is very important, Mr. Hechler,'' Mary said. ''Is there any way we can find out tonight?''

He hesitated, while seeming to make up his mind. ''Wish you folks could give me a hint what this is about.''

Realizing they might get more cooperation from the newspaperman if they satisfied his curiosity, Trace filled in the elementary details of their involvement with Milo King.

When Trace finished, Hechler shook his head and pushed his half-eaten food aside. ''So, old Milo's dead, you say? Too bad. But you know, now that I think about it, he's been a mite strange for the last month or two. Ever since he went north on that business for the union.''

''What business?'' Trace asked as the waitress cleared the table.

''Remember I told you Milo was the shop steward over at Collins Sportswear? Well, there was some big convention of union leaders in Washington a few weeks ago and Milo went as Collins's representative. I wondered a few times if something had happened up in Washington, because he came back...I don't know, different, somehow.''

Trace and Mary exchanged a meaningful look; the connection was made. Somehow, her path and Milo's must have crossed while he was in Washington attending that convention. Except...except, where did Martin King fit in?

"Matter of fact," Hechler continued, "I heard he took a leave of absence two or three weeks ago. Nobody's seen him around lately. 'Course, he never took a day's vacation or sick leave in the twenty years since his wife died, so I guess he had some time coming to him."

Again, Mary and Trace shared a glance that was full of unspoken meaning. Three weeks was just about when she'd first felt she was being watched. Everything dovetailed completely with Milo's activities. Only one question remained unanswered: Why? What had caused a seemingly honest, mild-mannered man to suddenly begin stalking a woman he'd never met?

And what did his brother, Martin, have to do with it? Or was Milo's warning simply the garbled thoughts and words of a dying man? Perhaps he'd only been trying to tell them to find his brother. Maybe in mountain vernacular "watch out for Martin" meant "look for Martin."

If so, then perhaps the nightmare was over, after all.

After Trace paid the check, the threesome walked in silence down the street to the newspaper office. Darkness fell early in the higher elevations. Kramer was one of those quiet little communities that apparently rolled up its sidewalk at dusk. All the storefronts were dark, a few shuttered. Kramer had settled down for the night. Mary only wished she could enjoy the same peaceful slumber she'd taken for granted only a few short weeks ago. Before Milo King had come to Washington on union business. And, shortly after, set about destroying her life.

Back in the *Mountain Crier* office, Hechler flipped on the microfiche machine and searched through a dusty carton for a particular roll of film. "Had the stuff put on film about five or six years ago. Keeping old copies of the newspaper took up all my storage."

Locating the roll he wanted, he threaded the film through the machine and began scanning several months of newspaper headlines. "Here it is," he said at last. "Yep, almost twenty years to the day. Still got my memory, at least."

Over the hum of the microfiche machine, Hechler read aloud the germane facts of Mrs. King's death. The story was essentially what he'd told them in the restaurant, the only new information was the detail that Mrs. King wasn't from the area. Martin had met her while on a business trip to Chicago. She'd been living in Kramer less than a week when she was killed in the tragic fire.

Mary and Trace stood in breathless silence while the genial newsman skimmed the stories. After a few minutes, he flipped off the machine and turned around. "Sorry. Not a single picture of Martin. Couple of his wife, but not one of him."

Trace leaned over his shoulder. "How about showing us the ones of Mrs. King?"

"Sure thing." Hechler flipped through the clippings until he located the shot that he wanted. "Let me use this newfangled contraption and see if we can enlarge this and print it out."

He pressed a few buttons on the computer-type machine connected to the microfiche reader and, a moment later, a sheet of paper rolled out bearing the fuzzy image of a fair-haired woman.

Hechler glanced at the photo and handed it to Trace. "Isn't that funny?"

"What?" Mary asked.

Both Trace and Hechler turned to stare at her, their faces set in identical expressions of bemusement. Wordlessly, Trace handed the computer-generated photograph to Mary.

Mrs. Martin King, deceased, bore an uncanny resemblance to Mary Wilder.

Mary's fingers trembled as she stared at the likeness. The woman's hairstyle was twenty years out of date, as was her makeup. Yet ... yet she looked enough like Mary to be her sister, if they had been contemporaries. Both had large dark eyes, with straight ash blond hair that fell to their shoulders. Mary's was styled in a contemporary blunt cut while Mrs. King wore her hair in a pageboy that was fashionable in her day. The two women even shared similar bone structure.

Folding the paper carefully, she slipped it into her purse. Once again, Mary felt those icy fingers of foreboding scrabble down her back. Was her resemblance to the dead woman mere coincidence? No, she couldn't believe that.

Somehow, Mary was linked to these King brothers, but she just couldn't imagine the connection. Nor did she know where to turn for more clues.

Here, in Kramer, she and Trace had reached the end of the trail and they knew very little more than when they'd arrived this afternoon.

After thanking Hechler for his kind cooperation, Trace and Mary walked out to the car. Stifling a yawn, he said, "I don't know about you, but I vote for getting a motel close by for the night. I don't feel like driving back down the mountain in the dark."

Mary nodded. She knew Trace was deliberately refraining from commenting on the amazing likeness. He must have seen that she'd absorbed all the shock she could for the moment, and she was grateful for his restraint. But then, Trace always knew the right thing to say or do to make her feel better.

Taking his lead and pushing the bewildering incident to the back of her mind, Mary said, "I'm bushed, myself. What about that place we saw on the edge of town?"

He started the engine. "It looked as good as any. Maybe if we get a decent night's sleep, we'll be able to think of another angle in the morning."

Mary waited in the car while Trace registered them at the Sleepy Time Motel. In a small, conservative village like Kramer, she knew the proprietor would be shocked at an unmarried couple sharing a room. She wondered if Trace would say they were married. She smiled wryly. They'd already been living in the same apartment for over a week and sharing a room for the past three days. Why did it suddenly feel illicit and delightfully sinful to be checking into a motel together?

When he came back out to the car, flipping the room key in his palm as he walked, she grinned. "Did you register us as the Smiths or the Joneses?"

Rolling his eyes, he hefted their overnight bags from the back seat. "I *have* checked into a motel with a woman before, you know. I'm not completely without experience in these matters."

Mary slammed her car door and moved to his side. "So what name *did* you use?"

Without breaking stride, he muttered, "Johnson."

Stopping in front of room eight, he unlocked the door and held it open with his foot while Mary walked inside. "Your honeymoon suite, Mrs. Johnson."

Deliberately keeping her back turned, she strolled over to the mirror. As she'd suspected, her cheeks were flaming.

TRACE LEANED BACK on the lumpy mattress and draped his forearm across his eyes, shielding himself from the provocative reflection in the mirror.

Completely unaware, Mary stood scrubbing her face in the tiny alcove that held the sink. She'd stripped down to her lacy bikini panties and bra, her honey-colored hair whirling like a cloud around her shoulders.

Even when she was dressed like an uptight society maven, she aroused him. Now, with her long delicate limbs exposed before his greedy eyes, Trace had all he could handle to keep from dragging her into his bed by that luscious blond hair.

He watched as, with a graceful economy of motion, she lifted her foot onto the counter and smeared body lotion over the length of her leg. At that moment, Trace would have traded Jonathan Regent's fortune to be that handful of creamy lotion.

For days now, the thought of making love to her had been a ceaseless, pounding fantasy. The woman was driving him nuts.

She straightened up and began smoothing the lotion over her arms, her shoulders, across the sweetly curved tops of her breasts. Lower. Her fingers massaged the liquid into her midriff, then lower still, onto her abdomen, dangerously close to the low-slung elastic waist of her panties.

Trace closed his eyes tightly, imagining his mouth gliding over the same skin her fingertips had just massaged. Breathing in the delicious, musky aroma of her.

Damn, he was going to lose it!

He turned over and faced the wall, but the image wouldn't fade.

Without true awareness of when he'd moved from fantasy to reality, Trace rose from the bed and crossed the room to stand behind her. She was smoothing the lotion across her shoulders. Suddenly, her eyes caught his in the mirror. The inky darkening of her brown eyes gave her away; she'd been aware of his watchful eyes all along.

Taking the small bottle of lotion from her hands, he whispered, "Here, let me help you."

He poured a small amount of the cool, slick fluid on his fingers and brushed his hand over the smoothness of her upper back. She sighed and leaned into his hard body, fueling the fires even higher.

With a small whimper of desire, she turned around to face him. Trace lowered his hands to the countertop on either side of her, capturing her in the circle of his embrace. He gazed down into the smoky depths of her eyes, as they pulled him closer, a shimmering, hypnotizing force.

"Mary-Mary," he murmured, raising his hands to cup her face. His fingertips sought and found the tiny scar at the edge of her mouth. With an infinite sweetness, he lowered his lips to kiss the old wound. "Tell me about this," he demanded gently.

"Now?" Her voice was a husky eloquent reminder of the white-hot passion sizzling in the air between them.

"Yes, now. I want to know everything about you, Mary-Mary. I want to know all of you. Taste all of you."

Flushing at the intimacy his words provoked, she breathed, "I was in my Tarzan phase. I slid off the grapevine."

He smiled and lowered his head once more, nuzzling her neck. "I won't let you fall anymore, Mary. I'll always catch you."

She bit her lip and plunged her fingers into his thick hair, drawing his face up to hers. Finding his mouth with her own, she demanded everything with her kiss. He willingly gave it.

Lightly skimming his fingers up the smooth, satiny plane of her back, he bent over and trailed kisses along the path his fingertips had just taken.

Mary shuddered in response and leaned back, pressing her gently rounded bottom against the hard vee at the crest of his legs.

Lifting his mouth from her shoulder, Trace gently turned her around to face him. He stared at her in awe. Never had he known a woman so gentle yet so strong; so warm yet with a core of solid steel; so innocent and so very, very desirable.

He touched her face, brushing her delicate eyelids, along the planes of her cheekbones and finally, pausing at the soft fullness of her lips.

Wordlessly, Mary opened her lips and pulled his fingertip into the sweet moist cavern of her mouth. Suckling gently, she moaned with delight and wrapped her arms around his neck.

Feeling a shaft of desire so strong it was almost painful, Trace lifted with an arm under her thighs and seated her on the edge of the countertop.

A wild, uncontrollable passion finally overtook them and he lowered his lips to her seeking mouth, replacing his finger with his probing tongue.

Somewhere deep in the hidden recesses of his mind, Trace knew what he was doing was wrong. Unfair to Mary. He was taking advantage of her vulnerability. He'd hate himself in the morning.

He didn't care.

Let the devil take tomorrow. Tonight, he had Mary. And that was enough for any man.

IT WAS STILL DARK when Mary awoke with the immediate sensation that something was wrong.

Shifting slightly, she felt the warmth of Trace's body lying beside her and, suddenly, she remembered their shared passion of last night.

What had she done?

Blinking away sudden tears, she inched off the bed and tiptoed into the bathroom. It didn't matter that she'd already decided to break off her engagement to Jonathan. In her heart, they were already finished. But she hadn't told him yet and, consequently, she'd broken a vow. Worse, she'd betrayed Jonathan's trust and her own self-respect.

As she stepped into the shower, she thought about the dinner she and Jonathan had planned for this evening. He was probably eager to hear the details of the extravagant wedding she'd arranged. The wedding that would never take place.

Mary knew she couldn't face that discussion. At least not yet. She had to get away from all the stress, go someplace where she could think. Where she'd be safe.

She wanted to go home.

Mary hadn't been home since her father's mild heart attack before Christmas, and she had a sudden, desperate need to cocoon herself in her parents' loving embrace.

Now that she'd made the decision, Mary could hardly wait to get started. She wanted to rush to Michigan where she would be protected and loved. Although it was still April and the weather was temperamental in the far north, conditions had been mild on the Upper Peninsula this year. Undoubtedly, her parents would be getting ready to move to their summer home on the shores of Lake Superior, a few miles outside Marquette. The place she loved more than any other on earth.

Dressing quickly, she hurried into the bedroom and nudged Trace. "Wake up! Hurry!"

Coming to his senses almost immediately, he grabbed for his revolver on the night table. "What is it? What's wrong?"

"Nothing. I . . . I just had an idea."

He flopped back down on the pillow and glared at the red glowing numerals on the bedside clock. "At 4:00 a.m.?"

"Yes." She sat down on the edge of the bed beside him. Ignoring the tantalizing rumple of his black hair against the white pillowcase, she slowly tried to explain. "I know what we did last night was wrong."

She held up a hand as he started to protest. "Let me finish. Please."

With a deep sigh, Trace locked his fingers around his wrists above his head and waited.

Mary fingered the coins he'd pulled from his pockets and tossed on the bedside table. "I'm breaking my engagement to Jonathan. I should have done it as soon as he returned from his business trip, but I...well, he was too busy to see me and I didn't force the issue. Anyway, after what happened between us last night—"

"What happened is that we made love," he interrupted. "Why can't you say the words?"

"Because I'm trying to forget it happened!" she snapped, angry with him for making her face her infidelity, her ultimate betrayal of Jonathan.

Trace didn't say a word, but a mask of cold indifference fell over his face as his jaw clenched. Wordlessly, he stared into her eyes, waiting for her to continue.

"Anyway," she said, shifting her eyes away from the icy aloofness of his, "I've decided to go spend some time with my parents. In Michigan. I want you to drive me to the airport."

Still without uttering a word, he pushed her aside and got out of bed.

Mary stifled a sudden yearning as she looked up at the hard-muscled beauty of his nude body, highlighted by remnants of moonlight. "Will you take me?" she asked, grimacing at the unintentional double entendre.

"I'll be ready in five minutes. Get your stuff together."

As good as his word, Trace came back into the bedroom in less than five minutes. Looking fresh and enticing from his shower, he stuffed his dirty clothing into his duffel and walked to the door. "Ready when you are."

Although Mary tried several times to engage him in conversation on the two-hour drive back to Asheville, Trace only muttered monosyllabic responses to her queries and initiated no dialogue on his own.

He stood silently while she settled the rental car bill with her credit card and, later, made a careful examination of his fingertips while she attempted to cancel her dinner with Jonathan that evening. When Bob Newland answered, she merely asked him to pass along to Jonathan that she'd gone home to visit her family for a few days. Even if Newland was completely innocent of involvement with the stalker, he gave her the creeps and she didn't want to divulge any information about her personal life to the man.

The first time Trace spoke of his own volition was when they approached the airline counter to buy a ticket to Marquette, Michigan. "Make that two," he said to the clerk.

She whirled. "That's not necessary."

"Maybe not. But it's all part of the job. Armstrong's bodyguard and escort service. We aim to please. Did I, Mary? Did I please you last night? Maybe you could write me an endorsement?"

"Stop it, Trace!" Catching the interested expression on the ticket agent's face, Mary grabbed Trace's shirtsleeve and pulled him a few feet away. "I tried to explain to you, but you heard only what you wanted. Don't diminish what happened between us last night. Please."

"Haven't you already done that?" he whispered.

"Ma'am? How will you be paying for these tickets?"

With a sigh of regret, Mary turned away from Trace to complete the airline transaction. More bereft than she'd ever been in her entire life, she felt alone and abandoned. She'd lost more than Jonathan, more than her heart, more than her self-esteem. The sharp stabbing pain in her chest was her undeniable reaction to losing Trace, as well.

They had to hurry to catch the first flight to Chicago, where they'd change planes. Trace slept most of the way, sitting up only when the flight attendant served the bland, microwaved breakfast.

After barely making their connection in Chicago, they made the short jaunt to Green Bay, where they changed planes once again for the final leg of the journey to Marquette.

Since they only had carry-on luggage, it took only a few moments to make their way through the small airport to the taxi stand outside. There was an icy nip in the air and the sky was gray and overcast. A complete change of climate from the almost tropical warmth in the south. But while others might bemoan the harsh northern climate, Mary gloried in it.

"I just can't wait to get to camp again," she enthused.

Trace swiveled his head quizzically as he placed their bags into the trunk of a waiting cab. "Camp? As in community cabins and arts and crafts?"

"No." She laughed. "Camp is what everybody calls their summer place in these parts."

Sliding into the back seat, she smiled at the driver. "Five-twenty-six Pine Street. That's off the Munising Road about four miles out."

"Camp," Trace repeated as he slid in beside her. "Does this place have indoor plumbing by any chance? I'm a city boy, you know."

Catching the cabdriver's eye in the rearview mirror, she rolled her eyes and laughed aloud. Not even Trace's good-natured grumbling could blemish her unabashed joy.

At long last, she was home.

Chapter Sixteen

Elizabeth Wilder stood in the doorway, wiping her hands on an ancient stained apron. "Mary! Darling! Why didn't you tell us you were coming home?" She pushed open the glass storm door and waved her daughter inside, like a mother hen gathering her chick into the nest. "Come in, come in. John, come here a minute!"

Wrapping her arm around Mary, the older woman hugged her tightly. "Your dad will be so happy. He hasn't been the same since...well, you know, his illness. But you'll sure perk him—Mary, for goodness' sakes, I didn't know you brought someone!"

Pushing open the storm door again, Mrs. Wilder ushered Trace out of the cold. "You must be Jonathan. Mary's told me all about you! Except she never said you were so handsome. Oh, Mary, this is a fine-looking young man. But, honey, somehow I'd gotten the impression that your fiancé was . . . was an older man."

Trace held up his hand, palm out, like a traffic officer stopping the flow of her words. "Actually, I'm not Jonathan Regent, Mrs. Wilder. Although I am pleased to meet you."

"Oh?" She looked questioningly at Mary.

"This is Trace Armstrong, Mother. I, uh, have a lot to tell you."

"I guess you do," Mrs. Wilder said mildly as she closed the front door behind them. "John? Are you coming? Mary's home."

An hour later, the foursome sat around the scarred kitchen table drinking Elizabeth's famous malted hot chocolate. Not wanting to cause her parents worry, especially in view of her father's heart condition, Mary had given her parents a heavily edited version of the events of the past few weeks.

Her mother's conversation had focused on the change in men in Mary's life and most of her queries had been channeled in that direction. John Wilder was simply so happy to see his only child that he just kept patting her hand and beaming, asking no questions at all.

Suddenly, Elizabeth jumped to her feet. "Oh! I'll bet you kids are starving. I'd better see to dinner."

She bustled around the kitchen gathering the ingredients for Mary's favorite, Cornish pasties, a local tradition of a half-moon-shaped pastry filled with ground meat, onions and vegetables and baked to an aromatic rapture.

John led Trace into the den, no doubt to show off Mary's fishing trophies and baby photos, and Mary was left alone for the moment.

The time had come, she knew, to make the phone call she'd been dreading all day. Slipping into her old bedroom, she curled up on her canopy bed and dialed Jonathan's office number. When his voice-mail message came on, Mary broke the connection. Next, she tried his home phone number. After four rings, his service picked up. "Yes, this is Ms. Wilder. Has Mr. Regent left a number where he can be reached?"

"Oh, hello, Ms. Wilder. Nice to talk to you. Where did I put that note? Oh, yes, here it is. Mr. Regent said he was sorry that you couldn't make your engagement and that he had to fly to New York this evening. He'll be in touch."

Couldn't make their engagement. Most men would have said couldn't make their appointment or couldn't make dinner, but in his formal manner, Jonathan had unknowingly identified the problem. It was true; Mary couldn't make the engagement.

After giving the operator the phone number at her parents' home, and leaving a message for Jonathan to return her call, Mary replaced the receiver. She should have been relieved that she had once more been spared the ordeal of breaking the news to Jonathan. Instead, she felt strangled, choking on the building tension, and wished it was over.

It was as though a razor-sharp guillotine blade was suspended over her neck and she didn't know when it was going to fall. Was the expectation worse than the actual blow?

She didn't know, but she did know that she was weary of her life being on hold. Although it had only been a couple of days since Mary had made her decision to break her engagement, it felt like weeks. She looked down at the enormous diamond still twinkling on her left hand.

It would, of course, have to be returned to Jonathan. But until she'd told him in person—or at least on the phone—she felt uncomfortable removing the token of his affection. What if someone noticed her ringless finger and told Jonathan? It would be so awful for him to find out from someone else. Yet the platinum band felt like a yoke of indenture and she yearned to be free of her commitment.

After dinner, they sat around the den talking until John yawned. Mary glanced at her watch. "My goodness, look at the time! Mom, don't worry about those dishes, I'll do them in the morning."

Mrs. Wilder had already shown Trace to the spare room, and joined her husband in their bedroom, when Trace rapped on Mary's door.

"Come in."

"Think your folks will mind if I make a long-distance call? I almost forgot that I wanted to check in with Harley Tobias."

"They won't mind at all." Mary pointed to the pink Princess phone beside her narrow bed. "Use this one. I want to hear what he found out."

She curled up in a wicker rocker and looked out the window while Trace phoned Harley in Virginia. She touched the pane with her fingertip. Even through the thickness of the dual pane windows, she could sense the bitter cold. Mary pressed her face against the cool glass and wasn't at all surprised to see clouds of light snowflakes drifting past.

Trace had finally reached Harley at his home and, as usual, the gruffly good-natured agent was one step ahead of them. By using his own sources, Harley had already discovered that Milo King had an older brother named Martin.

"Did you happen to get any photographs of Martin King?" Trace asked.

He listened to Harley's response. "Is there someplace local you can fax them to me?"

Again, a pause while Harley talked. Trace nodded. "That'll be great, old man. I sure appreciate it."

Hanging up the phone, Trace said quietly, "I don't know what good it will do, but Harley's going to fax me copies of the photos he was able to dig up of Martin King."

Mary frowned. "Tonight?"

"Yeah. I don't know why, but I've got this . . . this feeling that everything's coming to a boil. I don't want to wait until morning."

His manner toward Mary in private was still aloof, but at least he didn't seem as awkward with her as he had for most of the day. She took some comfort in his softer demeanor, yet missed the warmth and friendship that had been so much a part of their relationship. Before she'd spoiled it last night. "But where will you receive a fax this time of night? Nothing is open."

"Harley's going to call the local police and get their fax number. Where's the main station?"

"Downtown. But that's over ten miles away and it's starting to snow."

He crossed the room and looked out the window. "Son-of-a-gun! It's really coming down, too." He straightened up and let the cotton curtain drop into place. "Think your dad would mind if I borrowed his car?"

She thought about offering to drive him, but realized Trace might be glad of the opportunity to get away by himself for a short time. Besides, three mugs of her mother's malted hot chocolate had the same effect on Mary as an equal number of tranquilizers. She was almost asleep on her feet. "Of course you can use one of the cars. But take Dad's Suburban, it has four-wheel drive. Come on, I'll find you some warm clothes."

Keeping their voices low so as not to disturb her parents, Mary and Trace tiptoed downstairs. She found the spare keys to the Suburban on a holder by the back door. Next, she led the way to the mudroom, so she could find Trace warm clothing to wear out into the ever-building snowstorm.

Although Trace was a much larger man than John Wilder, Mary eventually found an insulated jacket, lumberjack cap and mittens that he could squeeze into. His feet, however, wouldn't fit into any of her father's snow boots so Trace had to wear his sneakers.

"Stay out of snowdrifts," Mary warned, "or you'll get frostbite. Those tennis shoes will be soaking wet in just a couple of minutes if you walk through heavy snow."

For the first time since she'd awakened him that morning, Trace gave her that familiar, crooked grin, causing her heart to lurch. "Yes, Mother Mary. And I won't slam on the brakes if I start to slide and I'll keep the flaps down over my ears and I won't play in the snow. Anything else?''

"No, smart aleck. I . . . I just worry about you."

Trace cupped her worried face between his mittened hands. "Don't worry, Mary-Mary. Everything is going to be just fine. Trust me."

Giving her a light kiss on the tip of her nose, he stepped out the kitchen door into the swirling snow. A moment later, she heard the garage door open, and she watched out the window until the Suburban backed into the street. A few seconds later, its taillights disappeared from her sight.

Mary turned away from the window, feeling suddenly alone and abandoned again. She'd thought she'd find sanctuary here in her parents' home, but her heart told her that Trace had been her refuge all along. Why hadn't she realized the truth before? Why hadn't she told Trace how she felt, deep inside where it counted?

Suddenly, she couldn't wait for his return. Filled with a strange surety that she and Trace could work out their problems, she was eager to talk to him. To tell him that she loved him.

But for now, as unaccustomed as he was to driving in heavy snow, she could do nothing more than pray he returned safely.

Too late, Mary realized she'd forgotten to give him a door key, so she left the back door unlocked and walked softly upstairs to the familiar warmth of her former bedroom.

MARY DIDN'T KNOW how long she'd been asleep when she awoke abruptly. For a moment, she felt disoriented until she realized she was back in her childhood bed. Safe in her parents' home.

She was wondering what had awakened her, when she realized she hadn't heard the Suburban pull back in. Hadn't heard the garage door close. Had something happened to Trace?

A vague creak in the hallway brought her to a sitting position. She recognized that creak; it always caught her when she was sneaking home late from a date. It was right past the landing by the stairs, almost impossible to avoid.

Her senses thoroughly aroused, she listened intently until she heard the soft thud of a footstep outside her bedroom door. "Trace? Is that you?" she called.

Only an echoing stillness responded.

The sense of foreboding that had been trailing her all day returned with a vengeance. Something was wrong; terribly wrong. She sat up and switched on the bedside light.

"Trace?" she called again.

Once more, only the eerie silence returned her call.

Suddenly, Mary detected a peculiar odor emanating from the hallway. A stinging, acrid odor, one she'd smelled before but was surely out of place now. She sniffed the air and got another, stronger whiff. So familiar, yet so elusive.

It reminded her of evenings at her parents' camp. Of cool evenings when they'd light the kerosene heater and—

Kerosene!

At that moment, the smoke alarm at the top of the steps blared out a warning. Immediately, the strong odor of kerosene was dissipated by another, even more frightening smell. The hot choking scent of fire!

As the piercing shriek of the fire alarm continued to scream in her ear, Mary sprang out of bed and ran to the door. Barely recalling her training, she placed her palm on the wooden door panel and was relieved to find it only warm. She pushed out into the hall into black suffocating smoke.

Holding her hand in front of her mouth, she started for her folks' bedroom and was relieved to see Trace, still fully dressed, shepherding her bewildered parents into the relative safety of the hallway.

Huddling together, the foursome started for the staircase, when Mary stopped, pointing in horror. Dancing, sizzling flames were already leapfrogging up the steps. Their primary escape route was cut off.

"Come on," Trace shouted, grabbing her arm. "We'll have to go out a window!"

Herding them into Mary's room, he took a precious moment to pick up the telephone by her bed. A shake of his head told her the phone line was dead. They wouldn't be able to count on any outside help. They were on their own.

"How steep is the roofline?" he asked her father.

The older man shook his head in confusion. "Not too bad. At least I don't think so."

Deciding to see for himself, Trace dashed toward the bedroom window. A popping sound struck their ears a split second after Mary's window shattered. Reacting purely by instinct, Trace dropped to the floor and shouted, "Turn out that lamp! Everybody stay down."

Mary blindly obeyed his command, but her attention was focused on the broken window. What had caused it to shatter like that? Heat from the fire?

Crawling on his stomach like a giant, slinky lizard, Trace moved away from the window and rose to his feet at Mary's side. "He's out in the yard. That was a rifle shot. He has every avenue cut off."

"He? Who? What do you mean a rifle?" Mary had been through so much trauma these past weeks that she couldn't absorb any more. She was dazed, punchy.

Grabbing her by the shoulders, Trace buried his face in her hair and whispered so her parents wouldn't hear, "The man who's been trying to kill you. We have to get your folks out of here."

Mary raised her gaze to meet his. "But the stalker's dead. Isn't...isn't he?"

The pained look on Trace's face was answer enough. He pulled her close to his chest and cupped her face between his hands. "I love you, Mary Wilder, and we're going to get through this. Do you understand?"

Trace loved her. Everything else faded into insignificance.

Suddenly feeling alive again, Mary snapped back, fully alert now. Giving her dazed parents a single glance, she knew her first responsibility was to get them safely out of the fire. "If he's watching the windows on this side of the house, we can go out the other," she said to Trace.

But when they led her parents out of her bedroom, Mary saw that the flames had already encompassed the rooms across the hall and were rapidly spreading. "Never mind!" she shouted above the crackling roar. "We can go up through the attic and still come out on the other side."

"Good," Trace yelled. "Get going. I'll be right there."

Leaving her to tend to John and Elizabeth, Trace darted back into Mary's room and yanked the covers loose. He carried the sheet and blankets to the adjoining bathroom where he threw them into the tub and doused them with cold water.

Carrying the dripping bedding in his arms, he followed Mary. She'd pulled down the retractable attic stairs and was trying to coax her parents up the narrow staircase.

"Here." Trace draped soaking-wet blankets around John's and Elizabeth's shoulders. "Keep these over your heads so a stray spark doesn't ignite your hair or burn your eyes." He pulled Mary beside him and covered them with the sopping wet sheet. Together, they eased her mother up the narrow stairs and turned to help her father.

Even in the dim red glow cast by the now-raging fire, Mary could see her father's face was ashen. Oh, dear heavens, please don't let him have another heart attack, she prayed. All thoughts of the peril they were facing, of the madman waiting on the lawn below disappeared beneath this more immediate and more frightening danger. She couldn't stand to lose her father. She just couldn't.

Feeling Trace's strong arm around her waist supporting her both physically and emotionally, Mary leaned forward and kissed her father's weathered cheek. "Come on, Dad! Just a little farther and we'll be safe."

John turned a dazed face to his daughter and nodded. Slowly, the trio climbed the steps and joined Elizabeth in the dark attic.

Taking a moment to get her bearings, Mary pointed to the brick chimney jutting up through the middle of the attic floor. "Over there! There's a gabled window on that side."

Wrapping an arm around each of her parents, she headed for their last avenue of escape.

Trace hung back, making sure the Wilders were safe. Holding the soggy blankets, he batted at the tiny spurts of flame that shot up on the plywood floor. The window Mary had led them to was painted shut. He was just about to rush to her aid, when she picked up a dusty brass andiron and wrapped it in the sheet.

Motioning to her parents to stand back, Mary swung the andiron in its percale sling and shattered the window. Grabbing a piece of wood, she cleared the fragments of glass from the window frame.

Trace couldn't help the thrill of pride. That was some resourceful woman he'd fallen in love with. Still keeping ahead in his battle with the encroaching flames, Trace watched out of the corner of his eye while Mary urged both her parents out onto the rooftop. Just as she lifted a paja-maed leg to follow, a section of the attic wall caved in, almost catching him beneath the debris.

As he raced to follow Mary out the window, Trace felt a sharp pain in his right hand and glanced down. A falling timber must have struck him. A gaping slash along the outside of his palm was oozing blood.

Ripping loose a piece of his shirt, Trace tied a makeshift bandage around the wound and scrambled through the window onto the roof.

As John had promised, this section of the roofline was gently sloped. Thankfully, it had stopped snowing some time ago, but the asphalt shingles were still slick and treacherous. Moving with great caution, Trace crawled to the opposite corner of the house from the gunman. A huge oak tree was nestled against the vinyl siding. If he could somehow get them into that tree . . . surely they could make their way to the ground.

One by one, while the others huddled together in the darkness as their home crumbled beneath them, Trace helped first the parents, then the daughter to the ground.

Trace held his fingertip across his lips in a signal for quiet as they raced across the snow-crusted ground to the relative safety of the garage. Although both the Suburban and the sedan were parked inside, they quickly discovered all sets of keys were inside the blazing inferno.

They were temporarily safe from the fire, but they were several miles away from town and outside help. Would anyone even see the flames in the night sky before it was too late?

And they couldn't forget a killer was still somewhere in the inky darkness, stalking them.

Trace had never felt more frustrated in his life. They were completely at that madman's mercy. His gun, the keys, everything that might be used as a weapon was burning up inside what was left of the house.

Keeping his fingertip over the light switch on the sedan door, Trace pushed Mary's parents into the back seat. "Get down on the floor and stay there," he hissed. "Don't move until Mary or I come to get you."

He knew better than to hope he could convince Mary to wait with her family. And, for once, he was grateful for her obstinance. He needed her help if they were to stand a chance of outwitting the gunman.

He looked over to where Mary stood just inside the garage. Trace knew she hadn't yet made the connection; she still didn't know the identity of the man who was outside waiting to kill her. Why the hell did Trace have to be the one to break the awful news?

Pulling her farther into the shadows of the garage, he kissed the top of her smoky hair. "I'm so sorry, sweetheart. Truly sorry."

Mary lifted her head and stared deeply into the golden eyes she so dearly loved. "What did you find out?"

Wordlessly, Trace reached into his jeans pocket for the fax he'd received from Harley. He handed it to her.

Moving slightly, to gain light from the blazing abyss that had been her family home, Mary held up the blurred photo.

Wife of Local Merchant Perishes in Blaze! the caption beneath the photo proclaimed. Slowly, her eyes drifted upward until they locked with the blank stare of the man looking back at her from the newspaper clipping.

Martin King's thick dark hair was cut in a full, collarlength style reminiscent of the seventies. His face was youthful and bland, the character in its features not yet formed. Nonetheless, Mary instantly recognized the blank stare of Martin King. The man she'd come to know as Jonathan Regent.

For a long time, Mary stared at the photograph. She wondered why she felt no surprise, no shock. Could it be that in the deepest recesses of her heart she'd suspected all along?

Martin King-Jonathan Regent. She almost laughed aloud. Regent was a none-too-subtle synonym for king. Martin/Jonathan must have thought he was so clever. Had he killed his first wife for the insurance money, as the newspaper hinted? Had he intended all along to kill her, as well?

Why, Jonathan, her heart cried, why did you want to hurt me so badly?

Trace's gentle finger wiped at her cheek and Mary realized she must have been crying. Taking his hand in hers, she lifted his fingertips to her lips. It was then that she saw the blood-soaked rag around his sooty hand.

Using her teeth, she ripped a piece of wet sheeting and rebandaged Trace's injured hand. The wound looked nasty. He definitely needed medical attention. But first they had to get away from Jonathan so she could lead them to a neighbor's camp, and hopefully find a telephone.

"We have to get him," she whispered fiercely.

"I know." Trace rummaged through a pile of garden implements until he found a sturdy shovel. "I'm going to circle around behind him." He pointed to a stand of trees about twenty yards away. "After I'm in place, see if you can call him, maybe lure him into that clearing."

Mary nodded. While Trace slunk close to the ground behind the garage, she looked at the family car with her parents huddled on the cold floorboards. Shifting her attention outside, she watched with a cold angry heart as the blackened timbers that had once been her folks' dream house collapsed in on itself. She thought about a dead man who'd only been trying to warn her. And she thought about the attempt on her own life.

Those hands at her back pushing her into the path of that bus were the hands of the man she'd meant to marry.

Jonathan Regent was responsible for all those horrible deeds.

There was no worse betrayal.

Stepping out of the sanctuary of the garage, she moved into the open as silently as a wraith. Sensing his nearness, Mary called out, "Jonathan? It was me you wanted all along. I'm here now. Come get me."

Crackling embers were the only response.

Deciding to try a different tact, she shouted, "Jonathan? It's me, Mary. I'm sorry. I never meant to..." To what? What had she ever done to him? Desperately trying to release her mind, to find something that might lure him into conversation, Mary gasped aloud when a shadow moved and Jonathan stood before her.

Holding the rifle centered on her heart, he stepped forward. "So, Jezebel, you've decided to own up to the truth." His voice was as cold and malevolent as death. "I should have known you'd betray me. You're a tramp. All women are tramps."

"Jonathan, I'm sorry."

"Sorry? I didn't want you to be sorry, I wanted you to be pure. Different from the others. For a while, you had me fooled. But then, of course, you proved my trust wasn't warranted. Damn you, Mary! Why couldn't you be pure?"

Mary stood quietly while his curses rained down on her. Martin/Jonathan was insane; why hadn't she seen it before? All the little clues came rushing into her consciousness. The way he'd always referred to her purity, to the virginal look of her fair hair and skin. Even her name, Mary, had delighted him. Now she realized it was because of the subliminal connection to that most pure, most innocent of women: the Virgin Mary.

"Are you listening to me, Jezebel? You must atone for your sins. Like my mother, who left my father for another man. But I found her and made her pay."

"Like you made your first wife pay?"

"Ah! So you know about her, do you? You and that bodyguard have truly been busy. Oh, yes, I know all about the two of you and your disgusting little affair."

Out of the corner of her eye, Mary saw Trace slip out of his hiding place. Shovel held high above his head, he stole quietly over the melting snow toward Jonathan. It was a horrible, eerie sight, one Mary knew she'd never forget. The sky had taken on a Halloween-orange glow from the ruins of her home. Charred timbers and the occasional hiss of a flame touching the melting snow made a stark contrast to the peaceful serenity of the snow-blanketed woods surrounding them.

Jonathan had paused and was watching her curiously. Terrified that he'd hear or sense Trace sneaking up behind him, Mary desperately tried to pick up the threads of the diatribe Jonathan would call conversation.

"I never meant to betray you, Jonathan. You have to believe that."

"Why couldn't you stay pure? I forgave you when you let Mark Lester seduce you, even though you denied it, because you seemed so virtuous. Of course, I thought my first wife was pure—until our honeymoon when she bragged about the other lovers she'd had. For the next twenty years, I searched for a woman who would be faithful. I thought I'd found her in you."

Trace was only ten paces away now. She had to keep Jonathan talking. Asking the first question that popped into her mind, Mary spoke softly so Jonathan would have to give her his entire attention. "How did you find out about us? How did you know that I'd betrayed you?"

"I've known all along, you stupid cow! That first night he was hired, I waited outside the apartment door. I heard you laughing with him. But I wasn't sure. I wanted so badly to believe that you were different. So I followed you. You really thought I went to Alaska, didn't you? Stupid tramp. But I followed you. And watched you. I saw you kiss that bodyguard on the beach. That's when I knew you had to die. No woman betrays Jonathan Regent!"

Five more paces. Her heart thumped in her chest as Trace drew ever closer to the crazed killer.

As Jonathan raged on, Mary tried to keep her fear for Trace from showing on her face. She couldn't believe that she'd once planned to marry this madman! She must have been so gullible, so desperate for love that she'd overlooked a thousand signs.

"Now it's your turn to die, lying Mary!" He raised the rifle until his eye was level with the sight.

Her heart shattered, Mary fought for control, Three more paces. "Wait, Jonathan! I have to know. What about Milo King? What about your own brother? Did you kill him?"

He lowered the rifle a fraction of an inch and sneered at her. His icy voice absolved Mary of any remaining guilt. In a voice totally devoid of emotion, Jonathan said coldly, "Of course I killed him. He was trying to warn you. The moment you mentioned that purple ball cap with the wolf insignia, I knew it was my interfering brother. He saw an announcement of our engagement. Saw the resemblance between you and that first tramp. I had to stop him. He was going to tell you everything."

Mary thought about the poor man who'd been afraid to approach her directly, so he'd tried anonymous notes first. When she'd misunderstood them, he'd set up a meeting, placing her welfare above his own. He'd known what his own brother was capable of.

Mary was so lost in her thoughts that she'd started drowning out Jonathan's ugly words. "You were so much help, Mary, you told me exactly where to find him."

Dear God, was that more guilt she had to carry? She'd told Milo's killer exactly where to find him.

Suddenly, Mary heard the click of the rifle being cocked. She saw the bright muzzle flash, but, miraculously, didn't feel the bullet punch into her defenseless flesh.

It was over in an instant.

Jonathan lay still on the ground.

Trace stood over him, the shovel raised high like a club, his breath coming in short, panting bursts.

Knowing Trace didn't have his full strength because of his injury, Mary rushed forward to help him. Kicking the rifle from Jonathan's reach, she took the shovel from Trace's hand and held the blade on Jonathan's throat.

Then, like the cavalry rushing to their rescue, the wail of sirens howled through the night.

LATER THAT MORNING, Mary and Elizabeth sat in the hospital waiting room, their hands clasped together. Trace's hand had been injured far worse than they'd first thought and he'd been in surgery for over two hours.

When the ambulances had delivered the bedraggled foursome to the emergency room, John Wilder had been hospitalized for observation. Only moments before, however, the cardiologist had told them that John appeared to have come through the ordeal without any further damage to his heart.

Mary had spent the last two hours giving her mother the complete details of the terror Jonathan had put her through these past few weeks.

Elizabeth patted her daughter's hand as a shudder claimed her body. "When I think about your almost marrying that man, it just makes me sick to my stomach. What about Trace, honey? How do you feel about him? I'm not blind, you know."

What about Mary and Trace? That she loved him, madly, deeply and eternally was no longer in question. But would Jonathan's ghost always stand between them?

One other question continued to goad Mary. If she'd been so wrong about Jonathan, what did that say about this overwhelming love she now felt for Trace?

Oh, why was love never simple?

Mary looked up as the surgeon, still dressed in green scrubs, stepped into the waiting room. "Miss Wilder?"

Mary jumped to her feet. "How is he?"

"He's going to be just fine. He's out of the recovery room now and wants to see you."

Her heart gliding through the air like the wings of angels, she followed the doctor to Trace's room. His arm was heavily bandaged and was hooked up to some kind of pulley above his head. Somewhere during their ordeal, he'd sustained a black eye, and it was now a bright purple and blue against his wan complexion.

He looked wonderful!

Rushing to his bedside, Mary took his good hand and held it against her cheek. She was truly lucky, blessed, in fact. After all, she'd found out about Jonathan Regent *before* she'd married him. Somehow, with Trace at her side, she knew everything was going to be all right.

As if reading the love mirrored in her eyes, Trace slid his good hand up to her wrist and pulled her into his arms. The kiss they shared was of infinite sweetness, as if they'd both finally realized how close they had come to losing their soul mates.

At last he released her and looked pointedly at the three-carat diamond still glittering on Mary's ring finger. "That ring's entirely too large for such a delicate hand," he whispered. "If you'd throw it away, I'll replace it with a much more suitable ring. One that will last forever."

HARLEQUIN®

Deceit, betrayal, murder

Join Harlequin's intrepid heroines, India Leigh
and Mary Hadfield, as they ferret out the truth
behind the mysterious goings-on in their
neighborhood. These two women are no milk-
and-water misses. In fact, they thrive on

MISCHIEF & MAYHEM

Watch for their incredible adventures in this
special two-book collection. Available in March,
wherever Harlequin books are sold.

HARLEQUIN®

I N T R I G U E®

What if...

You'd agreed to marry a man you'd never met, in a town where you'd never been, while surrounded by wedding guests you'd never seen before?

And what if...

You weren't sure you could trust the man to whom you'd given your hand?

Look for "Mail Order Brides"—the upcoming two novels of romantic suspense by Cassie Miles, which are available in April and July—and only from Harlequin Intrigue!

Don't miss

#320 MYSTERIOUS VOWS
by Cassie Miles
April 1995

Mail Order Brides—where mail-order marriages lead distrustful newlyweds into the mystery and romance of a lifetime!

On the most romantic day of the year, capture the thrill of falling in love all over again—with

Harlequin's

Valentine

Bachelors

They're three sexy and *very single* men who run very special personal ads to find the women of their fantasies by Valentine's Day. These exciting, passion-filled stories are written by bestselling Harlequin authors.

Your Heart's Desire by Elise Title
Mr. Romance by Pamela Bauer
Sleepless in St. Louis by Tiffany White

Be sure not to miss Harlequin's Valentine Bachelors, available in February wherever Harlequin books are sold.

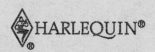

VB

Harlequin invites you to the most
romantic wedding of the season.

Rope the cowboy of your dreams in
Marry Me, Cowboy!

A collection of 4 brand-new stories,
celebrating weddings, written by:

New York Times bestselling author

JANET DAILEY

and favorite authors

Margaret Way
Anne McAllister
Susan Fox

Be sure not to miss Marry Me, Cowboy!
coming this April

HARLEQUIN®

Don't miss these Harlequin favorites by some of our most distinguished authors!
And now, you can receive a discount by ordering two or more titles!

HT#25577	WILD LIKE THE WIND by Janice Kaiser	$2.99	☐
HT#25589	THE RETURN OF CAINE O'HALLORAN by JoAnn Ross	$2.99	☐
HP#11626	THE SEDUCTION STAKES by Lindsay Armstrong	$2.99	☐
HP#11647	GIVE A MAN A BAD NAME by Roberta Leigh	$2.99	☐
HR#03293	THE MAN WHO CAME FOR CHRISTMAS by Bethany Campbell	$2.89	☐
HR#03308	RELATIVE VALUES by Jessica Steele	$2.89	☐
SR#70589	CANDY KISSES by Muriel Jensen	$3.50	☐
SR#70598	WEDDING INVITATION by Marisa Carroll	$3.50 U.S. $3.99 CAN.	☐
HI#22230	CACHE POOR by Margaret St. George	$2.99	☐
HAR#16515	NO ROOM AT THE INN by Linda Randall Wisdom	$3.50	☐
HAR#16520	THE ADVENTURESS by M.J. Rodgers	$3.50	☐
HS#28795	PIECES OF SKY by Marianne Willman	$3.99	☐
HS#28824	A WARRIOR'S WAY by Margaret Moore	$3.99 U.S. $4.50 CAN.	☐

(limited quantities available on certain titles)

	AMOUNT	$
DEDUCT:	**10% DISCOUNT FOR 2+ BOOKS**	$
ADD:	**POSTAGE & HANDLING**	$
	($1.00 for one book, 50¢ for each additional)	
	APPLICABLE TAXES*	$_____
	TOTAL PAYABLE	$_____
	(check or money order—please do not send cash)	

To order, complete this form and send it, along with a check or money order for the total above, payable to Harlequin Books, to: **In the U.S.:** 3010 Walden Avenue, P.O. Box 9047, Buffalo, NY 14269-9047; **In Canada:** P.O. Box 613, Fort Erie, Ontario, L2A 5X3.

Name:_____

Address:_____ City:_____

State/Prov.:_____ Zip/Postal Code:_____

*New York residents remit applicable sales taxes.
 Canadian residents remit applicable GST and provincial taxes.

HBACK-JM2